APOLLO

REBECCA F. KENNEY

Kenney, Rebecca F.

Apollo / by Rebecca F. Kenney—First edition.

NOTE FROM THE AUTHOR

This book is not intended to accurately represent the experience of everyone who struggles with depression. It does, however, reflect some of my own experiences as a creative person with periodic depression and ongoing anxiety.

DEDICATION

To all the souls struggling to shine through the darkness—
I see you.

To those who manage to do one small good thing
despite the crushing weight—
you are glorious and victorious.

And to my husband, who gives me the beautiful kind of
adoration and acceptance that Apollo offers Cassandra—

I love you.

TRIGGER WARNINGS

Death of an infant (in the past), suicide ideation, alcoholism, depression, brief mention of a mass shooting and a murder/suicide

SPOILER WARNING

This book contains significant spoilers for the Neverland Fae duology (*Wendy, Darling* and *Captain Pan*) as well as the *Hades* romance. For the best experience, I'd recommend reading the Immortal Warriors series in this order:

Jack Frost
The Gargoyle Prince
Wendy, Darling
Captain Pan
Hades
Apollo

(If you want, you can also start at *Wendy, Darling* and read forward from there.)

PLAYLIST

"**Adventure of a Lifetime**" Two Steps from Hell

"**Love You Like a Love Song**" Selena Gomez & The Scene

"**Make Me Believe**" The EverLove

"**Love Again**" Dua Lipa, Imanbek

"**You Get What You Give**" Glee Cast cover, New Radicals

"**Ever Ever After**" J2

"**I Won't Say (I'm in Love)**" The Lost Bros

"**Who Am I?**" Hugh Jackman, *Les Mis*

"**Symphony**" Clean Bandit, Zara Larsson

"**Broken-Hearted Lovers**" Somme

"**Luminous**" Alice and the Glass Lake

"**Make Your Own Kind of Music**" Cass Elliot

"**Maybe This Time**" Kristin Chenoweth, from *Cabaret*

"**Nothing New**" Taylor Swift, Phoebe Bridgers

"**Angel with a Shotgun**" The Cab

"**Stick with You**" Highasakite

"**Starlight**" Taylor Swift

"**Clean**" Hey Violet

"**Golden**" Harry Styles

"**Noble Blood**" Tommee Profitt, Fleurie

"**Shut Up and Dance**" Walk the Moon

"**Home**" Phillip Phillips

I

CASSANDRA

My mother had always fancied herself the tragic heroine.

Every day of her life was a new opportunity for something dramatic and doleful to happen, something she could sigh about to family and friends. She followed the news of fires and fatalities, pandemics and politics, trauma and tragedy, with an eagerness that was almost delight. It was almost like she *wanted* terrible, cataclysmic things to occur, though that couldn't be true, because she was a decent person. But every time I announced some fun or exciting bit of news to her, she injected her congratulations with caution. Her mind skipped instantly to *what could go wrong*. And so, over the years, I spoke with her less and less.

I was brought up on the sour skim milk of anxiety. It seeped into my blood, bones, and brain. My sister Meg and I tried to stop ourselves from thinking the way we'd been conditioned to think—leaping to the negative, living in perpetual caution. We tried to revolt. Meg did dare-devilish things like free-climbing and bungee-jumping with her girlfriend, while I did things like pursue a major in the arts when everyone told me there was no money in it.

Well. They were right.

Since I'd lost my job as a music teacher, I had been in the worst slump of my life. Depression, I suppose, though I cringed at the label. It sounded so dark, so final, so inescapable.

Then Meg called me about a day trip to Carowinds, the roller-coaster heaven of the Carolinas.

"You need something to shake you out of your slump, Cassie," she told me. "Some excitement, some fun."

"What if the harness breaks?" I said dully into the phone, picking lint from beneath my thumbnail. "What if I'm flung out of a roller coaster going sixty miles an hour? Will *that* be fun?"

"You sound like Mom," Meg snapped. It was the barb we threw whenever we wanted to sting each other's ego a bit.

I didn't respond.

"What, no comeback? Wow, you're really feeling low." Her voice softened. "You want me to drive over there? Because I will."

God, no. I stared around me at the towers of takeout boxes, the half-empty plastic cups of soda, the crumpled tissues scattered across the carpet like snowballs. "No, I'm fine."

"You're coming to Carowinds. I'm buying your ticket tonight, and we'll go next Saturday. It's fall, so they're only open weekends anyway. It's going to be cooler, too, so hopefully not many people. Short lines, no sweating—it'll be heaven."

Squalling babies, kids whining about waiting, weird smells, weirder people—

Damn it. I *did* sound like Mom.

So I agreed. I let her buy the tickets, and at 6 a.m. on the morning of the trip I exerted Herculean amounts of willpower to force myself out of bed, into the shower, and then into the car. I drove an hour and a half from my apartment, and I met Meg and Jessa at the park entrance.

But I ended up alone within the hour, because of course Meg and Jessa decided to do the Fury 325, the world's tallest and fastest giga coaster, and I was like *no way in hell*.

"We've got to do it, babe," Jessa squealed. "Cassie, you'll be fine, right? Look, there's the Afterburn—it's milder, you can ride that one! Meet you here later? Awesome!" And they danced off together, with Meg casting a sort-of-apologetic look back at me.

Meg was right about one thing—the lines were surprisingly short. I was able to breeze through the lower waiting area, right past the squiggly barriers where they channeled people in tight coils on busy days. I climbed the wooden steps nearly to the top of the platform before I had to stop and wait in line.

I was totally fine by myself. I was fine standing there, mindlessly scrolling through Twitter, while the mother ahead of me tried in shrill tones to convince her nervous nine-year-old son that he was ready for this kind of ride.

Somewhere above and ahead of me, I hear the rattling clank and the whir of the coaster, followed by a chorus of screams.

I closed Twitter and opened my Facebook app. I barely went on Facebook anymore, but when I did it was to stalk my ex. Because I was one of *those* women, much as I hated to admit it.

I'd met Ajax two years ago, when I first got the job as the music teacher for Mueller Road Elementary. I'd gone out with a few friends to celebrate, and one of them had brought him along. What was supposed to be a demure night of celebratory champagne had ended with me accompanying him to his apartment, where he explained his sexual expectations and made me scrub myself and shave *everything* before he finally nodded and said that I passed inspection. I'd thought it was strange, but really hot, in a kinky sort of way. Ajax had been charmingly addictive, and I had a bit of an addictive personality. Obsessive, I guess. I couldn't just like something a little bit—I always went all the way.

A soft tingle traced between my legs as I stared at Ajax's profile picture. Beautiful olive skin, glossy dark hair waving past his chin, a perfectly trimmed goatee. That glimmer of perpetual hunger in his eyes.

Movement in the line shook me out of my stupor. I swallowed and zipped the phone into my tiny backpack. What was I doing, getting turned on by a Facebook photo while standing in line with families and kids and stuff? What the hell was wrong with me?

I was nearly to the roller-coaster. Half a dozen dividers channeled people into different rows—four people per row. I shuffled into one of the holding areas and stared at the massive male back in front of me— huge mounded shoulder-blades packed with muscle, and a strip of bronze neck showing between the collar of the white T-shirt and a knot of golden hair. Not pale blond hair, not bleached—golden. Rich, warm, beautiful.

The short sleeves of the T-shirt stretched around the man's biceps. Despite the late morning sun, it was still a little chilly for short sleeves, but to each their own. His arms were perfectly sculpted slopes and swells of hard flesh, tanned a deep golden-brown. My gaze traveled down to the hands—relaxed at his sides, fingers arched. The backs of his hands were threaded with tendons and bold veins under that bronze skin. Damn.

The barriers swung open, and a bored attendant welcomed us to the ride and launched into a safety spiel. Dazed, I followed the bronze muscle-guy into the row of four seats. I avoided looking at him—he probably got stared at a lot. And I wasn't looking my best today, with my hair in two loose braids and a tiny bit of mascara. Why had I put my hair in *braids*? So juvenile. So dumb. I buckled myself and pinned my legs together, conscious of how weak and pale they looked. I'd been curled on my couch eating junk for way too long, only crawling out of my hole when I needed something I couldn't order online.

I hated myself for quitting on life. For not being able to get out of this funk. I'd been fighting the creeping sensation that I needed help, like maybe a doctor or medication, but I couldn't bring myself to make an appointment. I just couldn't manage to summon the willpower to find a doctor's number, or dial it. Which sounded silly, but it was agonizingly true.

Why was I even here? I didn't want to be on this ride, with my legs kicking helplessly, pinned into a padded cage. I glanced up at the massive contraption of metal and gears from which I dangled. Beyond all the bulky machinery arched the roof of the building, a latticework of steel rafters draped with fluttering cobwebs.

I didn't want to be here. I wanted to be back home, alone, where beautiful men couldn't make me feel terrible about myself.

Damn, the guy had gorgeous legs—perfectly shaped, calves ropy with muscle, completely hairless—

Hairless? He shaved his legs? Okay, he was probably gay. Or maybe a model. A gay model—

"Have you ridden this one before?" The rich male voice startled me.

Muscle-guy was freaking *talking* to me, and I hated him for it. I wished he'd disappear and let me experience abject terror and self-loathing in peace.

"Um, no. I haven't ridden it before," I said. "I don't usually do roller coasters."

The attendant checked our harnesses and took my little backpack, setting it aside with the other riders' belongings.

"I've never been on a roller coaster," said the man.

Without craning my neck, I couldn't see his face around the enormous padded shoulder-pieces of my harness, and I refused to yield to my curiosity. I stared straight ahead, at the painted metal of the seat in front of me.

"This is a vacation for me," he continued conversationally as the roller coaster jerked and moved forward. "A new experience."

"Uh huh." I wrapped my fingers around the handles on my harness and sucked in shallow breaths. My heart throbbed faster with every foot we ascended.

Muscle-guy said something else but I couldn't hear him over the panicked chant in my brain: *I hate this I hate this, no no no, I don't want to be here, I hate this—*

We ratcheted up, up, up—a breathless moment of suspension and then my body was flung forward—out and away—I was flying, weightless, breathless, shearing through space.

Sun crashed into my vision and my mind blazed white with shock, blank and gloriously empty, nothing but the bright glare and the screaming wind of our speed. I was whipped aside, flung upside down—my butt left the seat and for a second I was free-flying—another whip to the side, a shrieking loop, and I spun through space while my eyes filled with sunlight. Chilly wind blasted my face—pain and joy combined. I had never felt so excruciatingly alive.

With a jolt, we slid to a stop, and it was over.

Maybe I'd screamed, maybe I hadn't—I wasn't sure. I only knew that for a few blissful moments, my brain hadn't been chewing itself to pieces. I'd been *quiet* inside.

I couldn't remember the last time that had happened.

Dazed, I grabbed my backpack and filed down the exit stairs with everyone else. I didn't see Meg and Jessa anywhere around, and I was actually glad of it, because I needed *more*. More of that blinding sun, the speed, the weightlessness, and that blissful quiet in my mind.

I marched along the fence, circling around and getting back in line. The line was even shorter this time—I wouldn't have to wait more than a few minutes.

Up ahead I noticed a familiar white T-shirt and a pair of bronzed arms.

My stomach dipped and thrilled.

Muscle-guy was riding the coaster again too. Just a couple people between him and me.

When it was my turn to choose a row, I almost avoided him. That was my usual mode of operation lately—avoid anything potentially pleasant, lest it turn into something embarrassing or devastating.

But at the last second I darted into the row right behind him.

His head tilted, almost like he sensed me, and he turned.

Oh my god.

Yeah, he was way out of my league.

He had a lean, handsome face, with a regal elegance to the cast of his features. A tiny golden jewel nestled beside his nose, with more tiny gems sparkling at the tapered outer edges of each dark eyebrow and along his ears. He was clean-shaven, his long jaw bare and smooth, not a hint of scruff. But his eyes were the most captivating part of him—such a light brown they were nearly golden, and they seemed to glow faintly even in the shadows of the building. Some type of exotic contacts, maybe.

I had never seen such a beautiful man.

His perfectly carved lips moved, saying something to me. I had no idea what it was. My brain was skidding and resetting, like a scratched record.

Muscle-guy smiled at me then, a flash of brilliant white teeth. "Still a little dazed from the ride?"

I cleared my throat. "Oh, um—I guess so. Sorry."

"It was more fun than I expected."

"Same." I gave him a small smile. Despite the stupid juvenile flutters in my belly, something about his grin had eased me, loosened the knot that was tightening in my chest.

The gates opened, and we stepped into the row again.

"I'll put that aside for you," he offered, reaching for my bag.

I handed it over. "Thank you."

We didn't speak again. This time, when the roller coaster shot out and whirled us around and threw us upside down about six times, I did scream. And it felt amazing. I'd been wanting to scream all-out, full-voice, for so long—years, maybe. But people didn't take kindly to that when you worked at an elementary school and lived in a tiny apartment. The most I'd been able to do was release muffled shrieks into a pillow. But now— now I could scream, as loudly as I wanted, because everyone one was screaming and it was okay. I almost sobbed with the joy of it, as the wind whipped tears from the corners of my eyes and scoured them away.

When the ride came to its jolting end, I scrambled out, breathless, and grabbed my bag. I descended the stairs side by side with Golden Muscles Guy, and we both turned toward the line again at the same time. He looked down at me, grinning, and I smiled back.

Mutely we took our place in line, this time side by side. Standing next to him, I realized just how tall he was. My head barely reached his shoulder.

"It's like riding a chariot through the sky," he said quietly. "Only in shorter bursts, with more upside-down loops."

An odd thing to say, but a decent description. "You're not wrong."

This time, when we climbed into our seats, one of my braids snagged on the harness. While I was struggling with it, Golden Guy reached between my legs, collected the safety buckle, and snapped it into place. He did it quickly, respectfully, not a fingertip straying where it shouldn't—but heat flared through my core all the same. It had been way too long since any man had come that close to touching me there.

I screamed again as we rode, but this time it was less an expulsion of my inner torment and more a breathless venting of joy. When the ride ended, Golden Guy picked up my backpack from the storage area and handed it over. His warm fingers brushed mine.

"I like the way you scream," he said.

My breath stuck in my throat. From anyone else those words would have been truly creepy—but his golden-brown eyes were so open, liquid with light and sincere joy.

"Thanks, I guess," I murmured.

As we descended the steps, his arm brushed mine, hot and smooth, not a bit of hair. Damn it. Between the hairlessness and the piercings, I could pretty much guarantee he didn't play for my team. Not that anything would ever happen between us if he was straight, because he was so very beautiful, and I—I was—

"Should we go again?" he asked.

A flush of pleasure warmed my chest. "If my sister and her girlfriend aren't waiting for me."

But they were. Meg and Jessa stood by a lamppost, snacking on churros. They waved to me. Meg's eyebrow quirked as she scanned the tall man at my side.

"I have to go." My heart hollowed out, and the shadows dropped right back into it, filling me to the brim, weighing me with darkness. "But this was fun."

"Once more." Half plea, half command.

I narrowed my eyes at him.

"Sorry." He winced. "I'm used to giving orders."

"So you're some alpha-boss type."

His dark brows pulled together. "Alpha?"

"Top dog, leader of the pack."

"Ah. No, I'm not the leader of the pack. That would be my father."

"Family business?"

He grinned again. "You could say that."

Meg and Jessa approached, wearing telltale smirks as they glanced between us. "Hey, Cassandra," drawled Meg. "Making friends?"

I gave her a hard stare. "I was thinking I might ride this one more time. Where can I meet you guys?"

"At the Copperhead Strike," Jessa said with a wink.

"Take your time," Meg threw over her shoulder as they pranced away.

I rolled my eyes and turned back to Golden Guy—and nearly bumped into the broad expanse of his white-cotton T-shirt. When had he gotten so close to me? His pectorals swelled against the soft material, tiny points showing where his nipples were.

I'd always had a thing for guys in white T-shirts, and this man was pretty much customized to make my panties drop.

"Cassandra," he said.

Oh god. The way he said my name—hot damn.

I hurried away, toward the entrance for Afterburn. Only when we had climbed the steps and reached the back of the line again did I manage to remember normal human protocols. "What's your name?"

"Apollo," he said. And then he winced, as if he regretted telling me. As if the word had popped out against his better judgment.

"Apollo, huh? Like Apolo Ohno?"

"I'm not sure who that is."

"He's an Olympic speed skater, or he was. Now I think he does motivation speeches or whatever. He was on *Dancing with the Stars*, too."

"I've seen that," he said eagerly. "I enjoy music, and dancing."

"So do I—or I did, a while ago." Lately every song seemed to remind me of what I'd lost, so I'd kind of cut music out of my life. And I hadn't danced to anything in months.

Words welled up inside me—*I used to compose music. I'm a great singer and a decent dancer. I had dreams of composing a hit song that millions of people would love.* But I held the words inside, because no one should talk that way to a complete stranger.

"You still have music inside you," Apollo said. "I can hear it."

I frowned up at him. "Has anyone ever told you you're a little strange?"

"People around here usually do. Elsewhere I'm respected too much, and if they think I'm odd, they don't say it to my face."

So he was influential as well as handsome. Probably wealthy, too.

We shuffled forward, closer to the entry gates. Apollo braced his hip on the divider, his back to the roller coaster, facing me. Watching me with curious golden eyes.

"I used to write songs," I said, low. "I don't think I can anymore."

"Of course you can." He leaned in, his lean face sharpening with intensity. "When we ride this time, find the music in how you feel. The song already exists. You just have to uncover it."

The gates popped open again, and I followed him into the row. Once I was buckled, I closed my eyes, and I focused on the trickle of expectant voices, the thump and click of harnesses, the shriek of metal as we began to move. Our ascent was a rhythm, a clackety perpetual rattle that built and built until we launched into streaking speed—and as I flew out of myself into that liminal space of detachment, of flight, the song exploded through my soul—a strain of music more beautiful than any I'd ever composed.

I couldn't scream, couldn't think past the flow of the notes in my head, and the sheer joy of creation— something I'd never thought I would feel again.

I gripped the sequence of notes, playing and replaying them, terrified they would skitter away into the dark crevices of my brain. My fingers burned because I was clutching the harness handles so tightly.

When the ride stopped, I flew past Apollo, snatched my bag, and pelted down the steps. I plunked down onto a curb and opened an email to myself, typing in frantic notations. I'd uninstalled my composition app months ago, but I could make do with what I had until I could reinstall it.

A bulky male shape settled onto the curb beside me, but I ignored him until I finished jotting down the notes and cadence that blazed in my brain. Once the snatch of song was out, I could breathe again.

"Sorry," I gasped. "I thought of some music and I had to jot it down before I lost it."

"No apology necessary." He pulled the band out of his hair and shook it out. His golden locks were longer than I'd expected, reaching to mid-breast on him. As he redid the knot at the back of his head, I caught a whiff of fragrance—sunshine and honeysuckle and vanilla. I wanted to lean in and sniff him, but I caught myself just in time.

I tucked my phone away again and stared at my hands, at the bitten-down nails that so desperately needed better care. At my legs, left bare by my flower-print shorts—legs that were still slender-ish but blindingly white and not toned at all. I'd worn the shorts because the temperature was supposed to reach mid-seventies by early afternoon, but now I was wishing I'd chosen jeans instead.

A couple of Southern hottie types with glowing tans and sleek hair strutted past, casting admiring glances at Apollo. He didn't seem to notice them.

"Why are you sitting here with me?" I blurted out.

"Do you want me to go?"

I chewed my lip. Anxiety and self-doubt were gnawing at my edges again, pressing on my soul. But the sunshine bathed my skin like liquid gold, and a gorgeous man wanted to spend time with *me*. I felt purged and refreshed thanks to the screaming, and satisfied because I'd created a small scrap of beautiful music.

"No," I said. "I don't want you to go. In fact, I— look, I don't usually do this, but—could I have your phone number?" I darted a glance at him, my cheeks burning.

Apollo looked aggrieved. "I'm so sorry. I don't have a phone."

"What? Like, not at all? What about a home phone?"

"No."

"Email? Social media?" Okay, I was starting to sound stupidly desperate.

"No, none of that."

"You're saying there is no way to get in touch with you."

He grimaced. "I'm sorry."

I could feel myself closing up again, growing cold and dark. "It's all right. I understand." I got up, hitching my backpack over my shoulder. "Nice to meet you."

"It's not that I don't want to get in touch," he began, but I cut him off.

"This was fun. Thanks." Then I walked away as fast as I could, tears stinging my eyes. There was a women's bathroom up ahead and I practically ran into it. He couldn't follow me there.

I huddled in the stall, crying quietly into wads of cheap abrasive toilet paper, until I was sure he must have left.

Then I crept out of the bathroom and back into real life.

APOLLO

When the human girl fled from me, I thought my heart would explode through my ribs and rush after her, bloody and unbodied.

I could have followed her, but she ran into one of those spaces assigned to a specific gender. An odd concept, but I'd broken that rule on Earth before, and my innocent error had been met with shrieks of protest from the women inside. I wasn't about to repeat my mistake.

This trip to Earth was supposed to be my respite after months of helping Pan root out the remnants of Hook's fleet. Perhaps secretly I'd hoped I would meet the one who would free me from the Fae curse that bound my body and heart. But my primary motive had been rest, and fun, of the human kind. And according to human propaganda, the most fun one could have on Earth was at an amusement park.

In smaller or less populated realms, I could sense the presence of individuals with power—abilities passed down through the fruitful joining of gods with humans. But in a realm as large as Earth, so thickly populated, my senses were somewhat distorted. Many humans had faint traces of godly blood in them, but for most, their abilities were dormant, waiting to awaken in a different generation.

I hadn't expected to feel a storm of suppressed power while waiting in line to ride the humans' little metal train.

But there she was, a pale nondescript girl, soft and pretty and devastatingly sad. Usually I could discern the flavor of a human's gift and identify the god who was its source, but not this time. This girl's power was tangled, tormented, bound with chains of some kind. A geas, maybe? A geas was a Fae enchantment, stronger than the average curse. I should know—I'd cast a geas on someone myself, and I was currently suffering under a painful one that had been cast on me.

Most gods disdained Fae magic, but I'd always found it fascinating and useful. Blended with my natural gifts as an Olympian, Fae spells could be unpredictable, but they were always powerful. Perhaps someone had cursed this girl, bound her powers. The forcible suppression of her abilities was weighing her spirit in ways she might not realize.

I seated myself on a bench, planning to wait for her outside the women's room she'd entered, but then I saw a woman approaching—someone I recognized, dressed in a tie-dyed shirt and ragged jeans. Her hair spiraled from her head in iridescent rainbow curls. Her name was Iris, and she'd been Zeus's favorite messenger ever since Hermes left Olympus to serve Hook. Recently I'd discovered that Hook had cut off Hermes' wings and left him in some wasteland realm to die. Whether Hermes had actually perished or not was another question.

My father should have resented Hermes' defection enough to go to war with Hook, but instead he'd declared Olympus a neutral party and ordered me to stay out of the conflict.

I had generations of experience with Zeus's wrath. It wasn't a thing to take lightly. But I'd defied him and helped Pan anyway. I'd been lucky to get away with it this long. Judging from Iris's sudden appearance, I was in trouble.

"Iris." I gave her a grim nod.

"Sun god," she said. "Your father demands your presence."

"I'm on vacation."

"Vacation?" She snorted. "Such a human concept."

"Surprisingly enjoyable, after all the work I've been doing—work that would have been easier with more aid from Olympus."

"Ah yes, your obsession with altruism. Defying our High God Zeus by meddling with inter-realm conflicts."

"I prefer to think of it as a mission of mercy, freeing captive realms from Hook's rule, routing out undesirables who might bring harm to entire populations."

"Always the Averter of Evil and Bringer of Light, the savior and rescuer, the gracious Apollo." Iris smirked. "It's not for me to judge your motives, Phoebus. Your father demands your presence. Immediately. If you don't come with me now, he will send others to bring you by force."

I glanced toward the women's restroom. Even through the brick and concrete between us, I could sense the turmoil of Cassandra's power, the eddies of her distress.

If I left Earth now, there was no guarantee I'd ever find her again. With her power bound, I couldn't sense it without being in very close proximity. I had no idea where she lived. People traveled long distances to reach this amusement park, so she could be from anywhere.

But I could not disobey a direct order from my father. He still ruled the realm of Olympus, and he wielded greater authority and power than mine.

I followed Iris to a quiet corner of the park, behind a building. I could not disappear, but as Zeus' messenger she had limited capabilities of concealment, and she veiled us both before we leaped aloft, into the bright sky, she on rainbow wings and I with my gold-feathered ones. We did not speak as we sped over towns, roads, and forests until we reached Earth's realm gate, located near a human city called Baltimore.

A transient Fae like Peter Pan could take someone through their own realm gate into the In-Between, the vast space between worlds. At that point, the person must swallow the eyeball of a sluagh, one of the interdimensional monsters inhabiting the In-Between. The sluagh eye allowed one to perceive the realm gates, to move through the nebulous dark, and to stave off the madness that could overwhelm the mind in that liminal space.

Without a Fae traveler, I had to swallow a sluagh eye in order to pass through Earth's realm gate. I'd stashed a few in my temporary Earth residence, but Iris had some in a pouch she carried, and she handed one to me.

I hated swallowing the disgusting thing. But it was part of passing between worlds. The sluagh eyes were dangerous to obtain, practically priceless—I was fortunate to be an Olympian god with wealth and status enough to afford the privilege of inter-realm travel.

Sometimes I used my chariot to travel between realms. It was embedded with sluagh eyes, which meant I didn't need to swallow one—but the horses disliked the passage, and I'd used them far too often during recent battles with Hook's fleet. Instead of making them bring me to Earth, I'd left them at my estate in Olympus, so they could enjoy a well-deserved rest and romp.

The realm gates could be hard to spot, and Iris circled the same area of the sky several times before she spotted the glimmering slit, a gap in the fabric of this realm.

"You should have set beacons to mark the spot, like Pan does when he comes to Earth," I told her.

She snorted. "The day I take notes from a Fae will be the day I die."

"The Olympians' prejudice against the Fae has held back our understanding of magic, and of our own powers," I replied. "Why is it only the dark practitioners like Hecate who make the effort to learn Fae magic? If Zeus would explore the shared source of our power and that of the Fae, perhaps his own power would not be declining."

"Shared source?" Iris halted in mid-air, staring at me. "That's blasphemy. The gods are glorious descendants of the realm-makers. To be Olympian is to have pure, innate power, while the Fae are a bent people who scrabble magic from the dirt and roots in which they writhe. Conflating our power with their low magic is practically treasonous."

"Then why does Zeus allow Unseelie practices to continue unchecked in our realm?"

She glanced away, primming up her lips.

"You know what he lets the other Olympians do in the dark," I said. "The secrets that aren't secrets, the rot surging ever nearer to the surface."

"The rule of Olympus isn't your concern, and the decisions of the High Seat aren't yours to judge."

"Then I suppose Zeus will have yet another sin for which to judge me." I flew past her to the realm gate, and it sucked me right through into the In-Between.

The In-Between was darkness incarnate, a vast fathomless black filled with churning, amorphous, multi-eyed monsters. The sluaghs consisted of millions of wicked souls from every realm. The evil of those souls trapped them here in eternal limbo, while better souls passed on to the Underworld, ruled by Hades.

I'd seen Peter Pan dart up to a sluagh and pluck out its eye with deft ease, springing away before it could engulf him—but for those not gifted with the magic of a Fae traveler, even brushing against a sluagh could cause horror, madness, and paralysis, after which the victim would be swallowed into the sluagh's body, trapped for eternity.

Yet despite the danger posed by the sluaghs themselves, I loved the In-Between. In the limitless expanse I could see a myriad glimmering realm gates, like stars, more numerous the longer you looked. It was beautiful, truly.

But the real reason I loved it was the way my power affected the place.

I had no qualms about causing pain to the sluaghs. So whenever I passed through the In-Between, I released my power. Every mental chain I had looped around myself, every veil I'd cast over my glory to protect others from its brightness—I could let it all go in that cosmic emptiness.

My radiance shot outward from my body, a sphere of pure golden light expanding, racing away through untold leagues of blackness, dispelling the dark and bathing the universe in my glory.

In moments like these, I wondered if my power was truly lesser than my father's. He'd spent countless centuries telling me how weak I was compared to him. Every five hundred years I went through a renewal, a regenerating sleep that refreshed my mind, body, and powers. Like all Olympians, I came out of each renewal with certain personality traits enhanced or suppressed. In each lifetime I might be slightly more hedonistic, or cruel, or warlike, or studious. Renewals helped Olympians like me deal with the wear and tear of an eternal existence. And when every renewal began, and I emerged from sleep, my father made it a point to greet me with open arms and many expressions of pity for the fact that I'd been born so much weaker than him.

But here in the black heart of the universe, with power rolling off me in great golden waves, with the monstrous sluaghs squealing and squirming away as my light sliced through their smoky bodies—I wondered, not for the first time, if Zeus was the weaker one.

"Finished spewing yourself all over the In-Between?" Iris's voice jolted me out of my reverie.

I wasn't tired or empty yet. My powers felt supreme, inexhaustible, a bottomless fountain of light. But I closed myself off again and followed Iris to the Olympian realm gate. I didn't veil the natural glow of my skin as I did on Earth, and it felt good to walk into Olympus in my true godly glory.

Like the realm gate in Neverland and the one on Earth, the Olympian realm gate was in the sky. My people had built a massive marble staircase leading up it. A couple of guards stood by, but they barely nodded at us. They were posted to greet unexpected guests, not to hinder the coming and going of the gods and their messengers.

Iris and I didn't bother to descend the staircase, but flew straight to my father's gleaming palace on the Mount. The palace's hundreds of sharp spires glittered in the light of the setting sun, and I relished the same light on my skin. Nothing felt quite like the sun of my home realm. It blessed and refreshed me, and I felt power surging inside me anew, replacing what I had spent in the In-Between.

Not even during the wars with Hook had I revealed or used my full power. I preferred to rely on the strength of my arm, the wielding of my golden whip and my swords. If I ever lost control and let everything explode out of me, the resulting destruction could be devastating. When Peter Pan lost control of his magic after Wendy's capture, he'd nearly torn Neverland apart. I could control mine, and I used a percentage of it—but I never allowed myself to go full-throttle.

I soaked myself in the Olympian sun, letting my huge golden wings unfurl to their widest span. I swirled in the amber rays, my feathers sparkling and rippling. Out of the corner of my eye, I saw Iris watching me with grudging admiration.

With a mighty pulse of my wings, I shot far ahead of her. The gates of my father's palace opened for me, and I swept through, along colonnades threaded with cloud, until I reached the Court of the High Seat, a plateau atop sky-high pillars, with more pillars circling its edge. On a tall dais sat the alabaster throne, the High Seat itself, the throne of Zeus.

Hera sat in her own throne nearby, on a separate dais. When they'd ended their marriage one renewal ago, she'd insisted on continuing to rule at my father's side. And of course Zeus had agreed, because having her around to take on some of the responsibilities gave him more time for dalliances.

Speaking of dalliances—Zeus had a naked human girl on his lap. She lay draped against his shoulder, her face and body rosy with wine and wantonness. Her lips were swollen, and her lashes fluttered against flushed cheeks. Zeus was petting idly between her legs while she sighed and whimpered at his touch.

When he saw me, he dumped the girl off his thighs and smacked her ass. "Go."

She staggered away on legs wobbly with drink and desire. I watched her leave, and for a second I pictured the pale form of Cassandra lying across my lap. I'd tease a flush onto that white skin, bring a sparkle of delighted pleasure into those sad eyes. I'd make her scream like she did on the rollercoaster—

"What, not even a bow?" said Zeus.

"Apologies." I made my obeisance. "Your lovely toy distracted me."

"She's nothing. Boring." He snapped his fingers, and a nymph hurried to him with a goblet. "Drink?" my father asked, raising his eyebrows at me.

"Not now, thank you."

"I'd like to know something, Phoebus." He stood up, swirling the liquor. "What are you plotting, with all this flitting about between realms, all this currying of favor and generating of goodwill?"

"I'm not plotting anything. Simply helping out those in need."

"Is that so? Some in these halls think otherwise. They think you're looking for a higher seat. One of power." Zeus narrowed his eyes.

"The High Seat?" I sighed. "This again, Father? I've told you I'm not interested in your throne."

"Forgive me if I have difficulty believing it," he retorted. "Everyone else seems to want it. And these ridiculous rumors of my power fading—nothing but foolishness." He let lightning crackle along his hands and arms. Crooked glowing branches of it laced his golden crown. "You don't believe those rumors, do you, boy?"

"No, Lord Zeus. You are the High King, and you have my allegiance."

"Do I, though? Do I?" His voice lifted into a thunderous register I knew all too well. "Iris found you on Earth, yes? What were you doing there?"

"Amusing myself. Taking a break. Resting."

"The indefatigable peddler of protection and good works, resting?" Deep laughter rolled from my father.

"Not likely. I'll remind you that Earth is still mine, and its people our mine. They supply some of our best slaves."

"Oh, but Apollo doesn't believe in owning slaves," cut in Hera. Her long scarlet talons raked through her dark locks. Her ochre skin was as lustrous as ever, barely cloaked in a scanty chiton. "Isn't that right, my sweet?" Her smile was a beauteous poison. "You believe in such toxic and fanciful notions as the *equality* of the realms and their inhabitants."

"I believe no sentient being should own another," I said. "But we've discussed all these topics before, Sovereigns. Surely you had another reason for summoning me? Or perhaps you delight in wasting my time."

"Watch your tongue, sun-drop," crooned Hera. "I know where your mother lives."

An old threat, one I pretended to fear. Hera liked to remind me that my mother, Leto, was within her reach at all times. But Hera didn't realize how many layers of magic I'd woven around my estate of Delos. Not just Olympian wards and spellwork, but Fae enchantments too. I'd like to see her try to get through them.

I bowed, lifting my eyes to hers while I bent low. "Fair Queen," was all I said. Hera's fingers fluttered over her collarbone, and her throat bobbed lightly. Even my father's ex-wife wasn't immune to my golden charm.

"Are we to be blunt with each other then?" My father descended the steps from his throne. His dark brows cut savage lines above deep-set green eyes. "I require proof of your continued devotion, boy. You will go to the pocket realm of Gjöll for me and oversee the establishment of a new mine there, one whose ore will feed the forges of Hephaestus."

"You're having him make more weapons?" I frowned. "What use have you for them, when you are opposed to warring with other realms?"

"That is not your concern."

My mouth tightened. I had long suspected my father of selling weapons to the more unsavory types in the realms. Some of the weapons I'd seen during battles with Hook reminded me a little too much of Hephaestus's style, and packed too heavy an impact for a simple weapon made by human hands. If my father had sold weapons secretly to Hook, it would explain why he'd been so eager for me to stay out of the conflict—so ready to let the realms tear each other apart. Hephaestus wasn't the sort to ask questions about where his creations went. He'd always been a quiet, intent craftsman, focused on inventing ingenious new pieces rather than weighing moral issues.

"Well?" said my father impatiently. "You've been serving the leaders of a dozen other realms, yet you hesitate when your god, king, and father requires something of you?"

"I would think you'd jump at the chance to oversee this project," Hera put in. "You're always twittering away about better pay and safer conditions for human laborers. Just think, you'll be able to install the lighting in those mine tunnels—little sun-balls that never go out, to keep up the men's spirits and light them safely home."

She spoke sarcastically, with a mocking giggle, but a tension around her eyes and mouth made me wonder if she was altogether joking. And she had a point—the miners at the new site in Gjöll would be much safer if I oversaw the design of the place. But time flowed oddly in Gjöll, and I would be away from Cassandra for several weeks of her time, at the very least. She might forget me.

"Refuse this, Apollo, and you'll be banned from using the realm gate for twelve lunar cycles," Zeus barked. "I will have a spell set across it to prevent your passage."

It was a punishment fit for an unruly child, and my skin heated and glowed brighter at the insult. "You can't keep me confined to Olympus."

The moment I spoke, I knew I should not have said it. Zeus' green eyes went white, and lightning sparked from his lashes. "I can do anything I like to you, boy."

If I defied him, and he barred me from the gate for a year, I'd lose Cassandra for good. She'd be even harder to find once I returned to Earth—or she'd be dead. Her power aura had an edge of bitter hopelessness to it that concerned me. I had to get back to her and help her unlock her abilities so the heaviness could lift from her heart.

And I couldn't do that if I was trapped here in Olympus.

Zeus was nothing if not paranoid. Defying him now would only confirm his suspicion that I was plotting against him, and he might do worse than a forced confinement to this realm.

"Very well, Father." I bowed to him. "I will trust your wisdom in this matter. I am happy to serve you in Gjöll."

"Good. Watch yourself, my son. Give me no further reason to doubt your loyalty and obedience. And no more trysts and treaties with Fae renegades." He drained his cup and turned to a servant. "Bring the triplets to my room. And the boy too."

He stalked away from me without another look. I met Hera's eyes briefly, more sickened than usual by my father's behavior. A flicker of pain and revulsion crossed her face, but she turned away without speaking.

While overseeing the opening of the mine in Gjöll, I dreamed of Cassandra's face, sad and pale. I had nightmares of struggling to reach her while she drowned in the endless dark of the In-Between. I remembered the hectic, joyful brightness in her eyes after we shared the ride together. I desperately wanted to coax that brightness to the surface again.

When my sentence was served and the mine was running smoothly, I sent a report to Olympus detailing what I'd accomplished. I'd done good work, but I felt deeply unsettled about where the yield of that mine would go, and the purpose of the weapons that would be crafted with the ore. I didn't want to return to the High Seat, lest my father think up some other questionable task for me, so I swallowed a sluagh eye and left Gjöll through its blood-red realm gate, with some Earth currency, my favorite lute, and a few personal possessions in the bag I carried.

I needed to find Cassandra again, and to do that, I required the help of a friend.

After so much time spent in underground passages, creating eternal unquenchable lights for the miners, the In-Between felt impossibly vast, even to a mind like mine. It took me several minutes of hard staring at the other realm gates around me before I finally found the glimmering green-and-gold slit that would take me to Peter Pan's home. Neverland was small, classified as a pocket realm—an inheritance his Fae family had held for generations. Even among the High Fae or the gods, few could boast sole ownership of an entire pocket realm.

Peter was a powerful ally, and I considered him a friend. But this time I wasn't visiting him. I needed to speak with his partner and lover, Wendy.

As usual, I felt her power the moment I passed through the Neverland realm gate. I could feel the others, too—the Lost Kids who carried abilities of all kinds—some latent and some active. All of them had been coveted and pursued by Hook, rescued by Peter.

But Wendy's power was different—broader and brighter than the others, a pervasive atmosphere that encompassed the whole realm. As a descendant of Elpis and Tyche, her gift was the blessing of luck and hope on everyone around her, especially those she cared about. She had also learned to impart a focused dose of luck and hope to an individual.

To locate Cassandra, I would need all the luck and hope I could get.

The Neverland realm gate was in the sky, accessible only by flight, so I spread my wings and caught myself in midair before I could fall into the Never Sea. My wings could be banished completely, or I could make them invisible yet still tangible. Today I left them visible, with the idea of impressing Wendy just a bit.

As I flew toward Neverland, something enormous burst from the Never Sea with a rushing roar, barreling straight up into the sky toward me, jaws splayed wide. I conjured a long whip of light that snaked out and stung the monster on the nose.

"Down, Goliatha," I called. "Don't you recognize an ally of your master's?"

The giant crocodile bellowed, but her jaws closed and she sank beneath the surface in an explosion of glittering spray. I continued on to the isle, soaring across its forests until I landed in the clearing beside Peter's mansion.

A few of the younger Lost Kids were sparring in the meadow. Their eyes widened when they saw me, and they ran inside to fetch someone—Wendy, I guessed. I couldn't sense Peter's presence at the moment—he must be on an errand to another realm. Just as well, because if he found out I'd come to see his girl—well, he could be irrationally jealous.

Wendy and I had met at a Fae revel in Neverland, where we'd danced and kissed for a long time. Her mouth had been a delight. She was beautiful, strong—a warrior in her own right. I'd wanted her then, but she loved Peter, and I'd realized quickly she wasn't the one meant to break my curse. Since then, Wendy and I had fought side by side on many occasions, and we'd become friends.

When she came out of the house and her face lit up at the sight of me, I felt a surge of delight.

"Apollo!" She opened her arms for a hug. "I thought you were on Earth, taking a break."

"I was," I replied, embracing her. "My father summoned me for punishment."

"Oh." She pulled back, frowning. "Are you all right?"

"For now. But he has warned me against further defiance of his laws. His exact words were, 'No more trysts and treaties with Fae renegades.'"

"Shit." She winced. "Are you sure it's wise for you to be in Neverland right now, associating with us?"

"I can't stay more than a few minutes," I said. "I'm heading back to Earth, and I need something from you, if you're willing to give it."

"Anything," she said eagerly.

I couldn't resist teasing her a little. "Anything?" I asked, leaning closer.

"Except—well—certain things." Her cheeks pinked. "Watch yourself, okay? Peter gets jealous."

"I'm aware. All I need from you is a bit of luck. I met this woman on Earth, and I need to find her again."

Wendy's eyes widened. "You met someone?"

"Not like that. Her powers are blocked and she's in pain because of it. I just want to help her."

"Sure." Wendy gave me a wink. "That's the only reason."

I laughed, shaking my head. "Will you give me the luck or not?"

Her smile softened. "It's already done."

3

CASSANDRA

The weeks oozed past. I got a bad cold right before Christmas so I couldn't go to my sister's, and I was almost glad that I didn't have to fix my hair and dress nicely and pretend to be happy. Instead I stayed home and watched the "Die Hard" movies because I couldn't stomach any sappy holiday flicks. They pissed me off and made me nauseated with envy at the same time.

By this point I was living on unemployment and the dregs of my savings, dragging myself to the occasional job interview. There were precious few opportunities in my field, and I just couldn't bear the thought of going from teaching music to slapping greasy meat patties on starchy buns. Not that it was beneath me—I just thought it might kill my soul for real. Like I might give up and end things, if that was what I had to do to exist.

I'd had dark times before, even when I was a kid. The earliest one I could remember was around age four, right after—something I didn't like to think about, something I kept buried in the back of my mind. That was the year I'd had the first of the dreams. Nightmares, I suppose, except they felt different. Crisper, more colorful, and traumatic in a way that exploded sweat from every pore and left me shaking, crying, with my throat raw and the echo of my own screams in my ears.

Those dreams had their own taste, a special flavor—the flavor of death.

The nightmares could pop up anytime, but they were worse and more frequent during my depressive phases. After having one, I'd start frantically scrolling through local news feeds, or typing in keywords and scenarios from the dream. Within twenty-four hours I'd find some post or entry that described what I'd seen in the nightmare. A bus crashing into a ravine. A man dying from a brick that fell on his head. Someone walking at night and getting hit by a drunk driver.

Coincidence. It had to be.

Because the only other explanation—that I was some kind of prophetess who could see the future when she was depressed—was fucking ridiculous.

On New Year's Eve, I rolled off the couch and stumbled into the bathroom to stare at my limp brown hair and hollow eyes. I bundled my hair into a knot and scrubbed at the nacho cheese stains on my gray sweatshirt. Spritzed some perfume on the crotch of my leggings. Good enough.

Grabbing my keys and purse, I left the apartment to replenish my snack and drink stash. The hallway of my building smelled heavily of grease and stale cigarette smoke. The carpet was so thin in places I could see the concrete floors underneath.

In the lobby, I checked my mailbox and stuffed the few pieces of junk mail into my purse before shoving the glass front door open.

The night was cold, suffused with misting rain. The streetlights looked like golden smears against the charcoal blackness.

I hated the shortness of winter days. Hated Daylight Savings Time. Hated how the overcast winter skies always made me feel like I was indoors even when I was outside—the way the clouds lowered so heavily, like the oppressive concrete ceilings in a parking garage. I wanted to soar up and punch through them, a star blazing up and up into the clear brightness beyond. Somewhere, in some beautiful tropical place, the damn sun had to be shining.

I shuffled along the gleaming wet sidewalk, eyeing scraps of soggy paper and aluminum cans rolling gently in the chill breath of the night. A slow, eerie melody unfurled in my mind—pulsing bass notes paired with thin, haunting strings. A flute, maybe, ethereal and distant. A cello for dimension.

A flicker of joy in my heart, swelling, glowing.

I could hear entire bars of the song, all the layers of orchestration. My pulse picked up, and my head lifted. I almost walked right past the gas station, but the aggressive growl of somebody's truck grabbed my attention. Sighing, I crossed the parking lot, heading for the white blaze of the gas station doors.

A yellow BMW zoomed out of the mist, so close to me that I shrieked. "Watch it, asshole!" I screamed.

The car swerved up next to a gas pump. I stalked into the store and began angrily rummaging through their selection of chips.

Idiot freaks with fancy cars. Self-absorbed morons.

"I'm sorry I scared you out there," said a male voice behind me. "Please let me make it up to you."

Goosebumps stippled my skin, and my stomach fizzed with dreadful anticipation as I turned slowly around.

It was Apollo, golden hair curling unbound over his shoulder. He looked like freaking Thor, if Thor wore a men's peacoat of black wool and sported eyebrow jewels and a nose stud.

His anxiety melted into a glorious sunshiny smile. "Cassandra. It's you."

"You almost ran me over, asshole," I said breathlessly.

"It worked," he said wonderingly. "You see, I couldn't find you, so I visited a friend and got a dose of good luck—and it worked. Here you are."

"Good luck?" I snorted. "You nearly killed me."

"But you're all right?" His large hands cupped my shoulders, and a shudder of agonized shock ran through me. No one had touched me in weeks. I shrank away, and he immediately dropped his hands.

"I'm fine." With shaking fingers I tucked a stringy bit of my hair behind my ear. "I just came in here for some food and some drink, so if you don't mind I'm gonna get that and go."

I hurried toward the coolers, intent on snagging anything alcoholic and fruity. Try as I might, I couldn't stomach the hard stuff. My alcohol needed plenty of added flavor and sweetness.

As I reached for the cool door, I saw the towering reflection of Apollo behind me. Following me, of course.

"I have a phone now," he said proudly. "A friend of mine, Jack—he helped me get one."

"Is he the one who gave you the good luck?"

"No, that was Wendy."

"You seem to have a lot of friends." Another reason to hate this guy. Friends were people who pretended to like you until your life circumstances changed and they couldn't relate to you anymore. When you made them uncomfortable, they eased cautiously backward out of your life.

"I've helped a lot of people," Apollo replied.

"Yeah? Good for you." I snatched a six-pack of margarita bottles and let the fridge slam. This was so much worse than our meeting at Carowinds. I looked twice as sickly now, and probably three times as gross. Clutching my chips and booze, I headed for the checkout counter.

"Let me give you my number." A note of real pleading entered Apollo's voice. "I haven't forgotten you since we shared that ride."

"Really? Because I haven't thought about you once." A lie, of course. I'd thought about him every day. He'd even featured prominently in a few personal fantasy moments. But self-pleasure would probably pale in comparison to how it would feel to have him actually touch me…

"Ma'am." The girl at the counter stared pointedly at me. "Are you ready to check out?"

"Um, yeah. Sorry." I handed over the items and plopped my purse on the counter so I could hunt through it for my ID, which wasn't in my wallet where it should be. Finally I unearthed it and handed it over.

As I did, Apollo reached past me and plucked my phone out of my purse.

"Hey!" I snapped. "Haven't you ever heard of boundaries, or personal space?"

He smirked at me, and my insides morphed into fluttery moths. Swallowing hard, I jammed my credit card into the chip reader. At least he wouldn't be able to get through the lock screen—

But when I glanced at him again, he was definitely doing something on my phone. His fingers seemed to glow briefly golden. My imagination, maybe.

"How'd you unlock my phone?" I asked.

The girl behind the counter eyed Apollo with a mixture of admiration and suspicion. "This guy bugging you? You want me to call someone?"

"No, thanks. He's harmless." At least I hoped he was. I grabbed my phone, my purse, and my bag of snacks.

I'd never felt so humiliated, angry, and weirdly excited in my life. I marched out into the parking lot, intent on getting away from golden Muscle-Man and his dramatic coat as quickly as possible.

His voice drifted through the cold haze. "Call me, Cassandra. Anytime. Whatever you need."

"I don't need anything from you," I threw back at him.

Several minutes later, I locked myself safely in my apartment again. I was still jittery about the weird encounter with Apollo—it felt like Fate, though I'd never really believed in such things. Was it really luck that we'd run into each other again, an hour and a half from where we'd met the first time? Or maybe he was stalking me, like the guys in crime TV shows. Maybe he'd put some kind of tracking or listening app on my phone.

But when I checked, the only new addition I found was his number.

Sighing, I opened my composition app and added the snatch of song I'd thought of earlier. Luckily it hadn't floated out of my brain yet.

I ate my chips, drank my drinks, and drowsed off on the couch with the TV still running—a habit of mine lately. Not unhealthy at all, drinking myself to sleep every night while binge-watching some dorky show.

In the darkness of sleep a dream unfolded itself, a window opening into a roaring inferno of crackling flame. It hissed and spat around me, gnawing ever closer. I smelled the acrid stench of melting plastic and scorched fabric, felt the searing heat on my skin. In the nightmare I lurched off my couch and raced into the hallway of my building, only to be confronted with a wall of flame and the screams of my dying neighbors. The fire clung to me, excruciating agony clawing up my legs, and I shrieked aloud.

I woke up screaming, sweating, shaking all over.

That dream had the taste of truth.

It was real, or it was going to be real. I clasped trembling fingers over my mouth, trying to crush the keening sob back into my lungs.

How much credence did I give to my own visions?

Did I believe them enough to act on them?

A dark memory surged up, choking me—I crushed it back down. *No no no—don't think about that one, don't let it surface.*

Struggling out of my blanket-and-pillow nest on the couch, I staggered to the door of my apartment. My fingers shook so badly I could barely undo the lock and the chain. I leaned out into the hallway, inhaling deeply, sniffing.

I couldn't smell any smoke beyond the usual noxious miasma of stale cigarettes.

Maybe I was imagining things. Maybe this was just a fluke, a regular nightmare—nothing predictive.

But was I willing to take that risk?

My gaze landed on the small red square at the end of the hall. The fire alarm.

I could pull it, and no one would know it was me. Sure, everyone's sleep would be disturbed, but they'd be alive if, by some chance, my dream had been prophetic.

Barefoot I padded along the disgusting carpet and hesitated, fingertips grazing the handle.

I couldn't linger out here. Someone might see me. I'd pull it and run back to my room.

One quick jerk. I felt the handle give.

I sprinted back to my apartment and closed the door.

And I waited.

Nothing happened. No annoying blare of the alarm through the hallways. Nothing.

The damn thing must be broken. Or it had never worked in the first place. I wouldn't put it past the owner of this piece-of-shit building to find a way around the usual maintenance and precautions.

I chewed my nails, aching with indecision. Whenever I'd read a news story that coincided with one of my dreams, the timing of the event had been within a couple hours of my nightmare, sometimes less.

How much time did I have? And should I even try to do anything? What if by trying to prevent something, I triggered the events that caused it?

Yeah, I'd been watching way too much sci-fi TV. I pressed my forehead to the cool painted surface of my apartment door.

Fine. I would call 911. And say what? That I'd had a nightmare about a fire and now I was afraid one might start in my building? That would go over real well.

I could go to a lower floor and see if a different fire alarm would work. Yes, that was the better option.

I shoved my feet into some boots, grabbed my purse, phone, and keys, and quietly closed my door. I didn't bother locking it—I'd be back in a few minutes.

Better not take the elevator, just in case. I descended the clanky metal stairway down three floors to the lobby. Just as I reached for the stairwell door, a roach the size of my palm skittered across the floor.

I squealed and flew back up a few steps, my heart jumping.

Sucking in frantic breaths, I stood there, dizzy with fear and with the haze of the drink. I hadn't slept it all off.

Time to face facts. I'd been deeply depressed for months. I'd lost my boyfriend and my job, as well all the friends who were connected to my boyfriend and my job. My dad had left years ago, my sister was in another city, busy with her own life, and my mom lived a few states away—not that she'd be much support even if she lived closer.

To top it all off, I was inching closer to the alcoholism slope. No wonder I was having bad dreams. No wonder I was waking up in a panic, inventing dramatic scenarios where I was the hero. Maybe I was becoming my mother—craving tragedy, creating it for myself.

I should go back to my room and sleep.

Drawing in a deep breath, I turned to ascend the stairs.

A shrill alarm pierced the silence of the building—a pulsing, blaring, buzzing sound. Impossible to ignore.

Maybe the alarm I'd pulled had finally kicked in, a few minutes late?

No, that didn't make sense—

Which meant that somewhere in this building, a smoke alarm had been triggered. By an actual fire.

My brain blazed with the images from my dream. People trapped, screaming. Flames licking my skin—

Get out get out get out.

It wasn't my job to save anyone else. The alarm was loud enough to wake the dead.

I scrambled for the stairwell door and threw it open—raced to the front doors of the apartment building—dashed out into the snapping cold.

I hadn't brought a coat. No time to go back for one.

With a quick glance both ways, I crossed the street and stood in front of the Bojangles, staring up at my building. Orange light glowed and jumped inside three windows—no, *four* windows—oh god. I clamped a hand over my mouth and pulled out my phone to call 911.

Hours later, the firefighters were still trying to quell the inferno that had once been my building. The blaze had leaped through that rickety building like a rabbit through brambles, and saving the structure was pretty much hopeless at this point. I sat with a blanket around me, on a curb near one of the ambulances.

A paramedic approached me. "You should find somewhere to stay," she said kindly. "We've got your information—we'll let you know when and if it's safe to re-enter the building. Though from what I'm seeing, that could be a while, if at all."

"Did anyone die?" I asked hoarsely.

Her eyes told me the truth. *Yes.* But she only said, "We don't know anything for sure yet. But you should get out of the cold, away from the smoke. There's nothing more you can do right now. Is there someone you can call?"

"Um, sure. I'll call someone."

She nodded and moved on.

My brain could barely form coherent thoughts. Everything I owned was either burned or irreparably damaged by water and smoke. My sister lived four hours away in Raleigh, and if I remembered correctly she was on call this weekend anyway. I could drive to Raleigh, but my car was in the lot at the back of the apartment building, parked way too close to the inferno for me to access it. And I couldn't afford hiring a car to drive me four hours away. I needed to stay in town until I found out whether I'd be able to salvage anything from home.

A motel was a possibility. But my bank balance was dangerously low, at least until my next unemployment check.

I pulled out my phone, planning to skim through numbers until I found someone I could possibly ask for a favor. My contact list was full of people I hadn't spoken to in ages. Some of them had moved out of town— others were Ajax's friends, with no real connection to me.

Ajax's name was at the top of the list. Right above Apollo's.

I shifted my thumb, moving up and down between the two men's names.

Ajax, who had been wonderful until he decided he didn't want a girlfriend with mental health issues. *Too moody*, he'd said. *A real drag sometimes. You just bring me down, Cass, and I like to stay positive.*

And then there was Apollo.

I like the way you scream.

I've helped a lot of people.

I haven't forgotten you since we shared that ride.

Call me, Cassandra. Anytime. Whatever you need.

I tapped Apollo's name and called the number before I could persuade myself otherwise.

He answered after two rings. "Cassandra?" His voice was raspier than before, deep and throaty from sleep. It was the best sound I'd ever heard.

"I'm so sorry to call you like this. I don't even know why I'm calling, or where you live, or—oh hell, this was a bad idea—"

"Cassandra. I'm thrilled that you called. How can I help?"

"My apartment building—" A rumbling crash seized my attention, and I turned around just in time to see the top floors of my building collapse on each other. I released a short, harsh sob. "Yeah, it burned down. I can't get to my car, and I just need a ride to a motel, if you—I'm so sorry, I shouldn't have called you—"

"I'm coming to get you."

"I haven't even told you where I am…"

But he'd already ended the call.

The first responders made everyone move farther from the collapsed building. I found a new spot and huddled in my borrowed blanket, grateful that I had my purse, keys, and phone—though the keys wouldn't be much use with my apartment gone and my car probably demolished by falling debris. I held back my tears, though, because there were people wailing and sobbing near me—people whose loved ones hadn't made it out.

Was that my fault? Maybe if I'd moved faster, gone downstairs sooner and pulled the alarm on the first floor—

A screech of tires, and I looked up to see a yellow BMW jerking to a stop at the curb. Apollo leaped out, in short sleeves despite the cold. His bronze skin seemed to absorb and reflect the glow of the nearby streetlamp. In the frigid dark, he was a torch, a beacon of warmth and grace, and the anguished voices of my neighbors quieted a little as he approached. The golden beauty of him stopped my breath for a minute.

"Cassandra." He crouched, taking my chin and tipping my face up, inspecting my features. "Are you all right?"

"I'm fine. I got out." My guilt stuck in my throat and cut off my words.

Apollo took my hands and lifted me. The blanket slid off my shoulders, and he caught it and tossed it to a nearby family with a cluster of kids. Gently he ushered me toward the car, darting around me to open the door.

I slid in awkwardly, raking my purse off my shoulder and settling it in my lap. "How did you know where to find me?"

"I knew you must live somewhere near the gas station where we met. Within walking distance. And when I'm close enough, I can feel you."

"You can—feel me?"

He smiled, quick and bright, and closed the car door.

For a second, I seriously considered jumping right back out of the car. Why was I going somewhere with a complete stranger who said he could *feel* me when I was nearby?

But as strange and off-putting as the statement was, it was oddly comforting too. Apollo was the first person I'd met who talked openly about something that wasn't exactly rational. Maybe he believed in things that were a bit esoteric and inexplicable, like mysterious prophetic dreams.

Maybe he knew something I didn't. Maybe he could help me answer a few questions.

He hopped into the driver's seat. "I've studied the rules of the road for this area," he said. "And I've driven many different kinds of vehicles before, in many places—but if you see that I'm breaking the law of your land, let me know."

"Um, okay?" I stared at him. "You have a driver's license, right?"

"I got one a few days ago!" Eagerly he tugged a wallet from his pants and showed me the ID.

"Apollo Sol, huh? Age twenty-nine…" I peered at the card suspiciously, but it looked real. "Right, well… I just need a ride to a motel."

"Motel? That's like an inn—a place to stay?"

"Yep." Was he drunk? Foreign? Born in a bunker?

"I have a place to stay," he said, pressing the gas so firmly the car shot forward with a startling jerk. No wonder he'd almost run me over the other night. "You can come home with me."

And I was too stunned to refuse.

Apollo lived downtown, because of course he did. He seemed like the kind of man who had always had money, accepted it as normal, owned it carelessly and innocently. He parked in the garage behind the condo building and led me inside. He didn't take my hand, but I felt guided and encircled somehow as he beeped us in through the security doors into a lobby so elegant I felt like a grubby worm in a glimmering ballroom. My breath probably stank from sleep and alcohol, and I wore the same stained, ratty outfit I'd been wearing when I saw him at the gas station. I could smell the bitter smoke on my clothes and in my hair.

Clutching my purse, I stepped into the elevator and scrunched into the corner, as far from Apollo as I could get. Damn whoever decided to line this elevator with brassy mirrors. They reflected Apollo's rangy, long-limbed figure, his mane of golden hair, and his perfectly-cut profile about a dozen times, at a dozen slightly different angles. And they reflected me too—a shadowy scrap of tangled brown hair and pale skin and furtive dark eyes.

"I'm glad you called," Apollo said.

"I shouldn't have. I don't even know you—it's weird."

"Why?" He said it so gently I had to look up, to meet those honey-brown eyes of his. They were pools of compassion, affection, and honest delight. When I couldn't read anything creepy or lustful in them, my shoulders relaxed and lowered a little.

He kept speaking, quiet and slow, like someone might coax a scared animal. "People call me for help often. I'm a protector by nature, you see. I like to defend those who can't help themselves."

"That gets you off?" I say with a short laugh. "Feeling tough and powerful?"

His eyebrows, surprisingly dark compared to his hair, pulled together. "Gets me off?"

"Um—" Had he never heard that expression?

"Never mind."

The elevator doors opened and Apollo led me down a short hallway, where he opened another door. "This place is new," he said apologetically. "I rented it yesterday, already furnished. It's not exactly to my taste, but it's sufficient."

I stepped in, my jaw dropping as lights flicked on automatically. The place looked like something out of a magazine—a wall of windows with a view of the nighttime city, crisp modern furnishings, and abstract paintings that were unexpectedly soothing in their composition and colors.

"You just came to town yesterday?" I asked. I wanted to touch the creamy upholstery of the sofa, but my fingers felt too grimy to risk it.

Apollo shifted his weight and cleared his throat. "I've been looking for you, you see."

I turned around, my skin tightening with panic. "I think I should go."

"Not stalking you," he said quickly. "Well—maybe a little. But only because I thought we connected that day, and I couldn't stand the idea of never seeing you again. I was called away for a while by my father, but as soon as I could leave, I began searching for you."

"With the good luck from your friend?" I let out a tiny hysterical laugh.

"Yes. And with assistance from my friend Jack, who helped me get a phone and showed me how to look for someone on the internet. I couldn't find your address, but I managed to learn which city you lived in."

"You didn't know how to look up someone on the internet?" I crooked an eyebrow, trying to figure out if I could sneak past him and dart out the door. "Where have you been living, a survivalist bunker? Some kind of Amish settlement? Or—or prison?"

He grinned, a beam of white teeth. "I'd like to see the prison that could hold me."

"This was a mistake." My voice shook a little. "Please let me leave."

"Of course." He stepped aside, leaving the exit open to me. "But you're tired, and you have little money. Wouldn't you like to take a shower, at least? I'm leaving now, so you'll have the place to yourself."

Okay, that wasn't what I expected. "You're leaving?"

"What kind of person would I be if I didn't offer assistance to those displaced by the fire? I'm going back there to help as much as I can. I just need some of your currency first. Excuse me while I get that—and feel free to leave if you like."

He walked into another room.

I could leave right now. I could walk out that door and pay for a taxi to some cheap motel. That would be the smart, safe thing to do.

Or I could stay in this beautiful loft a little longer, and enjoy a nice hot shower, and find out why this man was so fascinated with me.

Apollo came back, flipping through a wad of cash that looked like all hundreds. My knees went weak.

"Are you going to murder me?" I asked. "Or tie me up and keep me prisoner? Or—assault me?"

He glanced at me. "Why would I do any of that?"

"That's what stalkers and serial killers do."

"Is it?" His mouth tilted up. "Well, murdering you would be an unforgivable waste. I don't kill women unless they're trying to kill me or my friends. And when I want sex, I can get it. I don't need to force anyone to be with me." He jammed the cash into the back pocket of his jeans. "As for making you my prisoner, I despise anyone who keeps another living thing in a cage."

"You could be lying."

"I don't lie."

"Everyone lies. Even if they don't mean to."

"Very astute. I'll be back soon. If you want to stay, the bathroom is through there." He pointed to the darkened doorway he'd just exited. "You should be able to find everything you need. Make yourself comfortable. What's mine is yours."

He left, and I stood frozen as the door shut behind him.

What's mine is yours.

During the brief time Ajax and I had lived together, he'd been careful to maintain the delineation between our possessions, even down to labeling the food in the fridge. "To avoid conflict," he'd said. And then, when we'd broken up, he'd kept the apartment, because I'd been foolish enough to let him put his name on the lease, even though I had paid the bigger share of the rent each month. And I'd had to move into the shabby hole I'd just lost.

I had nothing left now. Truly nothing, except the clothes I wore and the purse I still clutched in my hands. To have someone like Apollo tell me graciously and sincerely that what he owned was mine to use—well. I could feel the tears coming, and I knew this was going to be a big, messy cry. So I hurried through the bedroom into the bathroom, locked the door, and stripped off my grubby clothes.

I hustled into the shower, sat down on the glossy tiles under the blessed heat flooding from the rainfall shower head, and let myself break down.

For several long minutes I sobbed, until my stomach heaved so hard I thought I might vomit or crack a rib. Finally I pulled myself together and washed up. There was already soap and shampoo in there—lavender-and-honey-scented, just like Apollo. No razor, but I could deal with that tomorrow.

What was more pressing was my utter lack of spare clothes. Thankfully Apollo's bathroom towels were the deluxe extra-huge kind, so I wrapped myself in one and padded into the bedroom.

What's mine is yours.

Maybe I could find something to wear among his clothes. I'd promise to wash it later.

Apollo's wardrobe consisted mainly of white dress shirts, white T-shirts, jeans, and dark slacks. No fun graphic tees, no baggy sweatshirts, no stretchy pants. All of it looked brand-new. There were some fantastical-looking robes and stuff in his closet—costumes like you might see elves wear on the set of the Lord of the Rings. I hadn't pegged Apollo as the LARP-ing type, and my heart sank a little. Stalkerish and a cosplayer? Those were definitely warning signs.

But he had other things in his closet, too—three hard black cases. One looked like it might hold a lute or something of that shape. There was a guitar case too, and a flute case. A tall box at the back appeared to hold a keyboard of some kind.

The man loved music. A mark in his favor.

I didn't want to crease his fine dress shirts, so finally I pulled a white T-shirt over my head. It was the extra-tall kind, and huge to fit those big shoulders of his, so it draped long enough to conceal my lady parts, just barely. I hadn't been wearing a bra when I left my apartment, so that wasn't an option now. I grabbed a pair of Apollo's black boxers and pulled them on.

My other clothes reeked of smoke, and honestly I couldn't imagine ever wearing them again. I'd always associate them with the events of this night. Once I located the trash can under the kitchen sink, I stuffed them into it.

So now I was kind of stuck in the loft, since I couldn't wander around town in a borrowed T-shirt and boxers. I sat down on the couch and held my purse to my chest, trying to make sense of it all.

I'd lost every damn thing. No matter how many times I said it to myself, it still hadn't quite registered that my possessions weren't still out there somewhere, intact and waiting for me.

I'd had some important papers stowed in a fireproof box, but with the state the building had been in when I left, I doubted anyone could find them in the rubble.

Everything *gone*. My plastic container of childhood mementos. My clothes. My laptop. My TV, my dishes, my sheets and towels, my makeup, my movies, my furniture. The Tiffany lamp I'd loved. The guitar I hadn't touched in months. The paintings I'd purchased from an artist at a local maker's fair.

I pulled out my phone to call my sister and saw that it was four in the morning. A new year had begun, and I hadn't even noticed.

Last year I'd lost my boyfriend, my job, and my love of music. I'd used up my savings, and my apartment building had burned down.

Rock bottom.

Things could only go up from there, right?

I couldn't reach Meg, and when I finally got through to Jessa, she told me Meg had been called in to the hospital. "Are you okay?" she said through a yawn after I explained about the fire. "Need me to come get you?"

I wanted to scream, *Hell no, I'm not okay, and you should already be in the car on your way here.*

But instead I said, "I'm fine. I'm staying at a friend's house, and I'll call my insurance company later today. Tell Meg not to worry."

"Okay. Well, let us know if you need anything. So sorry about your place."

"Yeah, me too. I'll let you get back to sleep."

I ended the call and tossed the phone to the opposite end of the couch.

Insurance. I should have paid better attention when I chose my policy. I had the sinking feeling it wasn't going to cover much of my apartment's contents. Not that they were worth much anyway.

My body craved the cushiony softness of the sofa, and I gave in, stretching out with my cheek nestled on a satiny pillow.

4
APOLLO

When I returned from giving human money to the survivors of the fire, Cassandra was lying on the couch in my loft, fast asleep with her wet hair trailing across the throw pillows. The swell of her breasts through my T-shirt, the pronounced arch of her hip, the sloping lines of her long legs—and above it all, the plump curves of her parted lips—the image struck my heart and body like a blast of magic, and I stood motionless for a handful of minutes, staring at her.

Since our first meeting, several weeks of Cassandra's time had passed. It hurt my heart that she'd been in distress for so long, thinking I'd rejected her that first day. At least now she knew I cared. I could make it up to her.

I should go back to bed and let her sleep.

First I took the silky blanket from the arm of a chair and draped it over her. This place had come fully furnished, including accessories to make it more comfortable. It didn't feel like home to me, but I was used to wandering the realms, and I'd slept in far worse places.

Withdrawing to the bedroom, I closed the door, stripped off my smoke-scented clothes, and flung myself onto the bed. Humans designed excellent beds, and this one was especially comfortable. But I couldn't get Cassandra out of my head—I kept seeing the heavy curve of her breast, the tiny gap of white teeth between her lips.

My balls ached, a pain that I'd lived with since my last renewal sleep, a hundred years ago. An agony from which I couldn't find relief, no matter how hard I tried.

During my last lifetime I'd made the mistake of sleeping with a vindictive Fae who didn't take our breakup well. She accused me of using her to learn Fae magic—and perhaps she was right, though I'd made it clear from the beginning that my primary reason for being in Faerie was to learn Fae spellwork. Incensed, she'd banded together with her sisters, and by their joint power they'd managed to lay a geas on me—a curse preventing me from achieving sexual satisfaction or relief until the end of this renewal cycle—or until I met the woman with whom I'd spend the rest of my existence.

It was excruciating to feel all the same physical urges without ever being able to achieve a climax. The Fae who cursed me had told me about the geas when I woke from my renewal sleep, but I'd been in denial at first. I'd rutted into a beautiful nymph for three hours before I finally admitted that the geas was real. The nymph didn't mind—she came about five dozen times while I desperately chased the peak I couldn't reach. Something about the heat and intensity of my body tended to help women climax quickly and repeatedly. I could still accomplish that, at least, and I derived a milder kind of satisfaction by giving pleasure even when I couldn't have it myself.

I'd resigned myself to half a millennium without sexual pleasure—a torturous sentence for an Olympian. Our sexual drive was unusually powerful, and once we fixated on an object of desire, it was practically impossible to resist coupling with that person. The urge had resulted in many of the gods doing ridiculous and wicked things in the name of love. I'd been guilty of a few myself, in an early lifetime. But with each renewal came the softening of those ancient memories. I was a different person now, or so I told myself.

Since my last waking, I'd learned to focus on other things—specifically, aiding the helpless and downtrodden of every realm. I'd also managed to keep my inability to climax more or less a secret, feigning orgasm whenever I spent time with someone.

And then one of the Fates had told me my eternal mate would be from Earth, and that she'd have unique powers.

When I met Wendy, before I knew her name and her connection to Peter, I thought she might be the one to set me free. Of course she wasn't. And now, with Cassandra's life intertwining with mine—it felt like Fate. But I dared not hope for release from her—not yet. Seducing her at this vulnerable time would be cruel and wicked, something I used to be—something I'd vowed never to be again.

I writhed against the silken sheets, painfully hard, fighting the urge to stroke myself. That would only make things worse.

When I was in this tortured state, playing music was a blessed relief. I lunged off the bed and pulled on one of the undergarments humans called boxers. Then I opened the closet, seizing the case that held my lute. Other than a few clothes, a stash of Earth currency, and some personal items, the lute was the only thing I'd brought to Earth with me. I'd made a quick stop at Jack Frost's to arrange for identification documents, a phone, and something called a credit card. He and his life-mate Emery had been eager to help me out—as eternal frost Fae, they were well-versed in identity fraud. I'd played all my favorite melodies for their children while I waited for my "identity kit," as Jack called it. Emery had snapped photos of me for the driver's license and passport.

"Is it possible for you to take a bad photo?" she'd asked afterward, staring at the images.

"We could try," I told her, grinning. Then followed a photo session in which I had let Jack and Emery's children pull my face into various awkward shapes while Emery snapped pictures and laughed helplessly at all of us.

I smiled at the memory and tucked the lute into my lap, wincing as it grazed my erection. Gritting my teeth, I began to play. And I loosened the veils I'd laid over my glory, letting myself glow brighter, relishing that slight release, that minor indulgence.

I played the softest melodies I could think of, not wanting to wake Cassandra. I wove long rippling lines of notes, letting them soothe and sate me. Certain songs of mine had power, especially when I used this particular lute, made by the Muses. I could put someone to sleep, or inspire them to bravery and heroism. I could soften their anxiety and ease their pain. If I wanted to, I could even send myself to sleep with the music, thank the Fates.

My eyes closed, and I sank deep into the song.

5

CASSANDRA

I dreamed of music, delicate and winsome, crisp and wild. I dreamed of a man with golden skin and eyes of clear sunlight.

When I woke, I was so comfy I didn't want to move, so I stayed perfectly still, embraced by pillowy softness. The room I was in smelled unfamiliar— lavender and honey and vanilla.

A sound slithered into my consciousness—the pattering of rain, with the occasional *ting* of drops against metal. My eyelashes fluttered open.

Beyond the wall of windows, rain streamed from the lip of an overhang. We must be at the top of the building if I could hear the drops on the roof.

I hadn't heard rainfall in so long. I hadn't even realized I missed it.

In my mind a soft song began to form—rippling piano notes with an undercurrent of whispering strings. I fought the urge to look for my phone so I could write the music down. But the melody kept unfurling, so finally I lunged for my purse on the coffee table and extracted my phone. I noted down the delicate melodies and breathed a sigh of relief once I'd recorded them. I could go back to the song later, polish it, and finish it.

Released from the compulsion of the muse, I relaxed again.

The room in which I lay was softly gloomy—not depressing, somehow—just a cool gray ambiance that soothed my mind. In this elegant space, with the susurration of the rain beyond the windows, I could barely bring myself to worry about anything.

But I couldn't stay here, in a stranger's loft, when my life was in such a shambles. I had to begin putting it back together.

Tomorrow, murmured my body and mind. *Put it back together tomorrow.*

Either way, I needed to pee.

When I moved to sit up, a silky blanket slid from my shoulder. I definitely hadn't pulled it over myself, which meant Apollo was back, and he'd covered me up.

I sat upright and glanced at his bedroom door. Closed. I wasn't sure there was another bathroom. Pressing my feet to the cool hardwood of the floor, I padded along the edges of the space and determined that no, there wasn't another bathroom. I'd have to go through Apollo's bedroom. Maybe I could sneak through without waking him up.

Or maybe he was already awake. Vivid yellow light shone through the crack under the door.

Gingerly I tapped on the door.

When he didn't answer, I eased it open. "Apollo?" I said softly.

And then I froze.

He lay sprawled on the bed, on his stomach, with his head turned aside and his golden hair scattered. His long fingers were draped over the neck of a beautiful polished lute that lay beside him.

The sight of his magnificent bare back would have been enough to paralyze me. But he wasn't just a gorgeous, nearly-naked man. He was *glowing.*

Not "I-just-visited-the-tanning-beds" or "I-just-came-back-from-the-Bahamas glowing." Not "I-surfed-all-summer-and-got-this-rad-tan" glowing.

Actually *glowing.* With an inner light that shone through every cell of his skin, infusing the very air of the room with glimmering beauty. As if he was made of molten gold saturated with sunlight.

I should have been frightened. But my heart gave a great, triumphant leap.

Not a stalker, then—not exactly. Someone like me. Someone different in a way that couldn't be logically explained.

Someone who might be able to explain *me* to myself.

Either that, or he'd been dosed with lethal amounts of radiation and we were both going to die.

But no—there could be nothing healthier than this glow. I felt drawn to it, to him. I had the urge to bask in his radiance—like the craving for spring sunshine on my face after a long, bleak winter.

I slipped into the bathroom and used it quietly. When he didn't wake to the sound of the flushing toilet and the running water, I approached cautiously and sat on the edge of the bed.

Apollo. Glowing like the sun. The mythical connection was fairly obvious, and I didn't waste time debating the improbability of Greek gods being real—

because somewhere deep down in my musical, moody, esoteric soul, I'd always wanted them to be real. I'd always believed in something beyond—in the spirit of music, or magic. I'd always wondered about the concept of "the muse" and its origins. Add to that my scary propensity for dreaming about events before they happened, and yeah—I was primed for something like this.

Sure, there was a second where I started to panic, where I felt like maybe I should curl in on myself and start hyperventilating, freaking the fuck out.

But after the literal garbage fire that was last year—I could use a miraculous man in my life.

Apollo muttered something in his sleep and rolled over. Eyes still closed, he swept a hand over his face and moaned quietly. A thrill flooded my chest and stomach. My hands trembled. We were about to have a very weird conversation.

Apollo's dark lashes blinked, unveiling his amber eyes—and if I hadn't been convinced before, the sight of those luminous eyes would have sold me on his being the sun god. They swirled with yellow light, like stars trapped in transparent orbs.

He turned those eyes toward me. And his handsome features went taut with horrified realization. "Shit," he said quietly. Even as he said it, his light dimmed until he looked normal again.

But there was no unseeing what I'd witnessed.

"Shit is right," I said. "Who are you?"

"Apollo."

"The sun god Apollo."

"Yes." He sat up, every muscle of his stomach flexing as he moved. When he dragged his fingers through his wavy hair, his bicep swelled tight. *Hot damn* he was beautiful.

"Why are you here? Do all the gods still hang around incognito among humans?"

"I'm on vacation. Usually I live in the Olympian realm, with the others."

"Realm." I closed my eyes for a second, trying to acclimate to the concept. "So there's a *realm*, another world besides Earth."

"Many realms, actually."

"Oh my god—no. Just, *no*. I can only handle so much at once, okay? And I think I'm managing the 'sun god' idea really well, so let's wait on the other stuff."

He smiled. "But you look more excited than scared. Happier than I've seen you since the Afterburn."

Impossibly, illogically, I found myself smiling back at him. I couldn't stop it.

Embarrassed, I jumped off the bed. "I shouldn't be smiling. Not after everything that's happened. Not after discovering that you're not just some hot human stalker, but a literal *god*."

"We call ourselves *gods*, but we're merely immortals with good looks and power to spare," he said.

"Sounds godlike to me." I turned to face him again, clamping both hands along the edge of the dresser behind me. "So—what do you want from me? And don't say sex, because there are girls way hotter than me. I'm pretty sure I'm not your type."

"You don't know my type," he said, low. "Or anything about me. What I want is to help you. That's it."

I narrowed my eyes at him. "In exchange for what?"

"Whatever you care to give. Friendship—conversation—information about your world."

"So you want to help me get back on my feet after the fire, and in return I chat with you and answer your questions about my world? Don't you have friends for that? What about the guy Jack who got you your phone?"

"He lives far away, and he's busy. And frankly, Cassandra, you're the one who needs me. You've been sorrowful for a long time, yes?"

Sorrowful. The word sank into my soul and resonated, deep and true.

Sorrowful.

"I'm not sure why," I murmured. "I mean, I went through a breakup and lost my job, but other people go through that stuff too without getting this low. I don't know what's wrong with me. And I don't think it's something you can fix."

"Nothing is wrong with you," he said. "I may be able to give you some relief, but you might never be as light-hearted and carefree as other humans. That is your burden, and your gift. The truest music is birthed from the clarity of despair."

"Why can't it be birthed from the giddiest neverending happiness?"

Apollo grinned. "Sometimes it can."

"And how exactly do you think you can help me? By your very presence? Do you exude vitamin D or something?"

"Maybe. I am rather wonderful." His grin broadened briefly, and then he sobered again. "Before I can help you, though, I need to know what your power is. I can usually get a general sense of a human's godly ancestry and identify their power, but with you, I'm not sure. Your aura has been twisted, tangled, suppressed. Pushed down." He stared into my eyes, as if he was trying to read me.

My palms turned clammy. "I don't have special powers," I whispered.

"You need to admit it, Cassandra," he said gently. "That's the first step, realizing that you're different from other humans. Have you noticed any unique tendencies or abilities? Anything about yourself that surprises or frightens you?"

I gripped the dresser harder, aching for physical contact—a hand on my shoulder, a hug. No one had hugged me in so long.

Apollo rose from the bed, sympathy pooling in his beautiful eyes as he drifted toward me. He reached out, grazing my arm lightly with his fingertips.

But he was too pretty, too regal, too strange—I shrank away.

With a resigned nod, he dropped his hand. "Come into the kitchen. I'll make you some tea. I know how to use the microwave." He said the last sentence with a faint kind of pride, and I couldn't help a tiny smile.

"You say that like it's a big achievement," I said, following him out to the big room. I perched on a stool while he took a white porcelain mug from a hook and began filling it with water. "You know, some people think microwaves kill your brain cells, or cause sterility."

"Sterility?" He snorted. "Not likely. Olympians are notoriously virile, and we can heal from almost anything."

"Must be nice." I examined my ragged fingernails. "So...do you have a Mrs. Apollo? Kids?"

Apollo set the mug in the microwave and started the timer. With his butt propped against the counter, he crossed his sinewy golden arms and eyed me. I swallowed, self-consciously tucking a strand of hair behind my ear. Why couldn't he look a bit less like a cover model?

"I've had lovers and children, in past lifetimes," he said. "All my progeny have passed to the afterlife, along with most of my ex-lovers."

My heart cinched tight as I imagined so much loss. "I'm so sorry. That must be painful."

"Sometimes it saddens me," he said. "But it isn't as painful as you might think. Every five hundred years or so an Olympian enters a renewal sleep, where their body and personality are reset. Memories aren't erased, but they're blurred, and the emotions associated with them are softened. It's like waking up as a new person."

He took the mug of hot water out of the microwave and handed me a small woven basket filled with tea packets. "Pick your poison."

"Ooh, blackberry acai." I snatched the packet out. "This one."

Apollo opened the packet and dunked the tea bag in the hot water. Then he set a saucer over the top. "And now we wait." He leaned on the edge of the counter again, watching me.

"You're staring," I said.

"Yes."

"That's not polite, you know."

He tilted his golden head, and his lips curved. "Maybe I don't care. You fascinate me, Cassandra."

"Stop saying my name like that." I slid off the stool and walked to the big windows to watch veils of glimmering gray rain sluice off the lip of the balcony overhang. The sight and sound calmed my jittery nerves—until I felt the warmth of the approaching sun god behind me.

"How do you want me to say your name?" Even his damn voice was golden—and a Harry Styles song started unfurling through my mind, a luscious melody curling around the word. *Golden.*

"How bright can you get?" I asked, sidestepping his question.

"Dangerously bright."

"Like, you could kill me with your sheer radiance?"

"Yes."

I whirled, scanning his face. He wasn't kidding. "God. Wow. Okay. Maybe I should find a motel."

"You're not really afraid of me." He shifted a step nearer, and my gaze dropped to the bronze slopes of his stomach.

"Yes, I am," I whispered. "Don't you own a shirt? Or—pants?"

"Don't you own a bra?"

I sucked in a breath, suddenly conscious of how tight and full my breasts felt, pebbled against the soft shirt—and how the space between my legs had warmed, buzzing faintly with a sensation I hadn't planned for and didn't want. Apollo hadn't done anything but exist, make me tea, and talk to me, and here I was starting to melt for him.

"You know I lost everything," I said. "Including my underwear."

"Then I have only one question." He leaned closer, bracing a palm on the window glass, half-caging me against it. Yet I didn't feel trapped. I could slip out easily, but I didn't. I stayed, with Apollo's powerful tanned body arched over mine, and his yellow hair nearly brushing my cheek.

"What's your question?" I breathed. Pretty sure I'd say yes to anything he asked me…

"Do you like shopping?"

6

APOLLO

Cassandra stared at me. "Do I like shopping? What kind of question is that? You know I don't have any money, either."

"But I do. An endless supply, more than I know what to do with. It would be a privilege to give you some."

"Um…" She hesitated, pinching her lower lip between her teeth. My body yearned toward her, trembled with the desire to close the distance between us, and it was all I could do not to yield to the impulse. I wanted to catch her up in my arms, carry her to the bed, soothe every delicate secret space with my tongue, cherish every curve of her flesh with my fingertips. I wanted to coax her to tremulous ecstasy, tease her over the edge, watch her thrill and arch and gasp. I wanted to ease her down from the height with my kisses, and then start all over again.

"Your neighbors seemed eager enough to accept my charity," I said.

Her eyebrows lifted. "That's why you went back? To give them money?"

"I figured it might soften the blow for some of them."

"Not the ones who lost people."

"You'd be surprised." I winced, dropping my hand from the window and leaning back. "Humans say that money cannot buy happiness—but not having to worry about finances during a time of sorrow can certainly ease the healing process."

"How much did you give them?" She frowned. "I mean—never mind, it's not my place to ask."

I named the human sum I had delivered to each household, and Cassandra's eyes flared wide. "Oh my god. Yeah, that would definitely help ease the process."

"I'll give you the same. You can spend it on anything you like." I walked back to the island and removed the saucer from her tea. "Milk and sugar?"

But Cassandra stood paralyzed by the window, her cheeks flushed pink and her eyes bright. I couldn't look at her too long—the way the soft material clung to her luscious curves—Zeus's balls—my dick lifted, hardening, and I was glad of the bulk of the kitchen island between me and the girl. Forget her body—that face of hers was exquisite, whether it was softly sad or vibrantly excited. And she *was* excited at the prospect of money and shopping. She tried to hide it, probably because of some human social obstacle to her accepting money from me—but she didn't succeed.

"Are you trying to be my sugar daddy?" she asked.

My brow furrowed. "Sugar daddy? You want sugar in the tea?"

"A sugar daddy is someone who spoils a woman with gifts in exchange for sexual favors."

"I believe we've had this conversation. I don't need to pay for sexual favors."

"Right, because you're sex incarnate," she said faintly. "God, I said that out loud, didn't I?"

I shrugged. "Don't be embarrassed. I get that reaction from most mortal women—and many men, too. And no, this is not about buying favors. It's only fair that as another survivor of the fire, I give you the same amount I gave the others."

"Only fair," Cassandra echoed. "Um—well, I haven't been shopping for fun in a long time, but—yeah, I'm game. But I can't go like this." She indicated the clothes of mine she was wearing.

"I'll get you something to wear." My arousal had calmed a little, so I carried the mug to her. "Drink this. I'll get dressed and buy you some clothes for the day."

When I came out of my room after getting dressed, Cassandra was snuggled on the sofa, sipping her tea and watching a concert on TV. The music was of the genre humans called "classical," but with a rhythmic, raw edge and a heart-stirring vitality to the performance that drew me in. Entranced, I stood behind the sofa for a few minutes.

"I was in a couple musicals in high school and college," said Cassandra. "And I was in a band for a while, too."

"What did you play?"

"Keyboard. And I sang. People said I had a beautiful voice."

"Did you enjoy it? Performing?"

"I loved it. You'd think my anxiety would be worse with performing, right? But weirdly, no. I mean, sure, I got nervous sometimes, but the experience was awesome."

"You should do it again."

"Ha." She snorted. "No."

"Why not?"

"My depression is worse now, and if I'm not at my best, I might bring everybody down," she murmured. "I could ruin the performance."

"That's a load of shit."

She looked up at me. "You know, you're too golden and good and beautiful to say words like that."

I leaned down. "Words like 'shit'?"

She watched my mouth, her own lips parting. "I mean, you look like an angel, so hearing you curse is… well…"

"Exciting?" I smiled. "What else am I too pretty to say?"

Cassandra shrank down, still watching me, and sipped more tea. Her lashes blinked at me over the rim of the cup.

"Fuck," I said softly, holding her gaze.

"Go away," she whispered. But her mouth twitched up at the corner.

"I'm gone." I pushed myself upright again. "And when I come back, you'll teach me all the foul human words you know. And I'll teach you some in the language of the Fae."

"The Fae?" she gasped. "What the hell?"

But I didn't answer. I just left, smiling, and I smiled like an idiot while I chose a few clothes for her at a nearby shop. I was a fair judge of the female form, but just to be safe, I bought three different sizes of each clothing piece. Too much, probably.

When I returned, Cassandra was still on the sofa, but instead of watching the TV, she was staring disconsolately at her phone. "I took care of some insurance stuff while you were gone. Basically my coverage sucks. I won't get much for my stuff or my car."

"Um…" I frowned, shifting the bags in my arms.

"And you don't even know what insurance is, do you?"

"No."

"Never mind. The money you mentioned will help me get a fresh start—if you're still offering?"

"Of course." I tumbled the bags onto the sofa beside her, and she began eagerly pawing through them. "But I'll want something in exchange."

Her features shifted, hardened into desperate resignation. "Something more than conversation and information about my world?"

"Nothing salacious." I seated myself on the end of the sofa. "I want you to tell me about your gift. I haven't forgotten our unfinished conversation."

"Fine." She sighed, running her fingertips over the sweater dress I'd chosen for her. "I have dreams."

"Dreams?"

"Nightmares. They show me things that are going to happen. Like last night—I saw the fire before it started. I was going to warn everybody, but I wasn't sure if I—if it was—" She clutched the sweater tightly. "I've told a few people about my dreams over the years, and no one ever believes me. They think the bad things that happen are just a coincidence, or that I'm trying to get attention and make myself look special."

"Get attention? Who said that to you?"

"My ex-boyfriend, Ajax."

"He sounds like a dick." I clasped my hands together, forcing my glow back down as it resurfaced, rage-fueled.

To many people, including Cassandra, I came across as the good god—the calm, golden, angelic god—and I tried to make it true, to live up to my reputation—but I had rivers under the surface, rivers of molten unrest and unfocused anger. Well, perhaps it did have a focal point—my all-powerful father. And now some of it shifted to Cassandra's ex-boyfriend.

"I'm a lot to deal with, honestly." She tugged the sweater against her chest, like a shield over her heart. "He was right to leave me."

"What you're saying is he was too childish to handle an adult relationship, one with depth and complexity."

"I was *not* saying that, but I like your version better than mine." She gave me a small smile.

I live for those little smiles. The unbidden thought startled me, thrilled me. Frightened me.

I rose quickly. "You can change in my room. We'll do some shopping, anywhere you like, and then I'll contact a friend of mine. He's good with nightmares. He can help us figure out the source and meaning of yours."

Cassandra gathered an armful of clothes and stood up. "All I heard was 'Shopping, anywhere you like.'"

With her guidance, we headed to a place called "the outlets," a market filled with purveyors of all sorts of merchandise. I hadn't spent time on Earth in centuries, and once again I marveled at the misplaced ingenuity of this planet. Their efforts seemed to be entirely focused on making life easier for the wealthy, while driving the less fortunate mad with a constant ache for things they would never be able to afford. Apparently the merchants at "the outlets" offered bottomless wells of credit, represented by small colorful cards like the one Jack had given me—so I used the card rather than my wads of Earth money. But I donated extra paper currency to every merchant we encountered, and they all seemed excessively pleased with my generosity.

"You don't have to tip everyone so much, you know," said Cassandra as we left one shop.

"I like the joy on their faces."

"Where did you get all this cash, anyway?"

"I gave an inter-realm money-changer some of my Olympian gold, and she asked me which country on Earth I'd be visiting first. I wasn't sure, so she said if I wanted modern convenience and hedonism, the United States was the place to start. Then she gave me stacks of paper money. She deals in currencies of all kinds, from Wonderland chips to Valhallan ingars."

Cassandra stopped walking and gripped my arm. "You keep doing that. Casually throwing things like 'the Fae' and 'Wonderland' and 'inter-realm moneychanger' into casual conversation."

I lifted an eyebrow. "Yes?"

"So there are a whole bunch of realms? Storybook realms? And Faerieland?" Cassandra started walking again, faster this time.

"We just call it 'Faerie,' and I'm not sure about the term 'storybook.' But yes, there are countless realms in the universe. Earth is rather insular, but rumors of various realms have leaked into your culture over the centuries. My race used to visit here often and exert authority over humans, as you know. The Fae did as well—their influence predates the Olympian era. Most Fae who visit Earth now are Unseelies, popping in to capture humans for nefarious purposes. And my people occasionally take human slaves from Earth or other realms."

I glanced at Cassandra again. Her face was paler than ever.

"I've told you too much," I said apologetically.

"Do you have human slaves?" she asked, low.

"No. My servants are happy and well-paid for their work."

"Servants?"

"At my home in the Olympian realm. My estate is called Delos."

"I need food," Cassandra announced abruptly. "Look. Food." She pointed ahead to a series of vendor stalls lining three sides of an open square dotted with metal chairs and tables. "Olympian gods eat, right?"

"We do." Experimentally I sniffed the air, inhaling the mingled scents of sizzling grease, processed sugar, and baked dough. Interest sparked in my soul—and in my stomach. "And I want to try everything."

1
CASSANDRA

When Apollo said he wanted to try everything, he meant it. He ordered an embarrassing amount of food from every restaurant in the food court, and we laid it out on a table for eight. Families stalked past us, frowning because we were taking up so much space for just the two of us. At first I gave them apologetic smiles, and then I just stopped caring, because it was so much fun watching Apollo try the food. He wasn't shy about rejecting anything he didn't like, which included the meatlover's pizza and the Philly steak sandwich. He pronounced the Greek gyro "nicely flavored but oddly textured" and pushed it delicately toward me.

I watched him, munching my spring rolls and teriyaki chicken, and I realized that I felt genuinely *happy*. Happy, for the first time since Carowinds. I shouldn't feel happy, because my apartment burned to a crisp yesterday. I should be freaking out, calling the police or the fire department or somebody for updates, pestering my sister and her girlfriend for help. But I weirdly just—didn't care. Sure, I was still sad about the loss of some keepsakes—but the more I sat in the chilly sunlight watching Apollo shovel food into his mouth, the more I felt—liberated. Released. As if the old, grimy, grungy rags of my past life had been burned to ash and

I'd been given a bright, fresh, new life in which I could be anyone—including the shopping buddy of a curious and charming Greek god.

It was odd how quickly the rain had disappeared. Granted, we'd driven half an hour from my city to reach the outlets, so the clearer weather could have been a natural thing—but there was a crisp brightness to the afternoon that seemed slightly unnatural. Like maybe a certain sun god had adjusted the elements just for our outing.

Apollo's face froze after a bite of chili cheese dog. A look of horror swept through his eyes, and he carefully spit the mouthful into a napkin and pitched the whole thing into a trash can several feet away. Perfect aim.

I giggled. "This is fun," I told him. "I've always liked shopping. It makes me feel better, finding things I really love. There's this little rush of delight. And I don't even have to feel guilty today, because there won't be any credit card bill." I patted my shopping bags, sighing with pleasure as I remembered their contents.

Apollo was inspecting a mozzarella cheese stick and didn't answer. He bit into it with his perfectly white teeth, and the cheese began to stretch, longer and longer. He snapped his fingers and a tiny bolt of sharp white light sliced the string of cheese neatly in half.

Frantically I glanced around, but no one seemed to be watching us. "You can't do the powers thing here."

"No one noticed."

"You shouldn't risk it, though."

"Why not?" He gave me a golden half-smile. "What are they going to do to me?"

"Um… nothing, I guess. Just how powerful are you?"

"Cosmically powerful. I could destroy this whole market if I wanted to."

"Oh."

He inspected me, lips still curved. "And I have wings."

My jaw dropped. "Seriously?"

"Want to see?"

"Hell yes, but not here!" I caught his wrist, fearful he might leap up and produce a pair of fiery wings on the spot.

"So much anxiety in that beautiful body," he murmured. His other hand settled on top of mine.

A keen thrill lanced through my chest. "I inherited my mother's anxious nature."

"Parents and their unwanted contributions to our makeup." He winced, caressing the back of my hand absently. "I can understand that."

"Your mother?" I asked.

"My father."

"Your… father…" The enormity of exactly *who* I was eating with seized my mind in that moment. "Your father is Zeus. *The* Zeus."

"Yes." Apollo shifted in his seat, raking the food court with his eyes, as if the mere mention of his father made him nervous.

"Are you afraid of him?"

"Not afraid, exactly. Afraid of being forced into a confrontation with him, I suppose. Lately he keeps reminding me that he's in charge. He's afraid I'm trying to take over Olympus."

"Are you?"

"Of course not." He pulled his hands from mine and crumpled up some wrappers, pitching them into the trash can.

"Why not? From everything I know about Zeus— Earth myths and all—he sucks. He's cruel, vindictive, and disrespectful to women. Plus you said he allows slavery among the Olympians—something you don't believe in, right? And I'm betting there's more." I peered at Apollo, trying to interpret his tense expression.

"Why should you care who rules Olympus?" He laced his fingers together, rubbing his thumb over one of his gold rings. The little amber jewel tucked beside his nose glinted as he moved.

"I guess I don't really care. Just wondering why someone as powerful and generous and kind as you would allow a guy like Zeus to rule for so long. I mean—he's had his turn, right? He should let somebody else take over." I slurped my drink, blinking innocently at Apollo, and his tense features relaxed, humor sparking in his eyes.

"You're cute," he said softly, taking the drink from me. He tucked the straw between his lips and sipped experimentally. "Delightful. What is this drink?"

"Horchata."

"I love it."

"You can have the rest. It's the least I can do, after everything you've done." I touched my shopping bags again. Weird how I had to keep touching them. Maybe I had some deep-seated fear that I'd lose all these things too. "We should probably head out. It's getting late, and I need to find somewhere to spend the night."

Apollo's dark brows contracted. "I thought you were coming home with me again. I promise I won't try to seduce you."

I wanted to tell him his mere *existence* was a seduction—but that felt like too much objectification, and also I should have more damn pride than to let him know how deeply he affected me, how my underwear had been in a constant state of dampness since I put it on earlier.

Hot as he was, and as much as my body craved him, I couldn't seriously entertain the idea of sex with him. No way. If I started engaging in little fantasy scenarios, I just forced myself to picture my very average, pale, untoned human body contrasted with his magnificent tanned one, and the nausea that surged at the image drove all my desire away.

Every time I'd had sex with Ajax, I'd had to shave and pluck first, wash myself and apply perfume, fix my makeup, check my hair, brush my teeth—while he just came to the bed unshowered and ungroomed. He'd lie there, appraising me, before he'd nod and pat the space beside him. During our lovemaking, if he noticed a bit of stubble, or if my stomach gurgled, or if—heaven forbid—there was any kind of smell, no matter how slight, he'd let me know, and I'd promise to do better next time. I had to be perfect for him—a pristine pleasure doll. It was his kink, he said, and I submitted to please him.

If I had to be pristine for Ajax, who was so much less than perfect—what would someone like Apollo expect from a lover? Certainly much more than I could give. So I couldn't let myself imagine actually being with him. It wasn't an option.

"I have money now, thanks to you," I told him. "So I thought you'd want me to find somewhere else to stay."

"Not at all. I've already sent a message to my friend Icelos, and he's coming this evening to speak with you about your dreams."

"Oh, right. This is the nightmare expert you mentioned?"

"Yes. Icelos, King of the Nightmare realm."

My eyes widened. "Um… that sounds scary."

"He's very frightening. But he's also kind."

I shrank, clutching my shopping bags. "Still not sure I want to meet him."

Apollo chuckled. "Cassandra."

Oh my freaking god. His voice—honey and liquid flame—

"You saying my name like that isn't going to change my mind," I breathed.

"I'll be right there with you the whole time."

"Honestly, I don't know you much better than this Icelos guy."

He leaned across the table toward me, tenderness shining in his eyes. "Don't you, though?"

I held my breath, caught in the mesmerizing incandescence of his gaze, sinking into a molten, glowing universe that consisted only of him—and the aura of that universe was as familiar to me as my own soul. If I was blue-velvet sadness, he was rivulets of gold tracing along my veins, lighting me up, the gleaming foil to my beautiful dark. And I could hear the music of us, the pure liquid notes of him blending with the dark bass notes of me. Drums and soaring strings, golden brass and a trickling piano.

Apollo's eyes widened, still locked with mine, and he sucked in a sharp breath. "I can hear it," he whispered. "The melody in your mind—the orchestration."

"That's not possible." Tears formed at the corners of my eyes, but I kept holding his gaze, terrified that if I broke it, the music would vanish.

"You have to write it down, Cassandra, and quickly," he breathed.

"I have an app on my phone." I took a moment to play through the opening bars again, reinforcing them in my mind, and then I looked away from him. He gasped, short and harsh, and sagged back in his chair while I fumbled in my purse for my phone.

He didn't bother me while I made extensive notations on my composition app. When I'd dated Ajax, he'd always hated it when I got inspired at random times. He'd talk to me incessantly, try to snap me out of it, tell me I was being rude and inconsiderate. I'd explained to him over and over how I *had* to write things down as soon as they came to me, or they'd vanish from my brain, never to be heard again.

"So what if they vanish?" he'd grumbled. "It's not like you're doing anything with your music."

That had stung, especially because he was right. I was teaching music classes, and jotting down my own music in my spare time; but I'd never submitted my pieces anywhere. A bunch of them sat unfinished in a folder on my cloud drive. At least most of my compositions were saved there; the fire hadn't gotten to them, though it had destroyed my paper-only records of my earliest work. No matter, because if I kept hanging out with Apollo, I was going to have more new music than I knew what to do with.

When I completed notations for the main melody and most of the orchestration, I finally looked up at Apollo. He was watching me with an entirely new expression, a blazing admiration so vivid and raw that I caught my breath. Sure, he'd flirted with me, complimented me—but this was different. His face was flooded with sheer wonder, edged with a desire so sharp it almost looked like pain.

"That's who you are," he whispered.

"Could you really hear what I was thinking?"

"I have a connection with some composers and creatives," he said. "I can hear echoes or eddies of their artistic minds at work. But I've never heard anyone's creative soul as clearly as I hear yours. And that music, Cassandra—" His eyes glittered wet, and he looked away, his jaw tightening.

"You must have heard plenty of beautiful music in your lifetime. And you make your own, too."

"I do. But every artist has a place, a passion, and a vision that no one else can match. I've never heard anything like the song you played for me just now."

"Yeah, that's my problem." I grimaced. "My stuff is too different. It isn't marketable, see. It's not highbrow, and it's not pop. It doesn't fit neatly into a specific category. It's kind of weird. Back in school, the few professors who heard my compositions always urged me to lean more into an established genre and stop mixing it up. They said if I didn't change my style, the best I could hope for was a small fan following on social media."

"I don't know what that is, or what those idiots were thinking." Apollo's tan grew a shade more intense; he was losing control of whatever magic concealed his glow and made him look normal. "But in all the realms, I've never heard a song like that. I want to hear it again, live, in the open air, with a thousand musicians playing it in the biggest stadium the realms have to offer. I want to soak that music into my soul and live in it always. I want to *be* that song."

He was gripping one of the food trays as he spoke, and it snapped with a loud *crack* under the pressure. Heads turned our way.

"You're getting very intense about a piece of music," I said under my breath. "And you're starting to glow, Apollo."

"I don't fucking care. And don't pretend you don't feel the same way." He shoved the fragments of the tray aside and gripped my hand. "No soul who produced *that song* can be casual about music."

I trembled, the threads of my soul vibrating, because I knew exactly what he meant about wanting to live in a song, to *be* the melody—I'd felt that way before about some of my favorite songs. I regularly got chills from music—certain combinations of notes pleased me exquisitely and thoroughly, somewhere deep down where nothing else could reach. Specific rhythms just filled me up and synced with the cadence of my being. I had teared up at everything from a Disney song to a pop anthem, from a dark indie melody to a piece of beautifully executed chamber music.

I'd always felt a little embarrassed by the depth of my reaction to music, even among the other musicians in high school and college. Sometimes I wanted to sway and cry and move with a piece, or huddle in a corner and simply experience it over and over for hours, marveling at the mind that produced it. But that wasn't acceptable. We had to dissect the pieces, take them apart and critique them, learn what we were supposed to like and what "shouldn't" be done.

Apollo's reaction to my music was the kind of naked, visceral emotion I'd always longed for in an audience. It didn't matter that he was an audience of one—he was the damn god of music, and *he loved my song*.

"I want to play something else for you," I said suddenly. "Not my own music, but some songs from my playlists. On the way back. Is that okay?"

"A person's favorite songs are pieces of their soul," he answered.

"I'll take that as a yes." I gathered my bags and stood up. "Just don't laugh at my 'guilty pleasure' songs."

"If they please you, don't feel guilty about them," he said. "Why should any other human get to dictate what brings you happiness, as long as it harms no one else?"

"Yeah, well…humans seem to enjoy telling each other what they should and shouldn't like."

He scoffed, sweeping up the rest of our trash and leftovers and throwing it into the garbage can. "What do they do with all this?" He bumped the can with his foot.

"Put it in a landfill, where it sits and smells until it decomposes."

"In Olympus we repurpose our castoff items as raw materials. And we send the extra to Faerie to be remade. Fae magic can separate materials into their elemental particles and use or alter them to create something new."

"Magical recycling. Probably a lot more energy-efficient than the way we do it." When he reached for a few of my bags, I let him take them. "Tell me more about Faeries."

Apollo seemed to have a fascination with all things Fae, particularly the way their magic worked. He'd studied it for decades, he said, and he'd learned how to blend some of it with his Olympian powers. On the way to the parking lot he talked non-stop about Faerie, until my mind was pretty much blown. It would take a while for me to process it all.

When we reached his rental car, I synced up my phone via Bluetooth while Apollo watched me curiously.

"I know a little about human media devices from my stay at Pan's house," he said. "The ingenuity of your race amazes me. Yet you seem to employ your talents mostly to create entertainment and to craft various paths for enjoying that entertainment."

"We design important things too," I said, bristling. "Medical tech and stuff."

"You don't have to defend the importance of music and the arts." His smile soothed away any offense I'd felt. "I am the god of music, dance, and poetry. But I'm also the god of healing, so your medical technology interests me as well."

"That's not my area of expertise, but my sister works in the medical field. Maybe you can talk to her sometime. And of course there's the internet."

"Yes." His eyes brightened. "All the information and knowledge of your people, centralized and accessible for all! Brilliant."

"Accessible to *most*, not all," I corrected. "Now stop talking, and listen." And then I flushed hot, because I'd basically told the great and powerful Apollo to shut up.

But he didn't seem to mind.

I'd tried sharing my playlists with Ajax when we were dating. I quickly learned the kinds of songs he'd appreciate and the ones he'd sneer at. So as I queued up music for Apollo via Spotify, my palms started sweating. Why did I so desperately want him to like these songs? He was from freaking Olympus and had probably heard all sorts of amazing divine music—not to mention *Faerie* music. How could a bit of paltry Earth music compete with that?

I started with "Make Your Own Kind of Music," by Cass Elliot. I felt that song in my bones—it could have been the anthem of my life as a composer. Next, "The Whole of the Moon," by the Waterboys. We went from Emma Blackery to Highasakite to Halsey, and from Crowded House to Erutan to the Chainsmokers. Gradually I slipped in a Glee cover or two, and some Taylor Swift—and Apollo didn't roll his eyes or start complaining. He had a complimentary word to say about every single song.

"Good to know that the muses are still at work," he said when we finally pulled into the parking garage behind his building.

So the muses were a real thing. "Do I have a muse?"

"Muses aren't assigned," he said. "They come and go among people with talent. And they aren't all-powerful, either. It's up to every talented human to keep practicing their art and honing their craft, even when a muse isn't influencing them directly."

"Are you a muse?" I stared at him through the blue-shadowed dark of the car. "Because I've been especially prolific with the composing since I met you."

"I can have that effect, yes. But I'm not giving you the ideas—merely easing the way. Unblocking the channel, so to speak. I do it unconsciously, by my presence." He met my eyes. "Does it bother you?"

"Does it bother me that I'm suddenly able to compose again, and that the stuff I'm writing is pretty damn good? Hm, let me think—nope, doesn't bother me at all." But my cheeks warmed again, and I couldn't bear to keep looking into those golden eyes. "What does bother me is depending on you like this. The money, the place to stay—"

"And in return, you introduced me to 'the outlets' and shared your human music."

"Things you could have discovered on your own."

Apollo looked down at his hands, still curled around the steering wheel. When he spoke, his tone was darker, with a hollow timbre. "When you've lived as long as I have, in a family like mine, you realize the value of a friend with whom to share new experiences.

I'm the one in your debt, Cassandra, not the other way around."

Caution tightened my nerves. My childhood with my mother had taught me that danger and darkness crouched beyond every corner. My adult life hadn't really proved her wrong—I'd lost my job because of the "last in, first out" rule, I'd been rejected by a man I loved, and my apartment building had burned down.

Glorious, rich, lonely, magical men didn't just walk into a girl's life without a bunch of strings attached— strings like *other realms*, and asshole god-fathers like Zeus, and creepy nightmare guys who could poke around in my head and identify my "powers." As much as I wanted to like Apollo, and despite all the things he'd done right today, I couldn't let go of that innate tension, the suspicious part of me that was poised, waiting for misfortune to show up. I was expecting disaster—almost craving it, because then I'd be proved right. He was too good to be true, and therefore he must be bad for me.

No one could be that generous, that handsome, that intelligent and artistic and *perfect*. No one. Not even Apollo.

Apollo's fingers had tightened on the steering wheel. "You're very quiet. Did I offend you?"

"No. I'm sorry, I was thinking."

"You don't have to apologize."

"I'll stay tonight, to meet this nightmare expert," I murmured. "And then I think I should find my own place." Too late I realized how cruel my words sounded—he'd just told me how much he valued having a friend, and I'd responded with "too bad, I'm moving on."

"We can still hang out," I amended. "I'm not ditching you. I just think some space would be good."

"Space. Of course." He threw me a wry, pained half-smile. "I know I must seem very strange and dangerous to a human woman. I wish you could believe that I mean you no harm."

"It's not that." I touched his arm lightly. His skin was unnaturally warm. "Sometimes I need alone time. Time to just be me, without having to be all put-together and polite to someone else."

His brow furrowed. "I've seen you at your worst, Cassandra. You don't have to pretend with me."

I opened my mouth to protest—but it was sort of true. He'd seen me at the gas station, gathering my supplies for shame-eating and binge-drinking. He'd seen me in my filthy pajamas, wan and broken from the loss of everything I owned.

"That wasn't quite my worst," I whispered. "But close."

"What was the worst?"

The memory rose in my throat, choking me into silence.

"Never mind," he said gently. "You're under no obligation to tell me, of course. But believe me when I say that I've endured horrors too, and participated in them. My worst days were long ago—lifetimes ago, but the echo of them stays with me like a stain, like a brand, like a sad song in the back of my mind, one I can never really forget. I understand some of what you feel. And you, Cassandra, could never be an unwelcome presence to me, no matter what state you were in."

"You can't say those things," I said, trembling. "People on Earth don't talk to each other like that, not when they're brand-new acquaintances. You barely know me."

"Time means nothing when you've heard a person's soul."

"You can't hear my soul. And if you could, you'd know that I prefer to be *alone*." I opened the car door and jumped out, hustling my shopping bags along with me.

Apollo grabbed a few more bags from the back seat and slammed the door. "You've been alone too long," he said, with more of an edge to his tone than I'd ever heard from him. "You're hurting yourself with all the *space* and *alone time*."

"And since you're a god, you know best," I snapped.

"I know because I've done it myself!" he exclaimed. "Most of the gods have isolated themselves in one lifetime or another, and it never ends well. I'm not my own sun, Cassandra. I can't cheer my heart with my own light. I've tried it. It doesn't work. Beings like us—human, Olympian, Fae—the one trait we share is that we aren't meant to be alone. We need companionship. Friends, family members, lovers. A soul like yours needs time and space to create, yes, but you also need balance. You have to temper that creative isolation with relationships."

"You sound like a therapist." I stalked through the lobby doors.

"I'm the god of healing. Not just physical healing—mental healing, too."

"Well, stop trying to fix me."

"I'm not. I'm trying to—"

"To help me, yes. Well, I don't need your help." I planted myself in the corner of the elevator.

He stormed in after me, and as the door closed he tossed the bags into another corner and stood over me, fists clenched, letting himself radiate power and pure beaming sun, until I had to narrow my eyes against the sheer brilliance of him.

"Why are you so frustrating?" he said.

"Lots of practice," I retorted, but a pang shot through my chest. I couldn't count the number of times Ajax had called me frustrating, annoying, depressing, exhausting, and a bunch of other delightful adjectives that hadn't contributed to my inferiority complex *at all*.

But Apollo looked closer at my face, his frown shifting from frustration to concern. "I hurt you just then. I'm sorry. I should be more patient. You've taken all this so well—better than I ever expected. My frustration is my own fault." He turned away, setting a fist to the mirrored wall. "I'm acting like my father." A heavy sigh. "Maybe you're right. Maybe we need space."

Not *we*. I. *I* needed space. I wanted to yell at him that we weren't a thing—not a couple, barely even friends. At best we were the strangest kind of haphazard acquaintances, tossed together a few times by Fate, if such a thing existed, which it probably did, considering that the god of the sun was riding in an elevator with me.

I glared at Apollo's broad back, so obviously well-muscled even through his T-shirt. And then, as my gaze traveled up to his face, reflected in the mirror, I saw something that sent a shock of horror blazing over my skin.

A figure in dark flowing robes, taller than Apollo, with a doleful gray face half covered by strands of inky black hair. Tendrils of shadow swirled outward from the cloaked figure, spiraling and curling along the mirrored walls until the reflection of Apollo's glory was neutralized, blotted out by thick, smoky darkness. Apollo himself still glowed though—a torch in the sudden blackness of the elevator.

"Apollo!" I shrieked. He turned and caught me as I leaped for him. I curled against his chest, and he wrapped both arms around me.

"Don't worry, Cassandra." Then louder he said, "Making a dramatic entrance, my friend?"

"Simply traveling in the quickest and most convenient way," replied a soft male voice. The shadows lessened—or rather they withdrew, like threads being rolled onto the spool again. A tall dark figure emerged from the mirror like a person resurfacing from water, pressing through the filmy veil between one dimension and the next. The next second he was in the elevator with us, solid and real, shadows drifting around him like enraptured ghosts.

"This is the nightmare expert I told you about," Apollo murmured to me.

"I am the King of Nightmares," said the newcomer. I'd never heard a voice like his, and my mind immediately started playing "Black Velvet" by Alannah Myles.

"Icelos is my name—Icelos, son of Somnus, brother of Morpheus and Phantasos, Prince of Screams and

Sorrows," continued the man. "Apollo communed with me earlier using an Unseelie spell—one not usually employed by a god so pure of heart." He gave Apollo a rebuking look, then yielded me a faint smile. "Forgive me for not coming sooner. I had some business to complete."

"We are grateful you came at all." Apollo bent his golden head. The elevator stopped then, and Apollo swept a hand to the exit. "After you, my lord."

Embarrassed by my freak-out, I stepped out of Apollo's arms and gathered my shopping bags again. Apollo and I put them in the bedroom and then sat down in the living room, where Icelos began to question me about my dreams. He asked dozens of questions—when did they begin, how often did I have them, what sorts of things did I see, how soon did the visions come to pass, and so on. Then he asked if I'd ever tried to prevent the things I saw from coming true.

"Before the apartment burned, I was going to warn everyone," I said. "But the fire alarm was broken, and then it was too late, I guess. And I didn't think anyone would believe me. They don't believe me, ever."

Icelos's dark eyes snapped to mine, and he tipped his head sharply aside, as if scenting the thing I had omitted—the thing I didn't want to talk about to anyone, ever. The first nightmare I'd ever had. I'd told him they started when I was seven, but that wasn't true, was it?

The dark came roaring up from the bottom of my soul and I smashed it down again, piling layers of denial on top of it.

"Apollo," Icelos intoned in his black-velvet voice. "Give me a moment to speak to Cassandra alone."

Apollo threw me a questioning glance, and I nodded. "I'll be fine."

I dreaded talking to the creepy Nightmare King alone; he reminded me of Jack Skellington crossed with some kind of super-tall, elegant, gray-skinned vampire. But if he could explain my gift to me—if he could unveil the secrets of this thing that plagued me—well, I had to give him that chance. I had to know.

Apollo went into the bedroom and closed the door. A few seconds later I heard a burst of frenetic music, and I couldn't help smiling. The sun god was trying not to eavesdrop.

"Lean forward," said Icelos, reaching toward me with unnaturally long, thin fingers. From his wrists draped wide sleeves that trailed down to the floor. His robes bore faint imprinted images—scenes of terror and torment, pictures of deformed and demented creatures, like monsters from horror movies.

The Nightmare King placed the tips of his fingers at my temples and closed his eyes. I stared at his solemn face, so lovely and yet so deeply sad it made my eyes water.

I couldn't tell what he was doing in my head. I didn't feel any different. If anything, the whole scenario was just kind of awkward.

At last Icelos let go of my skull and leaned back. "Your powers are not naturally associated with nightmares, so I cannot unlock them for you. Your suppression of your abilities has forced them into this channel, so they appear to you only in sleep. You've been pushing them down since a very early age, since a certain traumatic event—"

I physically recoiled, putting up my hands as if I could push the truth away. "No."

Icelos regarded me coolly for a moment, then said, "Your power is prophesy—future sight. But it is being crushed under layers of self-doubt, guilt, and sorrow. And there's another component to the suppression—this gift is extremely rare, and has not resurfaced for many generations. Even if you broke the emotional chains constricting your power, you would also need some additional intervention to fully access your abilities."

"Fully access? What would that mean?"

"I cannot tell you for sure. But your visions would no longer come in the form of nightmares. They would be clearer, and they would likely give you more time between the vision and the occurrence."

"Enough time to warn people and prevent the vision?"

"It's possible. From what you told me of the fire, it seems you were destined to burn alive, but you avoided that fate. You may be gifted with the ability not only to see certain twists of the future, but to alter them through careful choices."

"That sounds like way too much responsibility," I gasped. "What if I just want to stay like this?"

"You could," he said. "But your visions will grow darker and more painful, and your emotional trauma will only worsen as you repress your natural gifts. You will suffer greatly, without ever being able to change the tragedies you witness. If you unlock the ability, it's possible you could learn to control the visions—to either let them flow, or to turn them off altogether."

"And how do you know all of this?" I twisted my fingers together, forcing my gaze to stay on his beautiful, dreadful face. "Why couldn't Apollo tell me these things?"

"As King of Nightmares, I have unique access to the darker side of the mind," he replied.

I touched my temple. "What else did you see?"

"Nothing I'll repeat to anyone." He gave me a reassuring nod. As he rose, the images printed on his silky black robes seemed to shift, portraying new scenes of torment and horror.

"You said I need to fix my emotional trauma and guilt or whatever," I said grudgingly. "Not much chance of that—but you also mentioned 'additional intervention.' What would that involve?"

Icelos glanced at the bedroom door. "He wouldn't want me to tell you."

"If it's about my gift, I deserve to know." Nightmare King or not, I might slap him if he didn't answer me soon.

"Your powers come from an ancestor with Olympian or Titan blood," Icelos explained patiently. "Possibly a very distant descendant of the Titan Phoebe, goddess of intellect and prophecy, if I had to guess."

"Does that mean I get other powers, like healing or long life or something?" I asked. "Or is it just the sucky nightmare thing?"

"The long life and healing powers of Olympians and Titans fade from their offspring after a couple generations," said Icelos. "So yes—just the 'sucky nightmare thing.' Your gift of prophecy has been dormant for many generations, and it is struggling to resurface. Think of it as birth pangs."

I grimaced. "Okay…"

"To speed the process and ease the emergence of your powers, you need to reconnect with the Olympian realm. You need a fresh infusion of its essence. Engaging with a pureblooded Olympian will help draw your abilities to the surface."

"Engaging with?" I faltered, because judging by the way he avoided my gaze, I could guess what he meant.

"Engaging sexually," Icelos clarified.

My cheeks flamed. "Did Apollo put you up to this? Is this some sneaky way of trying to get me into his bed?"

"Not at all. Your partner does not have to be Apollo—it could be any pure-blooded Olympian."

"Right. Like I have access to a bunch of those." I rolled my eyes.

Icelos shrugged. "If you would rather not sleep with him, ask him to take you to Olympus. You can choose someone there who is more to your liking."

"It's not a question of liking him or not, it's just—it's weird."

The Nightmare King quirked a slim dark eyebrow. "Many things are weird. This is not one of them. It makes perfect sense. Even some pure-blooded Olympians have found that merging repeatedly with a devoted partner—one who also possesses Olympian or Fae blood—unlocks new facets of their power. Why do you think Hera and Zeus stayed together so long? They made each other's power stronger, more multifaceted. And that is all I can tell you."

"So basically, if I don't want to get more miserable and traumatized than I am now, I need to get my emotional shit together, and I also need to screw an Olympian."

"Yes," Icelos said crisply. He glided across the loft to Apollo's bedroom door and tapped.

Apollo emerged a moment later, looking flushed and harried and very curious. But he didn't ask what we'd talked about, and neither Icelos nor I volunteered the information.

"I must go," said Icelos. "There are a few tasks I've been putting off in this realm, and it's time I dealt with them."

"Thank you for coming." Apollo clasped forearms with the Nightmare King. Then Icelos walked *into* the glass wall of windows and vanished.

"So he was—interesting." I pinched my lips together.

"Did he help you?" Apollo asked.

"He can't do anything himself. I have to deal with my trauma and depression first, I guess. Whatever." I flung myself onto the sofa. "I can't deal with it right now. I'm too tired."

"Of course you are. Your sleep was interrupted last night, and we've been shopping all afternoon. You'll take my bed tonight." He gathered all the bags and carried them into the bedroom.

"I'm not taking your bed. I'm fine on the couch."

"I only took the bedroom last night so I could hide my radiance from you," he called back. "Now that's not a problem, so you'll take the bed."

I walked to the doorway and surveyed the California king-sized bed. "There's honestly plenty of room if you want to share."

Did I just say that? Oh my god.

"We can stay really far away from each other," I added hastily. "No touching."

Apollo stared at the bed, his jaw flexing.

Wow, okay. Sleeping near me must be a really distasteful concept for him.

"Think about it," I said in the brightest tone I could muster. "I'm going to use the bathroom, if you don't mind."

"Hm." He nodded, so I gathered the toiletries and pajamas I'd bought and slipped into the bathroom.

While I was getting ready, my phone rang.

My sister. Finally.

I touched the green circle. "Hey Meg."

"Omigod Cass, are you okay? Jessa told me what happened. I had a really long shift and then I just *had* to get some sleep, and she said you were fine—are you fine? You're staying with a friend? What friend? I didn't think you had any friends."

"Wow, okay. Yeah, I have friends, Meg. I'm fine, but all my stuff is gone. Like, *gone*, gone. Most of the building collapsed, so it's pretty much all rubble and ash at this point."

"My god, Cass. You must be devastated."

"Weirdly, no." Again I went back through my mental inventory of the apartment, trying to drum up some emotion for what I'd lost. A few special books of sheet music, some jewelry I loved, vintage patterned plates I'd collected, my favorite leather jacket, my best shoes, my really nice vibrator, some art…yeah, I was sad about those things, but not devastated. "Everything is replaceable, you know? And it feels like it all belonged to my old life, the old me. The Ajax me. And now this is post-Ajax, post-recovery, so I get to start fresh. Does that make sense? Is it weird to feel like that?"

"Maybe?" I could hear the wince in Meg's voice. "But I'm honestly relieved. I thought after all this I might have to put you on suicide watch or something. But you sound good—are you good? What about money, do you need money? Jessa and I—" she hesitated, and I could hear Jessa's voice in the background, a long string of protesting words. "Um, yeah, Jessa and I are saving up for our next trip so we can't really help out a lot, but we could maybe spare—" more background chatter from Jessa, and then Meg's voice again. "I'll let you know if we can help out."

"Honestly I'm fine." I felt a rush of anger at Jessa, and then gratitude welled up inside me—gratitude for Apollo and his eager generosity with his "human cash." What would I have done without him? Crawled into a ditch and died maybe. But I couldn't tell Meg that the man I met at Carowinds was bankrolling me to the tune of tens of thousands of dollars. So I said, "I started a GoFundMe thing, and people have been giving. It's really cool."

"Oh good." Relief colored her tone, and I bit back a savage reply. I wanted to tell my sister exactly what I thought of her performative phone call and her careful concern. I wanted to tell her how much I really didn't like Jessa, how much Meg had changed since they started dating. But could I really fault her for wanting a separate life, a life with a cautious amount of space between her and the past? I was doing the same thing, honestly—moving into a new zone, crafting a new place for myself. Shifting away from a past that involved my mother, and Ajax, and the job I'd loved and lost. Meg and I had been through the same things in our childhood, after all—with one key difference.

She'd heard my whispered account of that first terrible vision, when I was four and we were lying in bunkbeds in the dark of our shared room.

She'd heard it, and she hadn't believed me—seven-year-old that she was, so wise and logical, so brave, even back then. The dream hadn't scared her.

"It's just a silly nightmare," she'd told me. "Nightmares aren't real."

We'd both endured the loss that followed. And we'd never talked about my dream again. Maybe she didn't even remember I'd told it to her.

And that was the difference between us. She'd only *heard* about our baby brother's death.

I'd seen it coming.

8
APOLLO

Sharing a bed with Cassandra would be the most difficult thing I'd done in this renewal—harder than my battles against Hook and his monsters, alongside Peter Pan. It would be harder than dealing with my father and his poisonous ex. Harder than stealing a tiny child and placing a geas so that everyone would forget her. The geas had been for Persephone's own safety, but I had the nagging sense that I should have found a better way to protect her. She seemed happy in Neverland, a seventy-year-old Olympian in a child's body—but she couldn't stay that way indefinitely. Eventually I'd need to discuss her situation with Pan again.

I pressed a hand to my forehead. Persephone wasn't my problem right now—it was the luscious, curvy human girl with the soul made of music. I'd heard her inner song from the moment we met, but the strains of music she'd imagined while we ate in the human marketplace—those were more exquisite and incredible than anything else she'd created. I'd felt my innermost being unfurled, layers peeling back and splaying open, exposing the naked core of my self. I'd been helpless, sensitized to the point of pain, stricken with the desire to blend my own existence with the music of hers.

Her sadness was still there, flavoring the melody, but it had lightened since she'd come to me, and that made me vehemently joyful. I was helping her, at least temporarily. But my fascination with her was shifting into a need so intense I could barely manage it.

Olympians loved quickly and violently, and we had a tendency toward obsession. If I wasn't careful, I would slip into a full-blown fixation with Cassandra.

One of the shopping bags had tipped over, and a silky shirt had slithered half out of the tissue paper. I stooped and collected the slip of material, letting it glide through my fingers, imagining how it would cling to the swell of Cassandra's breast. Her breasts—I ached to see them uncovered, to cup them in my hands. I thirsted to taste her. But merging with her sexually wouldn't be enough—I needed *her*, needed the soul-song I'd heard at the food court. I needed her to open her heart to me, to love me. The love of a soul that magnificent would be the most exquisite happiness imaginable.

I slid the shirt back into the bag and set it upright.

"Apollo, you idiot," I whispered to myself. "You're already obsessed."

Obsessed, and painfully erect. I'd managed to keep myself under control during our shopping spree by thinking about the most horrifying sights I'd witnessed during Pan's war with Hook. But now, not even those gory images were helping.

I hated this. Hated being overruled by my traitorous body, hated my natural desires being harnessed as vengeance by that vindictive Fae. Hated the way my intelligence, my honor, my glory, and my creative superiority could be dulled by this animal instinct.

Gritting my teeth, I picked up my guitar and began to play—but the sound wasn't right, wasn't what I needed, so I took the keyboard out of the closet instead. Jack's partner Emery had suggested the instrument. I was somewhat familiar with the piano, and she'd said an electronic keyboard would take things a step farther, offering more sound possibilities. I plugged it in, balanced it across my knees, and began to play.

My powers gave me the innate ability to use any instrument in any realm to its fullest potential, and I unleashed myself on that keyboard, flooding all my tension and passion into it until it sang in sync with me, lashing the room with wild chords and fierce lyrical phrases. I sang to Cassandra through the keys, augmenting the limited sound quality of the instrument with my own powers, making it resonate and ring and roar.

Vaguely I became aware of her presence, standing nearby, watching me and listening. Her creative consciousness pressed mine lightly, tentatively, an occasional chime of answering notes in harmony with my song.

My arousal wasn't going away. If anything, it had gotten worse. It thrummed through my body, an incessant scream of need.

I stopped playing with a clash of notes, and I gripped the keyboard with Olympian strength, my fingers warping the plastic—

"Stop." Cassandra's trembling hands slid over mine. "You'll break it."

I let her loosen my fingers from the instrument. She didn't let go, even when my grip on the plastic relaxed.

"That was incredible." Her voice was tremulous with emotion. "What brand is this keyboard? I've never heard one that sounded so good."

"I embellished the sound," I muttered.

"You can do that?"

"With any instrument. Sometimes with voices as well. I can make the sound louder, deeper, more beautiful, more tuneful."

"So you're a magical soundboard. Like Auto-Tune."

I glanced up at her, ready to ask for details about those unfamiliar things—but she was directly in front of me, bending, her hands still pressed to mine. As she leaned over, the globes of her breasts swung against the thin fabric of her shirt—a scanty thing with tiny straps running over her shoulders. She wore soft thin pants of the same material, which hugged her hips and the cleft between her legs. Over the creamy slope of her neck spilled her hair, chestnut-brown and glossy and fragrant.

My gaze lingered on the tempting notch between her collarbones, then moved lower to the deep valley between her breasts.

Frantically I snapped my gaze back to her face. Long lashes dropped low over her beautiful eyes, such sad eyes, liquid dark in which I could sink forever. She smelled like delicate flowers and honeyed skin.

"Shit, you're beautiful," I croaked.

Her mouth fell open. Which was the worst possible thing, because then I pictured inserting my length between her lips—

"I think I should sleep on the couch." I set the keyboard aside, went into the bathroom, and closed the door.

I showered in icy water for a long time, so long that I expected Cassandra to be asleep when I passed through the bedroom again. But instead I was greeted with a cacophony of sounds from her mind—a conflicted searing scream of violins and saxophones, supported by an inexorable, doomful drumbeat. And I could feel her power aura—shifting and straining, struggling under layers of heavy sorrow.

"Having trouble sleeping?" I carefully avoided looking at her, lest the mere sight of her face trigger the desire I'd just managed to subdue.

"Too much in my head," she groaned. "It won't stop."

"I could put you to sleep," I offered.

She flounced upright in the bed. "Sleeping pills? Or is that some kind of weird sex offer?"

I laughed, hoarse and breathless. "It's an offer of music. I have songs that can put people to sleep."

I risked meeting her gaze, only to encounter a storm of suspicion and desire in her eyes. I wasn't surprised that she wanted me—women usually did. But I craved her trust and affection even more violently than I craved her body.

"You won't touch me." Her words were both a statement and a plea for reassurance.

"Not without your consent," I answered. "I didn't touch you last night, did I?"

"You didn't." She sighed. "Okay then, Apollo—put me to sleep."

I took a moment to put away the keyboard and guitar, and then I took out my lute, finding solace in the familiar curve of its smooth surface. My fingertips danced across the strings, releasing a delicate melody.

Cassandra lay back against the pillows. "Oh… that is nice."

I wove a somnolent peace over her body, soothing her frantic mind. In the process, my own eyes grew heavy, and by the time she was completely asleep, I could barely manage to lay aside the lute before I collapsed and sank into a dreamscape of my own.

I woke to the sensation of warm soft flesh against my arm.

In her sleep, Cassandra had crept across the expanse of the bed to nestle against me. Her flimsy shirt had slipped aside, revealing part of one perfect breast. I could see the delicate rosy nipple, and my pulse shot up like the Afterburn. I'd seen many breasts in my lifetimes, but Cassandra's were easily in the top ten. She had the milk-white, pink-tipped, perfectly round breast of a goddess. I wanted that breast in my mouth, under my palm. My fingers twitched, moving nearer.

Then I curled my hands into fists and closed my eyes, jaw locked tight.

I was no Zeus, no Dionysus or Poseidon. I was Apollo—"high-minded Apollo," Hades called me when he was in a good mood, and when he wasn't he dubbed me "a self-righteous pretty-boy with a savior complex." He'd said it to my face more than once. Others had less flattering terms to describe the moral standard to which I held myself.

After lifetimes of mistakes, I had made myself into the god I wanted to be.

Apollo, who could purvey disease, but who chose to heal.

Apollo, who could have lounged in the Olympian realm the way the other gods did, but who instead chose to travel the realms, aiding the oppressed and battling on behalf of the weak.

Apollo, who could have been famed and worshiped in any realm for musical skill and romantic prowess, but who gave his gifts of music and pleasure quietly, to those who most needed them.

Since the geas had been laid on me, I'd spent time with many women—weary women, unloved women, women of many shapes and forms who hadn't been able to achieve pleasure with those of their realm for one reason or another, and who craved the touch of another person. I couldn't achieve the peak myself, but I could help them crest it again and again. Some of them had cried afterward, weeping with sheer relief and gratitude.

I could have loved any number of them. But I was waiting for the one the Fate had prophesied. The one I was destined to adore. The one who could set me free.

Self-righteous I was, perhaps. And that self-righteousness kept me from pressing my palm to

Cassandra's bare breast and claiming her sweet mouth while she slept.

To lessen the temptation a little, I eased away and rolled onto my side, with my back to her. That way, when she woke, she'd be spared the embarrassment of knowing I saw her uncovered.

9

CASSANDRA

My sleep was tormented, filled with wrenching horrors—people careening toward the car accidents that would end their lives—a man collapsing on his living room carpet, caught in the throes of a massive heart attack—a child reaching for a bottle of toxic cleaner under the sink—a girl finding her mother's loaded gun—

I jerked out of the chain of nightmares, trembling and sweating, and I staggered to the bathroom where I curled up in the corner and sobbed quietly. I couldn't prevent all those terrible things. There wasn't enough time, or enough information. All the dreams had the acrid taste of truth. They were actual events occurring to real people.

If I unlocked this gift, Icelos said I might be able to change future events—prevent tragedies. Or I might be able to quell the visions altogether—turn them off, like I turned off the TV whenever the news got too depressing.

Continuing like this wasn't a possibility. No way. I couldn't survive more nights of these dreams, knowing that they were real, that they were *happening*.

I needed relief. To loosen the bands constricting my gift and let it out, whatever the consequences. The result couldn't be any worse than this.

I went back to the bed and lay still for a full hour, my brain whirling with a tornado of anxious thoughts. Getting it on with Apollo seemed like an easier way of unlocking my powers than sorting out my childhood trauma. Maybe one tryst with him would do the trick, and I'd come into my birthright, literally. The sex didn't have to mean anything. Greek gods weren't the type for long-lasting relationships with humans. Besides, Apollo had no plans to stick around permanently. He was on vacation, like he'd said—amusing himself with human culture. We could have a quick fling, which would allow me to unlock my powers. I wouldn't have to worry about being a perfect happy little sex doll for more than a week or so at most. Afterward, he'd leave, and I could go back to my usual moody self—maybe with a bit more control over my visions this time.

I slid off the bed, heart thundering, and ducked into the bathroom for a thorough brush-and-floss. Quickly I stripped off my tank top, shorts, and panties and ran a little water into the bath so I could shave everything perfectly smooth—not a bit of hair anywhere. I'd purchased Tom Ford Black Orchid perfume at the outlets, and I spritzed a little on my wrists and inner thighs.

I plucked my eyebrows and anywhere else that needed tweezing. Then I inspected myself, every inch, checking my heels for dry skin and calluses, my toes for ragged nails. I pumiced, filed, and moisturized.

Ajax had always wanted to examine me before sex. Inspection, he'd called it. And then, once I'd passed inspection, he'd let me know what position he wanted me in. Sometimes he would even pose me himself, like a pliable living doll.

I had always come hard during our sessions, so I had let him set the standard and take the lead. I'd considered myself lucky; I had friends whose guys were terrible in bed. But Ajax's dominance meant I didn't have many moves of my own to try. I'd only ever slept with him, because my mother was terrified of boys and men, and she wouldn't let me date anyone when I was a teen—not so much as a chaperoned movie. Her paranoia had kept me skittish and scared of boys until junior year of college, when I'd met Ajax and he'd told me he would let me sleep with him if I'd make a few changes to my personal grooming habits. When I'd passed inspection the first time, and he'd agreed to take my virginity, I'd felt honored.

Maybe all of that practice had prepared me to give pleasure to an actual god.

But as I stared at myself in the full-length mirror, my heart sank.

I'd let myself go, skimped on the exfoliation, masks, moisturization, and exercise; so I wasn't as fit and groomed as I used to be. Ajax would certainly have turned me down in this state.

I couldn't dream that Apollo would want me. A sun god would be even more exacting and demanding. No way was I signing up for *that* on a permanent basis.

But this wasn't about a long-term relationship—it was practical, purposeful. And maybe, just maybe, if Apollo would have me—it could be fun.

I pulled my scanty clothes back on and cautiously opened the bathroom door, letting the light wash over the bed for just a second before I flipped the switch off. Apollo was still asleep, thank god. And now the room was lit only by the soft glow of his golden skin.

Easing onto the bed, I inched across the mattress and draped myself against him, slipping down my tank top strap until one of my breasts was exposed. Maybe he would take the bait and start something.

A few seconds later he stirred, and I sealed my eyes shut, breathing slow and quiet. I could practically feel those amber eyes searing my skin with their gaze.

But Apollo didn't fall for my "naked boob" temptation. I heard his breathing quicken—and then he rolled away from me.

Damn it. Now I'd have to actually make a move. Desperate I might be, but I could hardly bear the idea of propositioning him openly. What if he rejected me?

A slow, melancholy ripple of notes unfurled through my mind, played low and soft on a flute.

Apollo inhaled sharply, and the muscles of his shoulders tensed.

"You're awake," he murmured. "I can hear you."

Damn my inner music-voice. "I don't know what you're talking about. I'm sound asleep."

He chuckled. But he didn't roll back toward me.

I moved away from him, heart racing. My gaze skipped to the bedside clock, a radio/alarm combination thing put there by whoever had furnished the loft. It read 6:35 a.m. Too early for a seduction.

God, what was I thinking?

For a moment I considered fleeing the apartment for good and never coming back.

But if I did that, my only real shot at getting a handle on my dream weirdness would be gone.

And I hated to waste all that sex prep time.

Better just go for it.

I slid off the bed and shucked off the shorts, panties, and tank top.

Entirely nude, I padded across the hardwood floor and circled around to Apollo's side of the bed. His eyes were open, fists clenched around the sheets.

When he saw me, his glow burst into radiant flame. I yelped and closed my eyes against the painful brightness.

"Sorry," he gasped, sitting up. "You startled me. Cassandra, what is this? What are you—"

Desperate, I stepped nearer, hushing him with my fingertips. "Please—just look at me, and if you want to have a little fun, then we can... or if there's anything about my appearance that you want me to fix first, I can do that."

His beautiful lips parted, and his eyes went wide with agonized wonder. "Anything to fix? What the Styx are you talking about? You're absolutely stunning. But you've been very clear that I wasn't to try any sort of seduction. You weren't interested in being with me that way."

"I changed my mind," I murmured.

"Why?"

"Why? Um—" I swallowed. "Just—because."

"That's not an answer," he began, but I moved in and kissed him quiet.

His mouth was as warm and soft and strong as I'd imagined. I cupped his golden head in my arms and kissed him deep, quivering with the fear that he'd push me away, but he gave a strangled moan and pulled my body to his bare chest. His big warm hands slid over my shoulder blades, my lower back, the curves of my ass, my thighs. He brought one hand around to fondle my breast, releasing another groan of tortured delight into my mouth.

Reaching down, I tugged at the band of his pants. He climbed off the bed without ever taking his hands from my body, and I raked the pants from his hips, pushing them down until he could kick them off.

Then, shyly, I began to touch him—the angled ridge of his hip, the flat plane of hot skin right below his navel, the smooth pectoral with its tight oval bud, the array of silky hard abs along his stomach. His skin flared incandescent with every caress, and his breath barked harsh against my cheek, my ear—he cupped my face, tilting it up, and he kissed me fiercely, possessively.

His erection burned hard and hot against my belly, and his whole body was rigid with constrained passion.

"You can take me right now," I whispered. "You don't have to wait. I'm ready."

His hand tucked between my legs, and I whimpered at the warmth and pleasure that radiated from that touch. Apollo slid a languid finger through the liquid pooling at my core, tracing slow slick swirls through my folds. "Beautiful," he whispered.

I couldn't breathe. The sensations were too vibrant, too exquisite. I could only mew helplessly and grip Apollo's shoulders while his fingers slithered along me again and again.

"I don't want to come yet," I whispered, shaking. "I want to come with you inside me."

"Get on the bed," he whispered back, ragged.

I lay down, nestling my head into one of the huge soft pillows.

Apollo's great golden body moved over me, and for a second I nearly forgot that this was a one-time thing, just a tool to unlock my powers. I had the weirdest urge to let him fill me up with his seed, put his child inside me.

No. That couldn't happen.

"Condom," I gasped. "In my purse. Do you know what that is?"

"Is it to prevent pregnancy?" he said hoarsely, sweeping a palm over my belly. "You don't need it with me. I can't achieve release."

"What?"

"It's a curse. Nothing you need to worry about. Trust me, you will have all the pleasure you desire, and more. I will ensure it."

Suspicion blazed in my mind. This could be a trick to impregnate me. Greek gods were notorious for that. "I'm not taking any chances. Condom on, or no deal."

"Most human preventatives don't work for Olympians. But I have a Fae spell that will prevent my seed from taking root inside you." At the words, his dick twitched and glowed brighter.

"All right," I hissed, and I pulled his face to mine, spreading and arching my legs. He settled over me, the heated silky length of him gliding inside me. I broke the kiss and arched, mute with exquisite delight, unable to breathe. Ajax had never felt like this. Apollo's length filled me, smooth and hard and vibrant—almost *vibrating*. There was a faint buzzing heat, a swelling glorious warmth.

He pulled back and slid through again, and I squealed helplessly at the intensity of the sensation. "God, your dick—it's—"

"It's designed for ultimate pleasure." He smiled. "I love watching what it does to women."

To *women*—of course he'd been with many women. This session between us wasn't unique or special to him, any more than it was to me. It was fun, pure and simple. Sex without any emotional entanglement.

He thrust again, harder, and I shrieked, because he'd stimulated a deep secret place I didn't even know existed. Apollo grinned with feral delight and swept my hair back from my face, cradling my head with his palm for a second. Then he planted both hands on the bed again and began to rut into me with manic desperation. Harsh groans escaped his throat with every thrust.

With my mind a mute blaze of bright sensation, I watched his glorious handsome face and the surge of his powerful body. My mouth was fixed open, my eyes flared wide—my consciousness centered on the burning, vibrant shaft rushing deep into my body. Every flowing stroke was its own keen thrill, sun-bright and rapturous.

Apollo was swearing in a language I didn't recognize, his voice breaking—with pleasure maybe, or emotion? I was too pleasure-dazed to tell.

"I'm so close," he gasped. "I think it's going to happen—Cassandra, you miracle—"

A lightning crack of pleasure burst through my abdomen, radiating outward, making every nerve quake and tremble with ecstasy. Short sharp gasps broke from my lips—I couldn't stop them, any more than I could stem the tide of the pleasure flooding my body. My mind exploded into a surge of melody, oceanic and wild.

My inner walls spasmed, pulsating around Apollo, and he cried out, his beautiful face twisting with tortured desire.

"Did you come?" I panted.

He shook his head. "I told you, I can't. But I can give you another."

I dragged his mouth to mine again, sliding my tongue between his teeth. Then I tucked my cheek against his, my mouth brushing his ear. My voice was still shaky, my head still swirling with music. I wasn't sure why I so desperately wanted him to come, but I felt I couldn't be satisfied unless it happened. "I want you to come for me, Apollo. Do you hear me?"

He groaned, his profile brushing mine, and he kissed my forehead with painful tenderness. "You're not the one. I was so sure you were... but I don't even care. I want you, I worship you. I'll give the rest of my existence to your pleasure."

My heart thrilled even as I panicked. *A one-time thing*, I reminded myself. *To unlock my powers.*

"Do you feel how deep you are inside me right now?" I whispered.

"Gods, yes," he panted, glowing brighter. The low humming heat of his length intensified.

"I feel every inch of you, and it's beautiful," I kept whispering as he thrust. "*You're* beautiful. You're the sweetest, most generous—" Oh god, I had to stop saying things like that. *A one-time thing.*

"Take me harder," I whispered. "Harder—my god—oh fuck—" And I came again, unexpectedly, a startling, radiant shock of pleasure. I shrieked with the sheer force of it, clutching the pillow with one hand and Apollo's arm with the other. My legs locked tight around Apollo's waist, pulling him deep, deep, while my body twisted and spasmed around him.

And this time, when I clenched around that burning hardness, he threw back his head and screamed, while waves of light shot from his body. The blaze of his orgasm rushed through my belly, bathing my insides in golden heat until I felt transparent, incandescent, euphoric.

I couldn't breathe for a second. Apollo was bowed over me, shaking, and his groans of bliss sounded almost like sobs.

"See?" I said, my voice as watery as my legs. "You can get there. Just takes a little effort."

Apollo choked a laugh. "You have no idea."

He lurched away and collapsed beside me, one hand cupping my breast. I thought about pushing his fingers away, but decided I'd allow it because it felt good.

A one-time thing.

Or maybe we could do it a couple more times. Just to make sure my powers unlocked or whatever. I didn't feel any different at the moment—except for a bone-deep, sated bliss throughout every cell of my body.

When I looked down, my abdomen was glowing faintly.

"Is your sperm *molten*?" I said. "It won't hurt me, will it?"

"No, no." His hand trailed down to my stomach. "I've slept with women of many races in a dozen realms, and none have ever been hurt in that way. Give me a moment to remember the spell, and I'll neutralize it. It's been a long time since I came inside anyone."

His eyebrows pinched together, and then he traced a symbol over my skin while speaking soft words. The faint glow through my flesh dimmed to nothing.

"You're generous with your body like you are with your money, huh?" I murmured.

"Yes. I enjoy giving others pleasure and relief."

"And you were serious about the curse? Not being able to—you know—"

He propped himself on one elbow and beamed, while his eyes gleamed wet. "I've been like this for a very long time—giving pleasure, never gaining it. The result of a Fae geas, a kind of powerful curse. And you broke it."

"How?" I whispered.

"I'm not sure you're ready for that," he murmured, squeezing my breast gently. "By the Styx, I love the shape of these, the way they feel."

But I wasn't going to be derailed from the topic. "Do I have a magical curse-breaking vagina?"

He laughed, rich and golden. "Maybe."

I wasn't satisfied with his answer, and I wasn't thrilled about the fact that I hadn't felt a tangible change. Were my powers released, or at least partly unlocked? How could I tell?

Frustrated, I sat up and swung my legs off the bed. I went to the bathroom and cleaned the traces of Apollo from my inner thighs. The creamy liquid he'd released was flecked with gold and smelled faintly like vanilla. Good grief, he was too damn dreamy. I'd have been far more comfortable doing this again if I could see a flaw somewhere.

I marched back into the bedroom, where Apollo was about to pull on pants.

"Stop," I ordered. "Don't get dressed yet. It's inspection time."

"Inspection?"

"I'm looking for flaws." I perused every golden inch of him, from the yellow hair curling across his brow to the neat arches and shapely toes of his perfectly formed feet. Even the nooks and crannies of him were tidy—clean and well-groomed.

I was gliding a finger down his spine when he said, with tight humor in his voice, "Are you done? Because if you are, I need a shower. A cold one."

A cold one? Did that mean he was already—I circled to face him and *yes*. Yes, he was hard again.

"It shines," I said softly. "It's kind of—pretty." Without thinking about it, I touched the tip of him, and he twitched against my finger.

When I looked up at his face, his features were calm, but the familiar glow rolled beneath his skin, intensifying. "Gods have incredible stamina," I said.

"We do. And as I said, it's been a very long time for me. My body is trying to make up for the lost pleasure."

"Then you probably want to find someone else to do it with," I replied. "Someone—better."

"Better?" He quirked a dark eyebrow.

Someone taller, prettier, more skilled, more pleasant— "Someone else," I repeated helplessly.

"I understand." He backed away, snatching the pants he'd tossed on the bed. "You'd rather not be with me again."

"We did say we were only going to be friends."

"Of course. Friends." He nodded vehemently, yanking on the pants. "I'll be your friend, Cassandra. But in that case you may be right—some space might work better for both of us. Maybe it's best that you find somewhere else to stay."

My chest felt like it was shrinking, constricting my lungs. "I'll start looking this morning. Might take a little while."

"You can stay here as long as you need to. But we can't share a bed again, do you understand?" He zipped his pants with a savage jerk and met my eyes. "I can't handle it."

"Can't handle it?" I breathed.

He huffed a sigh of frustration. "When I'm close to you—sometimes I think I'll go insane if I can't be touching you, everywhere."

I backed away, against the same dresser where I'd stood after I found out he was a god. "You can't talk to me like that."

"Why not?" he said, wretched and pleading. "I'm only telling you how I feel."

"And I only did this so I could unlock my powers. But it didn't work, and now I'm thinking it was a really bad idea." I splayed one hand across my face, squeezing my eyes shut. "I don't even know you, and you're talking to me like we're a *thing*—I can't even trust that I'm not clinically insane and just *inventing* all this Greek god crap to deal with everything that happened to me last year. This was such a terrible mistake."

Apollo crossed the floor and gripped my chin, forcing me to look up at him. "What did you say?" His eyes were manic fire. "About unlocking your powers?"

"Icelos said that sex with an Olympian would strengthen my connection to my ancestors, and maybe help release my abilities. He said I might be able to start seeing the future more clearly, with more time between the vision and the event. Maybe I could even change what's going to happen." My breath sped up, and I shuddered at the force of his hold on my jaw.

"You seduced me so you could unlock the gift of prophecy."

"Yes."

"Not because you wanted me."

"I think it's obvious I wanted you—"

"Not my body!" he cried out, agony in his tone. "Not my flawless carcass, Cassandra. Me! You didn't want *me*."

I stood frozen, shocked. It had never occurred to me that a beautiful man might hate being objectified just as much as a woman would. All the handsome men I'd known had been conceited and cocky about their looks, all too eager for women—or men—to fawn over them. But Apollo had been beautiful for centuries. He was clearly done with being craved for his looks alone. I'd hurt him deeply, without meaning to. And suddenly that angered me.

"Why can't I just have a one-night stand like a normal person?" I said, my voice shaking. "Of course the first time I try casual sex, it has to be with someone who takes it way too seriously. That's just my luck."

"And it's just my luck that you're the one—my *one*—and you don't want me." Apollo released my face and laughed bitterly.

"The one?" My voice shrilled. "I'm not your *one*! Don't you realize how ridiculous that sounds?"

His glow dimmed until he looked completely normal, like a toned, tanned human man in his late twenties. "You're right. It does sound ridiculous." His voice was calm, emotionless, smooth. "For what it's worth, I think your remedy worked, but only in part. Your power aura is stronger and clearer, less tangled and tormented. But there's still something oppressing it."

He strode into the bathroom and slammed the door.

I thought about leaving while he was in there. I had money now, a lot of it, in cash, tucked into the ragged lining of my purse for safekeeping. But I'd left a bunch of really expensive brand-new cosmetics in that bathroom, and I wasn't about to leave them behind.

So I curled up on the couch and reviewed what I'd done, objectively.

Okay, so maybe I shouldn't have used him like that. But he was totally overreacting. People slept together for dumb reasons all the time, so why not me? Why should my sexual activities have some great serious meaning attached to them? Why couldn't I simply get myself thoroughly pounded without being mired in emotional aftermath?

I could feel it descending again, the weight on my soul, the crushing sense that I was just a shitty person in general, barely worth the trouble of my existence. Dragging the blanket around my shoulders, I made myself as small as possible and sat there, staring out the loft windows at another gray day. The sun wouldn't be visible this morning, and I'd dimmed the light of the sun god himself. Yay me.

Apollo slammed out of the bathroom several minutes later and swept into the living room, towel-clad and golden and steaming. His hair was curly and dark with water, dripping onto the coffee table as he seated himself there, facing me.

"You didn't leave," he said.

"I thought about it."

He nodded. "Listen, I have no idea how to relate to a human woman—or any woman—the way I'm trying to relate to you. I've made so many mistakes, and I'll make more. But I don't want you to leave." He gathered my hand in his. "I'll stop saying things that make you uncomfortable. If you want to have sex again, just to work on unlocking your powers, I'll do it, and I won't demand any emotional connection from you. If you'd rather have sex with a different Olympian, I'll get Dionysus to pay us a visit. He'll be happy to oblige."

I opened my mouth to speak, but he pressed a finger to my lips. "One moment, Cassandra, and then you can say anything you like. I want to be in your life, however you'll have me. Friends, sexual partners, distant acquaintances, anything. I'll be whatever you need. I have so much I'd like to show you—my wings, for one thing. Olympus, for another—if you're interested. And I still want to learn about Earth. There's a list of places I want to visit, foods I want to try. I want to hear concerts and go to a movie. And I want to dance in one of your human nightclubs. Pan says they're fun."

"Pan?" My eyebrows lifted. He'd mentioned Pan before.

"Peter Pan. A Fae friend of mine."

"Nope." I jumped off the couch, hurried into the bathroom, and started tossing cosmetics into one of my shopping bags.

Apollo came after me, leaning a forearm on the doorframe, which made his half-naked physique even more noticeable.

"That's what does it?" he said. "You'll accept the existence of Greek gods, nightmare kings, prophetic powers and multiple realms, but when it comes to Peter Pan—"

"Peter Pan is a fucking children's story," I snapped at him.

"Based on truth."

"I can't accept that. Look, I've had a really rough few days—rough year, actually—no, rough *years*, and I don't have the bandwidth for this. I don't need supernatural godly Fae mythical shit, okay? I need *normal*. Yesterday was really nice, with the shopping and the food. I need more of that. Not 'Peter Pan is my buddy and he likes nightclubs.' Hell to the no."

Apollo started laughing halfway through my speech, and by the end of it I was doing some kind of half-smile, half-frown thing with my face—I glimpsed it in the mirror and it was not attractive, so I just let the frown part go.

"You big golden dummy," I murmured. "Why do I feel better around you? The badness was creeping in again while you were in the shower and now—" I took a quick mental inventory. "I don't feel the same heaviness. You're also the god of healing, right? Are you like—healing me?"

"Not you individually," he said. "My healing powers aren't targeted or specific, unfortunately. They function as an aura, an influence pervading the area where I'm residing. Everyone in this building and everyone for blocks around will experience better sleep and improved general health while I'm here. Some of them may find their bodies suddenly and inexplicably free of disease. I've often wished I could control or direct the ability, and I tried to find a way, through Fae magic. It didn't work. And my research earned me the curse—the one you broke." He grimaced. "If there's a physical component to your depression, and not merely an emotional one, my aura may be helping with that part of it."

"Like medication can help regulate chemical imbalances in the brain?"

"Exactly." His eyes brightened with interest. "What kind of medications do humans have for mental health problems?"

"I'm not well-versed in that," I said. "And I've never been officially diagnosed with anything. I guess I'm scared of a diagnosis. I've always been leery of medication."

"Even if it could help you?"

"I've had a couple friends who used antidepressants, and their experiences weren't great.

Sometimes it messes with the creative spark. And I couldn't bear to lose that."

"But when I met you, depression had robbed you of that spark anyway," he said gently. "There's no shame in doing what's necessary to get your body and mind back on the right track."

"I know." I hesitated, avoiding his eyes. I'd had the same argument with myself countless times, working up the nerve to go to the doctor about my mental health, and then talking myself out of it. Maybe if I stuck around Apollo long enough, I'd be healed for good or whatever, and it wouldn't be a problem.

Maybe then I'd never have to dig into those other parts of my psyche, the dark terrifying places that twisted my insides into tight coils.

"Let's do something normal," Apollo said, taking the bag of cosmetics from me and setting it on the counter. "Jack's partner Emery mentioned something called 'brunch'—a type of feast humans enjoy. Two meals merged into one."

"Brunch," I repeated, giving him a small smile. "I could be into that."

10

APOLLO

Cassandra explained "brunch" and various other human cultural concepts to me while we feasted on fluffy baked goods called "biscuits" topped with chicken, bacon, eggs, and maple syrup. We had something called "home fries," too, which sounded very warm and comforting. I liked the aura of the eatery—thick beams of honey-gold wood, broad heavy tables lined with stools, and pleasant lighting. The music was decent, though I could have done without the annoying twang that most of the songs seemed to have. One in particular grated on my nerves until I had to cover my ears.

Cassandra watched me, amusement lighting her dark eyes. Finally she motioned to me. "It's done," she was saying when I cautiously uncovered my ears again.

"Thank Zeus," I groaned.

"Country music ain't your thang, huh?" she drawled.

"It's abrasive."

"That song was. Some of it's decent, though. I don't like to diss anybody's taste in music, you know? Different music speaks to different souls."

"I don't want to know the soul that music speaks to," I muttered.

Cassandra laughed—a full-out, sparkling laugh that triggered flutters beneath my ribs. "Show me this list of human things you want to enjoy," she said.

"I have the list in my mind."

"Well, let's write it down." She pulled out her phone. "Start talking."

So I told her everything I wanted to try, and she wrote down my ideas and more besides. When we'd paid for our food, we wandered through the downtown streets of her city, visiting places and checking activities off the list. She said for some of the things I would need to travel, to go overseas; but I told her those items could wait. Inwardly I hated the idea of any significant distance coming between us, but I didn't say that. The honest admission of my thoughts and feelings usually seemed to disturb her.

We checked out a music store, visited a pottery shop, and crossed a bridge over the river that ran straight through her city's downtown area. We bought specialty coffee, ate gelato, and wandered through an art gallery. Twice we encountered street musicians, plying their talents in the cold gray air, and I gave them wads of cash so large Cassandra nearly had a heart attack. In return, both musicians played us beautiful songs, and by the looks on their faces I knew they were astounded at the quality of their own performances. My doing, of course. I shed inspiration and beauty wherever I went.

We bought last-minute tickets to a musical at a nearby theater—Cassandra called it the Peace Center. I liked the name. A little on-the-nose, but well-intentioned.

Next we had to buy clothes in which to attend the show. I chose a shop that looked elegant, and when Cassandra paled at the prices I knew I had chosen right. Somehow she managed to sweep her hair into an elegant updo with little more than a stretchy band and some pins, and then we stopped by a jewelry store so I could adorn her neck and ears with jewelry to suit the evening gown she wore.

We were overdressed for the performance—me in my fine suit, Cassandra in her evening gown—but neither of us cared. The musical was called *"Les Misérables,"* and with me in the audience, the performance was truly exquisite. I marveled at how far humans had come from the simple Greek plays of long ago, when my race ruled on Earth.

More than that, the message of the musical struck deep into my heart. I couldn't stop seeing the miners in the Gjöll realm, the human slaves in my father's palace, and the common folk of Olympus. Even the demi-gods and divine descendants lived as second-class citizens in my realm, while the pure-blooded Pantheon were worshiped and revered. Incongruity and injustice were major themes of the performance, and I found myself identifying uncomfortably with Jean Valjean. His tragic, triumphant song rang in my ears long after it was over: *Who am I? Who am I?*

And who was I, indeed?

Was I Apollo, the unquestioning servant of the High Seat?

Apollo, the loyal son of Zeus?

Was everything I had worked for, everything I'd striven to become, subject to the whim of a ruler I no longer respected, a patriarch I could not trust?

Was I damning myself, no better than him, if I stayed silent in the face of my father's wrongdoing?

During intermission Cassandra went to the women's restroom while I stayed in my seat, tearing at my program, struggling with a sense of gnawing unrest deep in my bones. I shifted my thoughts away from the affairs of Olympus and the cosmos, back to my relationship with Cassandra. Back to the immensity of what she'd done for me, by breaking the geas. Back to the ramifications of that moment, for both of us.

During that handful of minutes in the shower after our fight, I'd tried to come to terms with the breaking of my curse and what it meant. My mind was still stuttering over the reality of it—I couldn't grasp it firmly yet, couldn't truly accept that it was *over*, that I was free, and that I was also bound to her.

Cassandra and I had enjoyed a lovely day together, but we hadn't conversed seriously, or settled anything between us. My heart was still sore and tender from her admission that she'd only slept with me to unlock her powers. And my body was still adjusting to the aftereffects of the broken geas—a rush of sexual energy so strong I'd had to excuse myself several times throughout the day so I could go to the men's restroom and find relief. I felt desperate and pathetic, reduced to jetting my release into human toilets in filthy stalls.

I didn't want to spend myself over and over into empty air. I wanted to be with my life-mate. With

Cassandra, my destined partner. The person with whom I'd share the rest of my existence.

But she was cautious, wary, frightened of getting too close to me. She needed to move slowly, when all I wanted was to spend a solid week with her in my house at Delos, learning all the ways our bodies could fit together and give pleasure. No, a week wouldn't be enough, nor a month, nor a year. I'd never tire of her soul and its music. The body she wore was a beautiful shell, a wrap for the exquisite being within, and I loved both the gift and its wrapping.

I'd started loving her in the food court, when I first heard the full glory of her inner melody. Since then, everything she did was a tiny burst of fresh love, augmenting what I already felt until it was nearly unbearable keeping it all inside. But I had controlled myself. All day I'd been on my best behavior—the charming friend, the trusted companion. I played the role to perfection. After all, I'd had years of practice hiding the agony of my desires.

I had to remember my goal, the god I wanted to be.

Apollo the selfless.

Apollo the protector, the generous, the brave.

Apollo the peacemaker whenever conflict could be avoided. Apollo the warrior when evil reared up with bared fangs.

Apollo, calm and collected and reasonable, pleasant and kind.

Phoebus fucking Apollo.

"Apollo?" Cassandra stood over me, staring at my lap. "Um…you okay?"

I looked down at the shredded bits of the program, scattered like snow over my pants and the floor. "I am perfectly fine." I gave her my best beaming smile. "Why do you ask?"

"Because you turned the program into powder." She leaned in closer, and I averted my eyes from the tempting view of her cleavage. "And you're starting to glow a little bit."

Quickly I drew a fresh veil over myself and my power. "Better?"

"Yes." She pushed down the cushioned seat and perched on it. "We can leave if you want."

"No, the show is wonderful." I brushed paper flecks off my pants. "And you look so lovely in that dress. It would be a shame not to let the world see you. Shall we go to dinner after this?"

She opened her mouth to reply, but her eyes fixed on something beyond me, and she frowned slightly.

I turned to see what she was staring at—and looked up into the eyes of my sister Athena; standing in the row beside me.

She wore a long, shimmering gray gown, and her silver hair was done up with crystal combs. As always, she embodied queenly elegance and graceful wisdom.

"Phoebus," she said under her breath, seating herself in the empty seat beside me.

"Athena," I breathed. "What the Styx are you doing here?"

"Enjoying myself," she said dryly.

"You hate Earth."

"I really do." She sighed. "Though it has improved somewhat since I was last here."

"Apollo," Cassandra interjected. "Are you going to introduce me?"

"Cassandra, this is my sister Athena," I said. "Athena, this is Cassandra. She is—a friend."

"Of course she is." Athena spoke barely above a breath, for my ears alone. "One of your pleasurable charity cases, is she?"

"She's different," I hissed back. "She broke the geas."

"She broke it?" Athena's gray eyes widened. "But that means—"

I glared at Athena, willing her to be quiet about the life-mate part of the curse, and she read the directive in my eyes. My sister knew me well, especially in this lifetime. She'd often told me that this version of myself was her favorite.

"Cassandra." Athena leaned around me, extending a hand. "So delighted to meet you."

"I'm just—so honored to meet *you*," Cassandra gasped. "I'm a big fan. Of your wisdom. And your everything, really. You're just—you're awesome."

I hid a smile. I could hear the stately theme music Cassandra's mind was composing for Athena at that very moment.

But this was no time for teasing. Athena rarely ventured out of the Olympian realm, so she must have a very important reason for coming all the way to Earth.

"Is everything all right at home?" I asked.

"No," Athena said bluntly. "It isn't. Zeus is furious that you went back to earth after your errand for him, rather than returning to Olympus."

"I'm not a child. I don't have to report my comings and goings to him."

She shrugged. "You know how he is. Unreasonable bastard. And Hera has been sending flocks of Aeternae to pester your mother. Those bony birds are the only things that can get through all the barriers you've placed around Delos. Except for Artemis and me, of course. We can pass through—and Hera is so terribly mad about that," Athena's mouth curved with satisfaction. "Leto called me to deal with the Aeternae, and while I was there she mentioned you had received a letter from Hades."

"From Hades?" I frowned. "Why would he write to me? He doesn't like me."

"Maybe something's wrong in the Underworld? Maybe he needs to contact Pan and he's going through you for some reason?"

I shook my head. "It doesn't make sense."

"Has he ever sent you a message before?" Athena asked.

I frowned, retracing the paths of my memories back through decades, through lifetimes. "No, he hasn't. I've always contacted him first if I was planning to visit."

"I thought so. Between that message and our father's wrath, I thought I should come find you."

"Why not send a messenger? I know how much you hate inter-realm travel."

"I knew I'd find you faster than a messenger could." Athena sighed, flicking a bit of paper off my knee. "We're blood, Phoebus. Half-siblings, but still. You are dear to me, and so is Leto. I want both of you to survive this resurgence of Father's anger."

The lights in the theater flashed, a sign that intermission was nearly over. Athena rose, a slim column of shimmering gray silk.

"Stay," Cassandra said, with genuine warmth in her voice. "Enjoy the show with us. That seat isn't taken."

Athena looked her over, head to toe. "I suppose I could stay," she said softly. "If I'm not in the way."

"Please." Cassandra smiled, and my fingers curled tight around the armrests of my seat. Cassandra was so beautiful, smile or not, but that particular smile glowed with admiration and acceptance. I felt a little jealous that she'd shed it over Athena instead of me.

Athena nodded and resumed her seat gracefully. Before the lights went out, she leaned close to my ear and whispered, "Zeus thinks you want the High Seat."

"I know. But I don't."

"You should. You'd make a much better ruler of the realm than he ever has."

"I don't want the responsibility."

"Right. You want to run around the realm cluster, fixing all the problems of every race except ours."

"What about you?" I threw back. "Why don't you aim for the High Seat?"

"I don't have the inter-realm allies you have, or the battle experience."

"Is that so, goddess of war?"

"Goddess of *wisdom* and strategy. I haven't fought in any battles since the Earth days, and you know it." She shot the last words at me while the house lights went down and we were all submerged in impenetrable blackness.

"Olympus needs a guide, not a warrior," I whispered. "You'd be perfect."

She started to say something else, but I said, "Shh," and inwardly congratulated myself on having the last word. Athena and I usually ended up debating for hours whenever we were together, since both of us prized victory too much to yield ground on any topic. I heard her scoff quietly in her seat, but she didn't try to whisper back as the next act of the *Les Misérables* began.

Since we'd secured seats so late, our places were far back in the theater, where it was deeply dark. During one of the songs, Cassandra's small fingers crept over and wound themselves with mine. I sat paralyzed, galvanized, not sure what it meant.

After a minute her hand shifted, fingertips finding new places to travel. She stroked the notches between my knuckles, followed each bone of my hand from the wrist all the way to the tip. Then she tucked two fingers against the underside of my wrist, where my pulse quivered quick and eager under the skin. Her touch slid to the center of my palm and sent vibrations of nervous desire all through my body.

My face burned hot with arousal, and my dick pushed against the seam of my pants. Zeus have mercy. I pressed my other hand over hers to still her questing fingers.

What did she want? Officially we'd decided on being friends, but the entire day had felt like a balancing act—flirting gently with her without going too far and making her uncomfortable. And now *this*—

Maybe she didn't realize how much a simple touch could affect me. How much I ached for someone who would handle me tenderly. Not a bracing male grip by way of greeting, or a clap on the shoulder, or a quick hug. Not the greedy touches of women who craved my beauty and had been denied their pleasure for too long. No, I yearned for the casual, affectionate intimacy of partners, of lovers, of mates. I wanted someone to rub my back, play with my hair, hold my hand, kiss my cheek—all the things that humans never expected a god to want.

Cassandra pulled her hand from mine to applaud the end of a solo, and she didn't touch me again for the rest of the show, though I sat tense and trembling in the dark beside her, aching for another brush of her fingertips.

After the performance and the curtain call, we filed out with the other attendees. Athena gripped my arm and said, low, "You should come to Olympus with me now, and deal with the Zeus situation and the letter from Hades."

"I don't want to deal with Zeus, and Hades can wait," I retorted. "I'm having a good time here. I deserve it, after all I've done for the realms."

"I know you deserve it," she said. "But it is the unfortunate burden of truly good leaders to rarely receive the rest they seek."

My lips curled. "Spare me your pearls of wisdom. I'm no leader. I help other men, and support them. I do not lead."

"You could." Athena leaned closer to my ear. "We may need a great leader soon, Apollo. There is one more bit of news I did not tell you earlier—I've received word that the Maru Sealgair have been sighted in our realm cluster."

Alarm spiked through my heart. "The Maru Sealgair? What would bring those bounty hunters from their own realm cluster to ours?"

"I'm not sure. But they must be seeking a very valuable prize—someone or something of greater power than any we've seen in a long time. And you know who they work for."

I swallowed the surge of panic in my throat. There was one person I knew of who was powerful enough to tempt the Maru Sealgair. One person, untrained and inexperienced, with powers that I'd never fully seen, though I suspected their extent. The child I'd hidden with Peter Pan.

Persephone.

If someone had managed to circumvent the geas I'd laid on her, the one that made people forget her—if word of her origins and powers had traveled through our realm cluster, or even beyond it—

If the terrible entity holding the reins of the Maru Sealgair learned of her existence—

"You look pale," said Athena. "You know something, don't you? About what or who they're looking for?"

I glanced aside at Cassandra. She was watching my sister and me, drinking in our conversation. "Do you need to go?" she asked.

"I think so," I said. "But I can spare one more night." I glared at Athena, daring her to contradict me.

But she only shrugged, with a soft smile. "I look forward to seeing you at home soon, then."

She glided away through the crowd, a gleam of silver and shadow.

Cassandra laid a hand on my arm. "If you need to go now—"

"No," I said sharply. Then I softened the harsh word with a smile. "First, I want to dance with you."

II

CASSANDRA

The club was incredibly loud, full of jarring music and neon lights. Apollo got this pained look on his face, and he left me for a moment, making his way to the DJ station. Threads of golden light slithered from Apollo's fingers, curling into the DJ's hands and coiling around his headphones. My eyes widened with panic, and I glanced around the place—but no one seemed to notice, not even the DJ. And within seconds, the vibe of the music changed, shifting into one of the songs on my playlist—a nostalgic Selena Gomez number, "Love You Like a Love Song." The DJ gave it a wilder edge, sped it up and played around with the beats, but it resonated in my heart like it always had—stronger this time, pounding through my veins as Apollo made his way back toward me.

He'd left his suitcoat in the club's coat room, and he wore a dress shirt, wide open at the neck, with his deep golden tan glowing against the crisp white material. His bright wavy hair was tied back at his nape, and the strobing lights glinted on the tiny amber studs in his nose and eyebrow. Palm to my waist, he swept me into the dance.

I'd always loved moving to music, even if I was only a mediocre dancer. Somehow, with him, I was better than ever, as if the inner soul of me was finally able to express itself through my limbs. Apollo was all lean hips and lithe waist, rolling through moves that looked almost familiar—but every jerk and slither of his body was a little unusual, a little otherworldly. Which made sense—after all, he'd danced in the Fae realm, in the Olympian realm, and god knew where else. Slowly a space cleared around him as people noticed his beauty and his unique moves.

I started to back away, to melt into the crowd, to watch him—but then Dua Lipa's "Love Again" thundered through the room—another one from my playlist—and Apollo caught my hand and pulled me close.

I didn't even think—I just started to dance, locked eye to eye with Apollo, with the beat throbbing deep and violent in my soul. Heat swirled and spiraled between us as we moved, heads whipping, hips swiveling, my fingertips trailing along his arm, his palm gliding up my thigh through the slit in my dress. It was a tango, a foxtrot, a waltz, a crazed hip-hop chaos—all of them and none of them at once, and somehow I didn't have to think about how to move—I was utterly synchronized with him.

My skin heated, molten, a light sweat filming my cleavage and the back of my neck. My hairstyle fell out completely, and the loose waves danced around my shoulders as I twisted and whirled with Apollo.

We stepped and turned, and my fingers gripped the elastic band holding his hair. I tugged it free, releasing the golden mane.

With a snapping jerk, he yanked me against his chest—a single fiery instant—then he pushed me away again, twirled me—we were back to back, and I writhed against him, my arms outstretched parallel to his. He whipped me around again, until his mouth was a scant shivering breath from mine.

Faintly I heard people cheering and whistling for us—they might as well have been in another realm.

Apollo's lips grazed my cheekbone, and a manic tingle of desire traced between my legs. I couldn't speak—could barely breathe. All the things that weighed me down seemed inconsequential, like Ajax and my old job, like my childhood and my mother, like the apartment fire. They all curled up into a tumbleweed of darkness and rolled away into the cloudy distance, while I existed solely in the dance with the gleaming sun god and his tempting heat.

The song slid into New Radicals' "You Get What You Give." Apollo caught my wrist and pulled me through the hazy colored fog of the club, through neon-sliced air tangy with alcohol and sickly-sweet with a hundred blending colognes and perfumes. I didn't ask where we were going. My heart had swelled past the confines of my ribcage and it pulsed with the thunderous stamp of a thousand dancing feet.

Apollo tugged me past the bathrooms, around the corner into a shadowed part of the hallway. His desperate grip on my arm disappeared, only to be replaced by both hands on my shoulders, setting me against the wall. He released me and braced a palm near my head. I could feel the sun-warmth flooding from him, soaking into my body.

"You and I, we're friends," he said hoarsely.

"Yes."

"But not just friends, after all."

My breath stuttered, emotions bursting enormous and undeniable in my chest. I might be a fool in the eyes of most people—feeling too deeply and quickly, wandering past the careful guidelines of society—but suddenly I didn't care. Maybe what I needed was something absolutely ridiculous and gorgeous and wonderful.

"No, we're not just friends," I whispered.

His harsh exhale bathed my lips, and he closed his eyes for a second in fierce relief. "I lied before, though I didn't know I was lying at the time. I thought I could be satisfied with being in your life any way you'd let me, but—I can't, Cassandra, I can't. I need all of you—selfishly, foolishly, I know it's sudden—" He pushed away from me and ran shaking fingers through his golden hair. "But you need me, too. You don't fully realize it yet, but we are meant to be together. I won't promise to make you happy, because constant happiness isn't possible or preferable, not for an artistic soul like yours—but I will give you anything, everything. I will stand aside when you need space, and take you out when you need to wander. I'll bring you tea or fly you to the stars." He stepped into my space again, golden and earnest and beautiful—and he slid to his knees, clasping one of my hands. "All I want in exchange, Cassandra, my darling, is a little of your love. Anything you can spare."

Something unlocked inside me—I could feel it unfurling, like a flower opening its petals to the sun. I almost laughed then, because it seemed inconceivable not to love him—I'd been trying to convince myself that I didn't, couldn't, wouldn't—but he was everything, after all. Everything I wanted, and all that I needed.

Music exploded inside me, a glorious rush of song, and it carried all that I felt for the god on his knees before me. My sorrow and uncertainty were there, yes, threads of darkness in the shining melody, but they were all but overcome in the flood of emotion and connection, the truth that my soul and his shared a similar cadence, a quiet resonance. The god of music and I were made to harmonize together—my darkness to his light.

I knew Apollo could hear it—the song I poured out for him. And because we were alone, we could feel it all as intensely as we wanted, with no one to judge us—not his family, or mine, or anyone in this realm or another. No one to say we were being silly, or corny, or ridiculous. Just me and him and the divine cataclysm of the music.

Still on his knees, Apollo leaned into me, and I sank my fingers into his hair, gathering him close, trembling with the force of what I felt. When he pulled away and got to his feet, my dress and his lashes were wet.

"Come here," I whispered, reaching up to him.

He bent his face to mine, and our lips sealed, soft and hot. There was a tender urgency to the way he kissed me, and I remembered Athena, and her advice that he should return home.

"You have to go, don't you?" I breathed.

"Yes."

"Could I—could I come with you?"

"I would love to bring you with me, but I'm not sure what I'll encounter, especially from my father. And I have no idea what Hades wants. Olympus might not be safe for you right now. It's best if you stay here. You can have the loft to yourself while I'm gone, and there's plenty of money—"

"I don't care about the money. Apollo, what will I do when you're gone?" My fingers curled into his shirt as panic coiled in my gut. "What if I go back into that dark place?"

"Cassandra." He covered one of my hands with his own. "You have been strong on your own for years. Your happiness doesn't depend on me. Keep yourself busy while I'm gone. What's a dream you've wanted to pursue, but you've never had the time or money to do it?"

I glanced aside, flushing. The first thing that popped into my mind was a poster I'd seen in the concert hall lobby—open auditions at the Little Theatre for a production of *Cabaret*. I'd wanted to be in a musical again, but when I was teaching I had no extra time, and after I got fired I'd been too demoralized to try out for anything. Maybe now I could muster the courage.

Apollo placed two fingers against my cheek and tilted my face back toward him. "You have something in mind, don't you? You don't have to tell me what it is, but while I'm gone, you should do it."

"I'm not sure I'm good enough."

A grin illuminated his handsome face. "You're good enough. Better than anyone in this realm deserves."

"An endorsement from the god of music." I fanned myself. "Such an honor."

Apollo laughed and kissed me again, quick and light—then again, humming in his throat—and then again, deeper, slower, sliding his tongue into my mouth while heat pooled between my legs. I swept my fingers down his back, down to that neatly shaped ass of his, and I cupped and squeezed it like I'd been wanting to do since I first met him.

Apollo growled and crushed me harder to the wall, his fingers finding the slit of my dress and gliding all the way up, right to my heated center. The thin cotton panties were wet through, and he gasped into my mouth when he touched them.

"You've made women wet before," I whispered.

"But they weren't *you*," he hissed, nudging his fingers beneath the material. When he touched me, I whimpered, helpless with craving. Every little brush of his fingertips made me tremble and twitch.

"You're so sensitive," he murmured, his lips drifting over mine. "I love touching you like this."

My body responded with a fresh surge of liquid warmth, and he circled through the slickness until I was nearly crying into his shoulder. "Apollo—Apollo *please*—"

"I need to be inside you," he said hoarsely. "May I?"

The music in my head shifted, thinning to an anxious wail of strings. "But—here? I'm not ready—I'm sweaty from dancing, and I need to shave and wash, and make sure everything is—"

"What are you talking about?" He laughed, ragged and breathless.

"Ajax always wanted me smooth and sweet-smelling and clean—"

"What the Styx," he rasped at my ear. "Forget him. You're beautiful, and you don't have to do any of those things for me. I mean, sure, the occasional shower—"

I laughed, but the sound was raw with aching relief.

"—but you never have to conform to some unreasonable standard of perfection," he ended.

"But *you're* perfect."

"Maybe some people think so. But who's to say, really? It's all subjective." He dipped a finger inside me, and a shrill gasp broke from my lips. Apollo grinned and nuzzled his profile against mine. "I will always crave you, no matter what, Cassandra. Are you going to come for me, darling?" Another finger, plunging deeper, and I shuddered around him. But I didn't quite break, because I saw the tension in his face, the agony of restraint.

"Only if you come for me too," I whispered, and I cupped between his legs, stroking upward.

He gave a shuddering gasp. "Have mercy."

Carefully I unzipped his pants and pulled his length free. He was glowing, burning for me, and my body trembled at the memory of how he'd felt inside me the first time. Grateful, sensual music filled my thoughts, spiraling and swelling, and I knew he relished it as deeply as I did, because he threw his head back and sighed, yielding himself to the blended pleasure of body and mind.

The dark end of the hallway was still empty, no cameras that I could see. Before my first tryst with Apollo, I'd never had sex with anyone but Ajax—and never anywhere but our bedroom.

Apollo kissed me again, and then his smooth lips drifted along my cheek to my ear. "I'm going to fuck you now," he murmured. Breathless, I nodded.

The next thing I knew, he'd lifted me against the wall, my legs over his hips, my panties pulled aside, and he was pushing in, filling me up with that delicious glowing heat. I whined, shrill and tremulous, and he groaned deep with pleasure. "Cassandra, you feel so perfect." His voice broke, and he began to pump into me. I could tell he was trying to be gentle, and while I loved him for it, I was desperate, quivering on the brink of something—not just love or pleasure, but something else, something bigger.

"Harder," I whispered.

Apollo swore and kissed me, and then he let himself go. He braced me, cupping my body while he rammed into me, and his glow cut through the shadows, bathing the hall in yellow light. I didn't care if we were caught—couldn't think about it—I closed my eyes and gave in to the bliss of being thoroughly pounded by my divine lover. The heat of him, the rush of each stroke, the soft blurred vibration of his length through my folds—it all spiraled and coiled and burst in a nerve-shattering explosion of pleasure. At the first spasm of my body around him, he came, hard and deep, and he slammed his lips to mine, crying out in my mouth to muffle the sound.

But he didn't pull out. His hips kept rocking, a smooth, easy rhythm, and his hand slid over my breast, smoothing the flesh, fingertip circling the peak. I quivered, and jerked, and came again, gasping.

"That's it," he whispered, still pumping gently. "That's my beautiful girl. Next time I'm going to taste that sweet succulent nectar of yours, and I won't stop licking you until you come at least five times."

"Oh god," I whimpered. "Is that even possible?"

"With me, it is."

"And this is what you do for other women?"

Apollo thrust so deep inside me that I inhaled, sharp and startling. He was softening, but still hard enough to make me feel pleasantly full and comforted.

"It's what I did for other women," he said. "But from now on, I'm yours alone."

I laid my arms across his shoulders, twirling my fingers into his golden hair. "That's good." And I kissed him, while he traced the Fae symbol on my belly and whispered the spell to neutralize the seed glowing inside.

Voices from somewhere nearby made us both jump. Apollo quickly pulled out of me and tucked himself away, while I straightened my underwear and my dress, muffling a giggle. "I can't believe I just did that."

He grinned, and started to speak—but without warning, my hearing cut off and my vision went dark. Dimly I was aware of my body swaying, my shoulder crashing against the wall. But I couldn't see or hear anything. I was lost in a blank world, inky black and soundless.

In the center of the blackness a picture expanded—like a TV screen growing larger. I saw myself in a room, heard myself belting out "Make Your Own Kind of Music" in front of three people, delivering the best performance of my life.

The snapshot faded, and another took its place—a teenage boy walking into the Orchard Park post office with a semi-automatic rifle—I glimpsed the clock on the wall as gunfire and screams erupted—4:00 p.m.

Then a third image—Apollo playing a lute, sending a flood of music over a woman whose body was half milk-white, half ebony. As the two-toned woman keeled over in sleep, Apollo grabbed the arm of the girl beside her, and they hurried together toward a golden chariot pulled by flaming horses. I watched them soar through the air, past a handful of bored-looking guards, straight through an iridescent slit in the sky.

The vision vanished, and my hearing returned.

Apollo's voice probed the blackness. "I don't know what happened. Give me a minute with her—"

"Did you drug her?" A woman's voice, shrill and accusing.

"I swear I didn't." Apollo's reply was drenched with anxiety.

"I'm—I'm fine." I blinked, and the dark fog thinned and cleared. I lay cradled in Apollo's arms. A man and a woman stood nearby, peering worriedly at me. "I just blacked out for a second."

"I'll call an ambulance," said the man.

"No, no, I'm really fine." I struggled to my feet, and Apollo braced me with a powerful arm. He'd veiled his glory again, but I felt the comforting warmth of him permeating my skin. "I have these episodes sometimes. We've got it under control." I gave them a hard, bright smile as Apollo helped me along the hallway.

The couple let us go, but I could hear them muttering anxiously behind us. And I was starting to panic—to totally freak out—because what the hell was *that*?

We collected our things from coat check and burst out into the cold night air. Apollo held our bags, and he kept his hand in the center of my back, as if he thought I might keel over again.

"It's a long way to the loft," he said. "I'll call a car." He pulled out his phone and began fumbling around, clearly uncertain how to use the app. Gently I pushed the phone down.

"Let's walk, please," I said. "I think it'll do me good."

"Are you sure?"

When I met his eyes, the agonized concern in them made my heart twinge. Sweet sensitive god-man. "I'm sure."

We began to walk away from the nightclub, along a blue-shadowed sidewalk intermittently gilded with the glow of street lamps. The air had the frozen breathless stillness and the crackling spicy scent that precedes snowfall. In South Carolina, snow was rare, but we usually had one or two days of it each year, and those days were always magical. Just the thought of soft white flakes drifting from a chalky black sky or cotton-gray clouds was enough to soothe my spirit a little. I filled my nose and lungs with the clean air, exhaling slowly.

At this time of night, the chattering downtown crowds had dwindled to quiet weary workers headed home, or giggling groups of friends staggering along to the next bar. Apollo and I took a shortcut through an empty square, an expanse of damp gleaming pavers and the glittering metal skeletons of unoccupied chairs and tables.

"Can you tell me what happened?" His breath steamed more than mine, a swirl of white mist in the icy night air.

"I had visions," I told him. "First ones I've had during waking hours. I think having sex with you unlocked my powers, like Icelos said it would."

"But we've had sex before, and nothing happened with your powers." Apollo raised an eyebrow.

"Maybe it has something to do with the way we connected this time. The, um—the emotions." I blushed—and then I stopped walking, struck by a horrible thought. "Oh god—is this going to happen all the time now? Am I going to have random unpredictable visions? That would seriously suck. I won't be able to drive, because what if I black out while driving? Not that I have a car, but—oh, this is bad. This is really bad."

Apollo moved in front of me and cupped my face with his hands. "We'll work through it. Did Icelos mention anything else?"

"He did say I could maybe learn to control it…"

"Perhaps you can. We'll have sex all day, every day, until you master your visions." He grinned and winked at me.

"You're so not funny," I whispered, trying to hide a smile.

"I'm a little funny." He leaned down to kiss my forehead.

We kept walking, crossing another cold, empty street.

"Icelos also said I needed to deal with my childhood trauma," I muttered.

"Hm." Apollo collected my fingers in his. "A difficult path to walk."

"No kidding."

He didn't push me to say more, but after a few minutes I said, "I need to ask you about one of my visions. There was a woman whose body was divided right down the center, and one half was white while the other was black. She had a girl with her. You put the monochromatic woman to sleep and then you took the girl in your chariot, and the two of you went through this rainbow slit thingy in the sky. There were a few guards, but they didn't try to stop you."

Apollo halted and pulled me to a stop with him. "Hecate."

"Hecka what?"

"Hecate—a witch, part-Titan and part human, servant to Demeter. She had a girl with her, you say? How old?"

"Like early twenties?"

"It could be her," Apollo muttered. "Pan could have aged her up—"

"If there's a girlfriend of yours you haven't told me about—"

"Styx, no! The girl is someone I rescued from Demeter, long ago—or at least she might be. If the girl in your vision is the same person I'm thinking of, she's in serious danger. It would explain the presence of the Maru Sealgair in this realm cluster."

"The bounty hunters?"

"Yes." He began spitting harsh words in a language I didn't know—swearing, I'd guess.

"You need to leave," I said. "I understand."

"I don't want to go." He pulled my hand to his lips, a searing desperate kiss on my knuckles. "I can't leave, not now, not when your powers are so volatile."

"She needs you, though," I said. "I could sense it, in the vision—that girl needs your help."

"It sounds as if she's in the Olympian realm," he said. "Which means your prophetic powers have taken a huge leap."

"We can figure that out later. You have to go."

"I'll come back." His grip on my hand tightened.

"You'd better. Don't pull a Thor and leave me here for years while you're off gallivanting in Asgard—"

"I have no idea what you're talking about, but I swear I'll come back to you as quickly as I can. Time passes differently in some of the realms, so I can't predict exactly when, but I will come to you. I swear it."

We had nearly reached his building. The January cold burrowed beneath my wrap and poked its claws through the slit of my dress, chilling my bare legs. I gritted my teeth to keep them from chattering and instinctively leaned into Apollo's warmth.

"Are you cold?" He let go of my hand and wrapped an arm around me. "I'm sorry, I didn't realize. I stay warm wherever I am." Heat flowed from where he touched me, rushing through my flesh and blood, warming me within seconds.

"Before you go, can I see your wings?" I asked impulsively.

He flashed me a smile, then glanced around. "This way."

Together we ducked into the parking garage behind his building. He pulled me into the stairwell, an empty, echoing concrete space. "I can make them vanish when I'm flying," he said. "I'll do that tonight when I fly to the realm gate, so I'm not spotted. You wouldn't believe how many eyes are on the Earth sky these days. Jack Frost warned me about it, and so did Pan. Of course Jack is an elemental Fae of this realm, so he's invisible in his Fae aspect, but if he flies around in human form—"

"Too much information," I interrupted, with an apologetic smile. "I promise one day I will let you tell me everything about Jack Frost and all the realms and everyone's powers, but I'm a little overwhelmed right now, and I think I can only handle one supernatural revelation at a time."

"The wings." He nodded. "I'm usually shirtless or wearing a chiton when I do this—give me a second." He laid aside our belongings and unbuttoned his white dress shirt, tossing it to me. I tucked my fingers into the fabric, relishing the leftover warmth from his body as I watched, expectant.

Two enormous golden wings snapped out from his shoulder blades, shedding amber sparks. His feathers gleamed with a vivid, burnished beauty. When I reached out, mesmerized, I could feel the heat of them on my palm.

"May I?" I whispered.

Apollo nodded, and I trailed my fingertips along his feathers. They were stiff and soft at once, hardy yet pliable, a rippling brush of gold. "So pretty," I murmured. And then I backed away a few steps just to take him in—dark pants slung low on his hips, the rich tanned glow of his torso, so cut, so tempting—and his face—classic male beauty, with that halo of bright waves crowning his head, clustering against his shoulders. The wings framed him to perfection.

But best of all were his amber eyes, dark-lashed and luminous as he let himself shine. A sudden, violent pain wrenched through me. I couldn't let him go, because he was too good to be true. A beautiful dream. If he left, I'd begin second-guessing myself. I might start to believe that I'd hallucinated him.

Tears stung my eyes, and Apollo swept toward me, a rush of gilded skin and shimmering wings. "What is it? Is it too much? I can hide them—you've been through a big change tonight."

"It's not that," I choked. "It's—you're real, aren't you? This isn't some trick of my overwrought mind?"

"I'm real." He kissed my nose, both my cheeks, and finally my lips. Then he pressed his wallet into my hand. "You'll have the loft, my instruments, my money, everything we bought together. Where else would they have come from? And you can ask any of your neighbors from your old building. They'll remember me. Your sister and her girlfriend met me. I'm real."

"You're real." I crushed my mouth to his, tasting the fiery sweetness of him. "You'll be back."

"Zeus himself couldn't keep me away." He gave me one more fierce kiss and clasped me to his chest so that his heartbeat thrummed against mine. I sighed into him, reassured.

But it still hurt when his wings vanished, and he waved to me, and he walked out of the parking garage. A moment later I heard a whispering beat of feathers on the wind.

And he was gone.

Mechanically I gathered the bags, along with his suit jacket and shirt. I used his keycard to enter the building and I rode the mirrored elevator alone until I reached his floor. Again I tapped the keycard, and I stumbled into the loft, which greeted me by turning all the lights on automatically.

I kicked the door shut and let everything fall to the floor except Apollo's shirt, which I crumpled against my face so I could breathe in the honey-and-amber scent of him.

That scent was real. The shirt was real. *He* was real. And so were my visions.

Which meant that as much as I wanted to cave in on myself, and sink into an agony of missing him, I couldn't. Some afternoon very soon, a boy was going to walk into a post office with a loaded gun. And I had to stop him.

The morning after Apollo left, I walked to the downtown park and used a burner phone app to call the police and tip them off about the post office threat. I didn't dare drive myself to the spot, but I hired a driver to take me to a yogurt shop across the street so I could watch what happened.

Which was nothing.

Absolutely nothing happened.

The police cruiser was sitting right in the parking lot when four o'clock rolled around, but no gun-toting teenager turned up. He probably saw the police presence and got scared off.

Either that, or my vision wasn't about today at all. Maybe it was going to take place on some future day. Impossible to know, and that frustrated the hell out of me.

I waited for another hour, too anxious and nauseated to eat the frozen yogurt I'd ordered. It turned to soup in the paper bowl while I stared across the street, watching the post office long after the policeman had left. Still no sign of the boy from my vision.

I'd done the right thing, hadn't I? I'd prevented a shooting... maybe.

The kid from my vision was still out there somewhere, still angry and murderous. Still in so much pain he was willing to end lives. Why had I seen *him*, and not some other tragedy or accident?

And how had my visions leaped between whole realms? Could I only prophesy things in the Earth realm and the Olympian realm, or would my visions eventually extend farther, to other realms? Hopefully not—I didn't think I could handle that. Until now, my visions had always been related to events in my vicinity—local happenings, nothing in other cities or worldwide. If I had to guess, my vision of Hecate and the girl only occurred because of my very recent, very intimate link with Apollo.

Maybe my Earthly visions focused on the most horrific things happening nearby. And if that was true, should I move somewhere with higher crime rates and more natural disasters? Did I have a responsibility to live in a place full of death and trouble, so I could see it and try to prevent some of it from happening?

"Ma'am?" The chirpy voice of the yogurt shop girl pierced my thoughts. "Did you need something else?"

I could hear the real question in her tone: *Why did you order frozen yogurt only to let it melt while you stared out the front window for two hours, you weirdo?*

"I'm good, thanks," I said. "I was waiting for someone, but I guess I'll just call a car and go."

"Oh." Her face changed, shifting into a sympathetic smile. "I've been stood up before. It sucks. Take your time."

I didn't correct her. When the car came, I went back to Apollo's building and ordered food, even though it was only five o'clock. Auditions for *Cabaret* were going on all day tomorrow, and I needed to practice. I hadn't sung in front of people for over a year. Judging from the vision of my audition, I still had the skills, but was I good because I decided to wing it, or because I practiced a lot ahead of time?

I'd always been one to practice a lot and prepare. But with Apollo's influence so fresh, maybe I didn't need to. Maybe I could rely on his "god-of-music" aura to carry me through the audition.

An echo of his words came back to me. *The muses come and go, touching people with talent… It's up to every talented human to keep practicing their art and honing their craft, even when a muse isn't influencing them directly.*

No leaving it up to the muse, then. Time to practice.

For a second I stood in the center of the silent loft and felt the crushing press of my powers, the towering significance of what they might mean in terms of my responsibility to humanity. The thought of experiencing sporadic, unpredictable blackouts over and over, being lashed with the horror of human suffering again and again, being tethered to that responsibility for the rest of my life—it cascaded into my soul, a dark and familiar tide, weightier now, and blacker.

I didn't have to do any of this. Didn't have to respond to the visions or try to intervene. I didn't have to audition at all—I could stay here, cocooned in this elegant space, embraced by memories of Apollo. I could burrow down, and stagnate, and wait.

But if I let myself sink into that dark water again, it would be hell trying to get out. It would take Herculean amounts of willpower to claw back to the surface, to manage one small act of defiance against the dark. And then, if I managed one small act, I'd have to push and struggle harder to achieve a second act, a second tiny success. I'd been there before, so low that brushing my teeth or taking a shower was a monumental achievement, where each miniscule success was a new rung in a teetering ladder, one I could use to climb out of the deep well into the light.

I might end up down there again someday, against every bit of my will and hope. I didn't always have a choice. But today, I could feel that the choice was mine.

Apollo believed in me, and I needed to believe in him, so until he returned I would do things that scared me, and go after things I wanted. I wouldn't mope around and wait for him. He'd be disappointed if I did.

Or maybe he wasn't the one who would be disappointed. He'd probably be his typical sweet, understanding self about it. But *I'd* be disappointed if I sat around waiting on a man again, even if the man was the divinely awesome Apollo instead of Ajax the narcissistic asshole.

Decision made, I turned on the TV and flipped through channels, hoping there might be a concert or some kind of singing show on tonight—something to inspire me.

Instead I landed on a local TV news station with the headline, "Local teen shoots mother, then self."

And the face on the screen was the boy from my vision.

I stood frozen, stunned, even after the tiny sound bite about the incident had ended.

Maybe, if I'd done nothing, if the cop car hadn't been in that post office parking lot, there would have been a report about a mass shooting instead. Maybe I'd saved several lives by acting on my vision.

But I couldn't feel glad about that, not with the boy's face emblazoned on my brain. Eighteen years old, the reporter had said. So damn young.

I walked the apartment for the rest of the evening, practicing my audition song, working on breath control and phrasing, intermittently pausing to cry for the kid I hadn't been able to save. And I kept seeing the boy in my dreams that night. In a way it was a relief to have regular nightmares, not vision-y ones. When I finally dragged myself out of bed the next morning and showered, I tried to push thoughts of the boy aside. I couldn't do anything about his fate now, so what was the use of dwelling on it?

Instead I thought of Apollo. Had he found the girl he was supposed to save? Who was she, exactly, and why were inter-realm bounty hunters after her? And who did they work for? Must be someone really bad, judging from the way Athena and Apollo had looked when they were talking about it.

Around eleven, I walked into the Little Theatre building and followed the cardstock arrows taped to the wall until I located the audition signups. The whole place smelled vaguely musty, and a few of the tiles in the drop ceiling had rings of brown water stains. A large dead roach lay upside down under the signup table, and the carpet was a disgusting, greenish-brown, mottled mess. But music trickled along the hallways, and energy thrummed in the air among the couple dozen women auditioning for Sally Bowles.

I sat in a cold metal folding chair until my name was called, and then I walked into the audition room—not the theater itself, but a large backstage area with a piano in the center and some scenery detritus cluttering the corners.

"Hi," I said as brightly as I could manage. "I'm Cassandra—"

And then I stopped, because there were three people sitting behind the table in front of me. I'd seen them in my vision—glimpsed the backs of their heads, anyway. Now I could see their faces, and one of those faces—

It was Ajax.

Dark wavy hair, longer than when I'd last seen him. Same Josh Groban look, artsy and attractive, with a fuzzy scarf looped over his sweater.

It made a kind of sense that he'd be here. He'd studied music and theater in college, and he was active in the local arts community. He must be involved in directing this musical. Oh god.

Ajax blinked dark eyes at me. "Cass. I'm surprised to see you here."

"Um, yeah." I tried to scrape my scattered thoughts back together. "Well, you know I performed in musicals in high school and college, and I've always loved *Cabaret*, so I thought I might be a good fit for Sally. I'd—um—I'd like to sing for you."

"Sure, go right ahead." He looked down at the paper in front of him and wrote something, while the other two people just watched me, polite and expectant.

What had Ajax written down? Something about me? Something personal, something bad?

A nervous sweat broke out over my body, but I managed to hand off my sheet music to the pianist and take my place, hands loose at my sides.

When Ajax looked up again, every note of music inside me died.

I was transported back to the bedroom I once shared with him—naked, exposed to his inspection, raw and trembling. I heard the words he'd said to me during the breakup—that I was moody, I brought him down, I kept him from being happy. That I would never make anyone else happy until I got my shit together.

But he was wrong. Because I hadn't gotten my shit together, and yet Apollo cared about me anyway. I had the deep sense that I made the sun god happy—or maybe not *happy*, exactly—maybe there was something better than happiness between us. Deep-rooted joy, and trust, and the understanding that on some esoteric level we were *essential* to each other. Happiness and sadness might fluctuate, but Apollo and I were beyond all of that. He craved me—not just my body, but the essence of me.

Being with him settled me and soothed me in a way nothing else ever could.

Summoning a smile, I nodded to the pianist. And then I began to sing.

At first I thought I was singing for Ajax, in defiance of him. But I realized, halfway through the first line, that I wasn't singing for him at all. This song was for me. My anthem, my redemption, my glory.

I'd never sung so beautifully in my life, and I could see it on the faces of Ajax's companions. I'd given them the "wow" moment everyone wants to get during an audition. I had the part, I could feel it.

They asked me a few more questions and said they'd been in touch. "Thank you," I told them with a final brilliant smile.

I took the bus back to Apollo's building, worrying over how much time I might have to spend with Ajax if I got a part in the musical. He was one of the directors, so he'd be around all the time, interacting directly with me. Did I want the role enough to put up with his toxic behavior for weeks?

My thoughts snapped off abruptly as darkness began to wash over my vision. Desperate, I swiped the keycard across Apollo's door and stumbled into the loft just as my sight and hearing shut down completely.

The scene that emerged from the darkness was dim—warm lighting, the clink of bottles and glasses, the murmur of voices. A bar, late in the evening. Ajax and the other two people from the audition sat in a booth with a couple others.

"Most of them were quite good," a woman was saying. "But my favorite was the girl who sang the Cass Elliot song—Cassandra was her name, I think. She is so talented. I think she'd be perfect for Sally Bowles."

Ajax sighed heavily. "She would be perfect. It's too bad she's so unstable."

"Unstable?" the woman asked.

"I've known her for years," Ajax said. "She's a great girl, lots of talent, but really moody. Gets into these heavy depressive phases where she just won't do anything. And she refuses to take medication."

You always advised against medication, I screamed inwardly, but of course the Ajax in my vision couldn't hear me.

"I worry that she won't be reliable," he continued. "She also has these periods where she's super intense about creating her own music, and during those times she refuses to pay attention to anything else. I'm afraid we wouldn't be able to count on her to show up to rehearsals, or performances for that matter. Did you know she was fired from her teaching job?"

Not because of anything I did, my inner voice protested. *It was layoffs—last in, first out.*

"Sorry to hear that," said the woman who'd liked my song. "Well, let's move on to the other options then."

My vision cleared until I could see my own pale fingers, pressed against the dark hardwood floor of the loft. I could hear the faint whirr of the fridge and feel the soft breaths of air circulating from the vents.

My first impulse was to give up. To hide in the middle of Apollo's bed with all the blankets draped over me. To curl up in the dark where no one could find me.

Or…

Or I could fight. I could show up at the bar and confront Ajax. I could tell him he was being ableist, discriminatory, contributing to the ongoing stigma around mental health. But knowing him, he would take my rebuke and twist it around, gaslighting me and making me look even more unhinged in front of everyone.

Third option—I could succeed in spite of him. He might close this door to me, but there were dozens of others. I just needed to find the path I was meant to take.

There was one good thing about that vision. It meant I was gaining more control over what I saw. I'd been thinking about Ajax and the musical, and then a vision had appeared to let me know what I should expect. Maybe if I thought hard enough about a topic of emotional significance to me, I could trigger a vision related to that topic or person.

I tried it for a while, thinking hard about my sister, about Apollo, about my own future with music and performance. No matter what happened between Apollo and me, I couldn't just sit around and let him finance my life while I did nothing. I needed a purpose, some way to exercise my creative side and make my own money.

I was still amazed at how much he'd done for me, ever since we met on the Afterburn. With him, I'd composed my first bit of music since Ajax. I could still remember part of it—the rest was somewhere in my phone.

I grabbed the phone out of my purse and found the notes I'd made on the curb at Carowinds while the man I'd just met waited quietly at my side. The melody felt just as poignant now, just as exquisite—and I could hear more of it unspooling through my mind, new musical phrases revealing themselves. Not just notes, either, but words. Lyrics. Snatches of everything Apollo had meant to me since that first day.

Eager not to lose a single note or word, I kicked off my shoes, fetched Apollo's keyboard from the bedroom, and went to work.

12

APOLLO

When I left Cassandra behind on Earth, I hadn't planned on stopping a war.

I hadn't planned on helping Demeter's daughter escape from her *again* and turning the harvest goddess into my mortal enemy in the process.

I certainly hadn't pictured myself standing on Hades' side, defending the Underworld from Olympian invasion, facing off against my father and the entire Pantheon, minus Athena. My clever sister had stayed out of the mess.

Zeus was furious at my open defiance. Even as he spoke with Hades, I felt the pressure of my father's power creeping through the soil of the Underworld, winding around my legs, sucking at my energy. Few people knew that he could siphon energy from other Olympians or Titans—he did it subtly, secretly, invisibly, and I only knew of it because a drunken Hera had once threatened to have him use that power on my mother.

Along with his other abilities, that trick of his had enabled Zeus to maintain dominance over the rest of the Pantheon, and it had permitted him to control the Titan Coeus all by himself, a feat still whispered about in Olympus to this day.

But Zeus had never done it to me. So when the drain began, I was too shocked to react at first. I stood paralyzed and suffering at Hades' side, feeling my energy being sucked away into the body of my father. He was consuming me, weakening me so I wouldn't be able to help Hades and Persephone. He was using my power to fuel his purpose—a wicked revenge for my defiance.

My rebellion was no careless choice. I'd been loyal and subservient to Zeus for centuries. I'd focused on bettering myself and seeing kindness and justice done quietly, wherever I could, in the places he didn't care to look.

I'd tried to follow my father's directives. I'd gained the courage to defy him for the first time when I'd helped Pan battle Hook's army. And here I was, revolting again for the sake of Hades and Persie—for the freedom they deserved and the love they'd found.

And this was my reward for trying to be better than my past self, for trying to spread healing and light through the realms. My father was taking my birthright, sucking away all the energy and light inside me. He probably thought it was his for the taking—he'd given me life, after all. It was only by his grace that I'd been allowed to exist for so long.

For so long—the phrase triggered a memory. Cassandra's dark eyes, earnest and vibrant. Her melodic voice, edged with rebellion. *Why would someone as powerful and generous and kind as you allow a guy like Zeus to rule for so long? I mean—he's had his turn, right? He should let somebody else take over.*

And then Athena's voice in my head: *You'd make a much better ruler of the realm than he ever has.*

The woman I adored and the sister I respected. They believed in me. Trusted me.

Impulsively, I tugged at the power inside me, pulling against the sucking force of my father's magic. I pulled, uncertainly at first, and then, with Cassandra's words and Athena's reassurance flooding my mind, I revolted with all my strength, straining against the will of Zeus.

For a blistering second, I knew only pain. He was still speaking, still engaging with Hades and Persephone, but I thought his stance changed a little, as if he was bracing himself against me. I kept my face calm and my body still—by the will of the Fates, I'd had practice controlling my physical reactions. But inwardly I was roaring, hauling against the forcible drain on my magic. I couldn't speak any Fae spells, or use any tonic to augment my energy—this was me, alone, the purest test of my true power.

I thought of the In-Between, and I imagined myself in it—only instead of releasing energy in a great wave, I reversed the wave, and I sucked all the light and energy of the universe into myself. Not a black hole like my father, not one who would take and take yet give nothing in return—no, I was the unconquerable sun, giver of beauty and light, of healing and warmth, of music and peace.

My power reverted to me, rushing back out of my father, along the invisible channel he'd created, and straight into my body. The jolt of its return sent me back a step, but no one noticed. They were all watching

Persephone, watching Zeus as he raised a lightning bolt against her.

And then Peter Pan arrived, crashing through the realm gate with his usual flair for dramatics and awkward timing. He had an entire army of Lost Kids with him—reinforcements to help Hades in the defense of the Underworld.

While Pan shouted at the Olympians, I kept pulling the last eddies of my power back into myself. My father resisted, jaw clenched, listening to Pan's brash speech while he tried to regain his hold over my energy. But my veins were humming with the awareness of my own strength, and of the truth I had long suspected—that my power surpassed my father's.

"What will it be, Zeus?" Hades called out, when Pan finally stopped shouting. "We've existed here quietly for a long time without interference. Our way of life does not affect yours. And the realms just recovered from the terror of Hook's conquests. No one wants another war. Will you let us live in peace with the contented dead, or will you start a conflict that will only send more souls to my cities?"

He kept speaking, but I focused all my intent on one last effort—I reached through the channel between Zeus and me, and I latched onto the crackling light of his energy. With all my might, I summoned that energy to me.

He tried to resist me. But he was distracted, stretched thin—and old, so old—I felt the immense age of him, greater than mine. Energy gushed from him into me, white-hot sparkling power merging with my golden light. I drank it in, and then I tore the connection between us.

The bolt in Zeus's upraised hand guttered and vanished. He dropped his fist at once, pretending that he'd intended for it to disappear—but I knew better. My heart thundered while I stood silent, focused on veiling the radiance that wanted to burst through my skin.

"You speak well in your own defense, brother," Zeus said to Hades. "You may continue to rule the Underworld, for now. I'm interested to see how long this marriage of yours will last." With a sneer, he turned and strode through the realm gate. My fellow Olympians hurried to follow him. None of them wanted to move against Hades on their own.

But Demeter was beside herself. She'd lost her daughter and both of the realms she'd planned to claim—plans laid over the course of decades, now crumbling into dust. "This isn't over," she snapped at Persephone.

Hecate took Demeter by the shoulders and guided her toward the realm gate. "What your mother means is we'll come visit sometime, and try to rebuild the connection between you two. I'm sure we can find some common ground, a shared purpose—"

But Persephone said, "No."

My heart burned with pride. How far she'd come, the little girl in the cage, the one I'd rescued and delivered to Pan. Now she stood, fully grown, a glorious, powerful woman—and with Hades's protection and partnership, Demeter and Hecate wouldn't be able to hurt her again.

As Demeter left the Underworld through the realm gate, she turned back for a second and looked at me.

We'd been friends once, Demeter and I. But over the years, she had shifted, slowly, becoming more selfish, cruel, and vindictive with every renewal. I'd continued to feign friendship, if only to keep an eye on her. And now she knew I'd stolen her daughter twice—the first time seventy years ago, and then again just yesterday.

Not a trace of friendship was left in her eyes—only pure hatred. She'd be out for my blood, intent on revenge. The knowledge unsettled me, and I thought of my mother Leto back at Delos. The Fae magic and Olympian wards around my estate were designed to protect her, but what if Hecate found a way around them? Hecate had Titan blood and Unseelie magic.

I couldn't leave the Underworld immediately—there was Hades' and Persie's wedding to attend. Besides, I was fairly sure I'd be very unwelcome anywhere near my father at the moment. Best to let him calm down before I went home to the Olympian realm. Athena liked my mother—she'd keep an eye on her. And my mother wasn't entirely helpless herself. Her powers had waned, but she still possessed a few abilities. Hopefully enough to shore up the defenses at Delos until I could clear any threats.

I'd crossed a line this time—a point beyond a simple difference of opinion with my father. I'd stood against him, resisted his attack, and stolen his energy. He wouldn't tell anyone of it—of that I was sure. It would make him look weak. But he'd be after me now, as surely as Demeter was.

My anxiety mounted, even as I tried to enjoy the wedding, and it mounted still higher when Persie begged me to stay for one night. I agreed, of course—I owed her because of the memory geas I'd laid on her, the one she'd suffered under for all those years. It was to protect her, but I still felt I owed her a debt I could never repay. So I yielded to her request, and I helped her and Hades create a sun for the new realm she'd made.

Afterward she and Hades started kissing intensely, hands wandering to intimate places, so I left them to their lovemaking and passed through the realm gate again.

I'd poured a lot of power into the making of that sun, and when I left Persephone's world, I was tired. It took me a while to locate the Earth realm gate, but at last I saw it, flickering blue-green and beautiful. I aimed for it, using my wings and limbs to force myself through the emptiness of the In-Between.

My estate in the Olympian realm used to represent home and rest for me, but at that moment I could think of nothing but getting back to Cassandra. I wanted to lie on the sofa in the loft, with her sweet-sad smile turned on me. Maybe she'd let me put my head in her lap, and maybe she would lace her slim fingers through my hair. I'd tell her what I'd done, how the conflict with my father had escalated, and how I'd absorbed at least some of his energy—an unforgivable act in his eyes. She would help me decide what to do.

It was daylight when I arrived in the Earth realm, so I couldn't fly straight to Cassandra with my own wings. I had to land quickly and take human transportation to her city, which added several frustrating hours to my trip. But at last, around sunset, I arrived at my building. I didn't have my keycard since I'd given it to Cassandra, but I only needed to zap the card reader with a bit of my power and it let me in. I rode the elevator up to my loft, leaning against the mirrored walls.

I felt achingly weary in a way that was unusual for me, as a god. I only ever felt this exhausted after a big battle. Perhaps absorbing my father's foreign energy and creating a whole *sun* for a new realm had wrecked me more thoroughly than I'd realized.

When I reached the loft, I lifted my hand to rap on the door, not wanting to startle Cassandra by barging straight in.

The instant my knuckles met the door's surface, glowing red letters flashed into view—words in ancient Greek, a language still spoken by many Olympians.

I stared, unable or unwilling to comprehend the message at first.

As its meaning sank in, I fell to my knees, one hand braced on the floor, the other gripping my mouth to stifle the bellow of anguish that wanted to break out of me.

Demeter and Hecate had gotten here first.

And Cassandra was gone.

13

CASSANDRA

Someone was smacking me. "Wake up, little whore. Wake up."

I frowned, blinking against the aching blur in my head. The last thing I remembered was recording and uploading a TikTok video of myself performing my new song—nothing fancy, just me and the music. I'd set the phone aside and rolled on my back on the sofa, smiling and satisfied. Even if no one else liked it, I did.

I must have fallen asleep right there, on the couch. But then why was I sitting upright, with my arms pinned uncomfortably behind me while a woman smacked my face and called me a whore? Maybe this was a new kind of vision?

My sight cleared a little, and I saw a woman—tall, delicate, beautiful, with pale skin and long brown hair. She wore a gown of green and gold, and clasped an emerald-crusted staff in her hand. Behind her stood another woman, the one with two-toned skin, from my vision. The black-and-white witch, Hecate.

Panic flared in my stomach. In my vision Apollo had stolen the pink-haired girl from Hecate, which meant that Hecate was bad news.

"You're Hecate, right?" I said. "Why are you here?"

"The little wretch knows you," said the green-and-gold woman. "How strange. Have you had dealings with her before?"

"No, never," Hecate replied.

"She has power," murmured the tall woman. "It's half obscured by something. Maybe she's a Seer."

"Does it matter, my lady?"

"I suppose not." The tall woman probed her lower lip with a sharp fingernail. "She'll be dead soon anyway."

Oh god. Not cool at all.

The three of us were in some kind of cabin, from what I could tell—a cabin whose inner walls were coated with twisted vines and weirdly-colored foliage. It was like being inside a cave with Poison Ivy from the comic books.

I twisted as far as I could, examining my body. Apparently I was cinched tight to a chair by coiling vines, while the chair itself was knotted to the wall. No way to tip it over and get free, even if I'd been alone.

"I recognize Hecate," I said hoarsely. "But who are you?"

"I'm Demeter," said the woman.

I shrugged.

"Goddess of harvest and agriculture?" she prompted.

"Sorry, never heard of you."

She scoffed bitterly. "I knew humans had devolved, but I didn't think it was this bad. There's a pitiable lack of knowledge, a total dearth of respect for divine beings like myself. It's almost enough to make me want to stick around and teach these humans a few things."

"But your magic isn't the same here," said Hecate.

"Not quite as strong as it is in Olympus, but still very effective, don't you think?" Demeter plucked at one of the vines, and it shivered in response. "I'm so bored, Hecate. Why don't you torture the girl while we wait for Apollo to show up? That will amuse me. See if you can find out what her power is, and why Apollo is so fascinated with her."

"How did you even find out about me?" I asked.

"Zeus has his little spies, especially when it comes to his renegade children," Demeter said. "He has known about Apollo's weakness for you all along. And after what Apollo did to him in the Underworld today—the open rebellion—well, Zeus was all too happy to give me the information I wanted. He needs Apollo out of the way, you see. The glow-bug has been an irritant long enough. And while I despise Zeus deeply, for the moment Apollo bears the greater share of my wrath. We've called a truce, the god-king and I, until I've disposed of his son."

"Apollo is a god," I whispered. "You can't kill him."

"Maybe not, precious." Demeter approached me and tapped my nose with a sharp nail. "But Hecate knows Unseelie magicks that can douse his power like my fingers pinch out a candle. And then he'll be helpless, at least until his new master receives him."

"New master?"

Hecate threw Demeter a warning look, but the goddess kept talking. "I'm going to sell him off to some very angry bounty hunters. They're mad at *me* because they came all this way and now they can't get to

Persephone—not that I would ever have let them take her, but I don't mind pacifying them with an alternate choice. I've invested a lot of resources lately and thanks to Apollo I've got nothing to show for it—so this is the way he pays me back. His body and his powers will be delivered to the Garguignol, and I will receive the purchase price. Then the glow-bug will rue the day he decided to steal my daughter from me."

"You must have been doing something terrible to her," I retorted, though my whole body was shaking from sheer anxiety. "She looked pretty happy to be leaving with him."

"So you have visions, then," Hecate intercepted. She glanced at Demeter. "This girl could be useful."

"This piece of human trash?" Demeter arched a slim dark brow. "Don't say that! I was looking forward to taking her apart in front of him."

"I think we need her," Hecate continued, appraising me. "If she's an oracle, she could help us. We could plan a new future."

Um, no. Death would be preferable to existing as a prisoner, enslaved to these two. Five minutes with these Olympians and I already hated both of them.

"My powers are blocked," I said quickly. "They're pretty much useless. Apparently my trauma is too deep and multilayered—I'm of no use. I do get a few random visions, but they're mostly about Earth stuff. They wouldn't do you any good. I only had that one vision of Apollo because we—because I—"

"You slept with him," sneered Demeter. "Of course you did. Half the females of every realm have been with Apollo."

I knew she was lying, exaggerating, but the words still bothered me. I wanted to protest, to tell her that Apollo was mine now, no one else's—that he cared about me. But that would only confirm her belief that torturing me was the best way to hurt him, so I kept my mouth shut.

Demeter smirked, as if she could read my discomfort. She swirled around, and with a twitch of her fingers coaxed the vines to move and grow into the shape of a leafy throne. She sank onto it, sighing. "Proceed, Hecate," she said. "Dig into her brain and extract her most painful memory. Figure out what it is that's holding her back. Once her power is fully exposed to us, I'll decide whether or not she's worth keeping alive. Maybe we can sell her to the Maru Sealgair as well."

"No, please!" I writhed in my chair, trying to twist my hands free of the vines, but they only tightened painfully. "Please—"

But Hecate gripped my chin and began carving something into my forehead with her sharp nails—words or symbols. I could feel each one being marked deeply into the thin flesh, the tip of her nail grinding against the bone of my skull. And I screamed, trying to twist away, but when Hecate's claw raked dangerously near my eyeball, I decided to stop fighting. I let her finish carving my forehead, and then I sat sobbing through a haze of blood and tears.

Hecate fumbled around in a satchel, then brought out a bottle of green smoke, which she blew into my face. Then she planted her thumbs at my temples, her fingers clasping my skull painfully tight. I gritted my teeth, tasting the blood that ran over my lips from the wounds on my forehead, and I tried to stop sobbing, tried to be brave as Hecate dove into my mind.

When Icelos had read my consciousness, I hadn't felt him at all. He'd been so gentle, so delicate in his explorations. But where he'd been a breath of influence, Hecate was a pair of stomping boots, grinding her heels into my skull. I felt her invasion like the worst headache of my life, like the blaze of a bullet through brain matter. I shrieked, over and over, until Demeter said, "Hera's tits, would you shut her up?"

Hecate paused her invasion long enough to run a bloody finger along my lips. My flesh sealed together, gluing my mouth shut. I could barely inhale through the snot and blood and tears—I was forced to calm down and focus on breathing, or risk passing out from lack of oxygen.

"What do you see, witch?" said Demeter.

"She has locked it down, but I'm getting in," answered Hecate. And even as she spoke, I saw the bedroom I shared with my sister when we were growing up. I saw the bunkbeds, made of enormous chunky pine planks. I saw my thin pillow, and the peach-and-green quilt I used to sleep under. My consciousness sank into the bed, and then the vision began—the first vision I'd ever had. The one I'd tried to forget so many times.

I'd had a nightmare about my baby brother, alone in his crib. He'd managed to unswaddle himself, and his face was buried in a fold of the blanket. He was still—too still.

I'd surfaced from the vision, crying. My sister Meg, older than me and upset about being woken up, had told me to go back to sleep, that it was only a nightmare.

For several minutes I'd stayed awake, wondering if I should go check on my baby brother. But I was afraid of the dark, and I'd never had a vision before. This dream had felt different from regular nightmares—significant and vivid. But I had convinced myself it was nothing, and I'd gone back to sleep.

The next morning my parents told us my brother had passed away. And six months later, my father had left for a new life, free from my mother and her emotional wreckage.

That was what men did. They ran when things got difficult. My father had done it, Ajax had done it—Apollo would do it, too. He probably wouldn't come for me at all. This was so obviously a trap, and he must know it. He'd be a fool to step in. He should do what Ajax and my father had done—run from me and my mess.

But my anger at them was the surface issue, the one easy to see and deal with. The truth rankled further down, under the layers I'd spread over it.

Hecate's power scalded my brain, burning away those layers, searing down to the raw, bleeding truth until it blazed through my mind. Blinded by my own blood, with my mouth glued shut, I could see it clearly now—I had never really blamed my father, or Ajax. I'd blamed myself for everything, all the abandonment and pain. I was to blame—my visions, my inaction, my depression, my darkness. I was the problem. I'd always believed that. And I'd always been convinced that my visions were bad, and tragic, that they could never yield anything good, not really. Every single one had ended in tragedy or loss. Even my vision of the audition had ended badly—with yet another rejection of me as a person—a rejection that had nothing to do with my talent and everything to do with my wretched mind and my unstable emotions. My vision of Persephone's rescue had led to *this*—my capture and torture. If Apollo did show up to save me, he'd be bound with spells and delivered to this Garguignol person, whose very name sounded like rotting flesh and old bones.

All of it was my fault. Apollo's impending demise—my fault. The apartment building disaster—my fault, because I didn't act quickly enough. Ajax leaving—my fault. My father leaving—my fault.

My baby brother's death—my fault.

And that was the truth at the core of me—that I was a plague and a poison, worthless and wicked. That I didn't deserve to exist.

There was no reason for me to be alive, not if I couldn't prevent some of the pain and terror in the world. Not if I caused even more tragedy by my very presence on Earth.

Not even Apollo himself could fix me, or give me a purpose. It wasn't his place to do that. And soon he'd be tortured or enslaved—all because of me.

Hecate was speaking low, relaying everything I was thinking to Demeter, laying my pain bare.

The crunching pressure in my head eased as the witch withdrew. She wiped my eyes and nose with a cloth and unsealed my lips. "I've been in that place," she said quietly. "Best thing you can do is yield to the evil.

Embrace it. If you can't prevent pain, cause it. Hurts less that way."

I stared at her, helpless, emptied of hope. Unable to think of a single reason why she might be wrong.

"We can use her," Hecate said to Demeter. "She's an Oracle, and her powers are fully exposed now. She will have some control over them. I think her visions will change depending on the realm she's in and the people she relates to most closely."

Demeter rose from her vine throne and approached me. "We know the abandonment and evil of men, little Oracle," she said. "They see us as a threat, whether we are or not—so why not be the greatest threats we can be? If they view us as selfish and capricious, we shall be more self-serving and volatile than they could ever imagine. This is our creed, and it could be yours. After I use you to torture Apollo a bit, after we sell him, Hecate can heal you up, and we'll bring you home with us. Your visions can be useful. You'll be part of a family, a sisterhood where men serve our needs, not the other way around. And you'll have a purpose—aiding the plans of your future queen." She smiled, cunning and conspiratorial. "What do you say?"

I sucked in a deep, shuddering breath. "If this is the same sorry pitch you gave your daughter, no wonder she said no."

Demeter's hand flashed, and her palm smacked my face so hard my head snapped aside. "You'll be my prisoner then," she said. "My slave, existing only to spew out visions. Maybe Hecate can find a way for us to use your brain alone, disembodied. I understand Wonderland has some very interesting technologies for disassociation, and for viewing a person's inner thoughts in holographic form. We'll find a way to make your visions ours, while putting you through the greatest possible agony." She smiled, glancing at Hecate, as if for confirmation.

But Hecate only lifted her head and said, "He's coming."

Only a second's warning, and the next instant Apollo crashed into the cabin, right through the roof, gold feathers flashing. He had a massive gun gripped in both hands, and as his feet slammed to the floor he started shooting, spraying bullets at Demeter.

A few of them punched through her, but she was quick, throwing up a leaf-shaped shield of translucent green energy. The vines nearest her quivered and blackened as she sucked their life away to feed her defenses.

"Hecate!" she screamed.

Apollo began to turn, to aim at the witch—but she had a knife to my throat already, pricking my skin, releasing a thread of blood.

Apollo froze.

"Don't hurt her," he said. "Hecate—please."

"Put it down," she answered.

Apollo laid the gun on the cracked floor of the cabin and vanished his wings.

"Olympians don't use guns on each other," said Hecate. "I'm surprised you'd stoop to such a weapon, when you have other powers at your disposal."

"I thought you'd have the cabin warded to limit my powers," he said. "And you do, don't you? I can feel the wards—and something else—" He took a step toward me and wavered on his feet, his eyes turning briefly dark. "What is it?"

"The darkest of Unseelie weavings," Hecate replied. "Babes' blood and pixie heartstring, the eyes of hatchlings and the tongues of virgins—mixed together and used to write the words of the Unspoken Tongue, which you were too noble to learn during your stay in Faerie. Son of Zeus, your power is fully bound until you reach the lair of the Garguignol. I will give the Maru Sealgair the countercurse, so the Garguignol can unbind you when and how he sees fit."

Apollo's skin had lost its healthy tanned glow. He was paling before my eyes, his light crushed and dying. Even his hair was a duller blond, nearly white. He staggered, and fell to one knee, breathing slow and heavy.

"As for your little whore," said Demeter, dissipating her green shield, "she will be my slave. I plan to extract her brain and keep it alive—my own little vision machine. I hope your rescue of Persephone was worth it." She dug a bullet out of her flesh and tossed it aside.

"How did you know about Cassandra?" Apollo said hoarsely.

"Oh, your father has had you watched since you returned to Earth." Demeter's lip curl. "You angered him terribly, glow-bug. He's done with you. We'd barely left the Underworld when he pulled me aside and told me where I could find the person you love most."

Tears welled in my eyes as Apollo looked up at me. "Is that true?" I whispered.

"Yes," he said softly. "Cassandra, I love—"

Demeter kicked him full in the face with her pointy boot, and gold-flecked blood sprayed from Apollo's mouth and nose. He groaned, and then, with a massive effort, he climbed to his feet, teeth bloody and bared.

"Hecate!" Demeter shrilled. "What's happening? He's supposed to be weak!"

"His powers as the sun-god are suppressed, but he's still got the strength of a human male," the witch said. "Don't just stand there, my lady—restrain him!"

Apollo lunged for Demeter, and she recoiled into the vines clustered along the wall. They swallowed her into them, until her body was a faint bulge of rippling green. Then two great arms of entwined vines shot out from the wall, whipping around Apollo as fast as a snap bracelet. In half a second he was bound, immobilized in a thick wrapping of vines.

Cautiously Demeter emerged to inspect her handiwork. "That should hold him until the Maru Sealgair get here. Send word that we have him."

Hecate stepped to a corner of the cabin, sat down cross-legged and opened her bag. She began drawing a complex circle on the ground, laying stones and bits of herbs around its perimeter.

"Such slow work," Demeter grumbled. "So bored." She walked up to Apollo and took his jaw in her hand. "How long have we been friends, you and I?"

"Longer than we should have been, and not as long as you think," he replied.

"So self-righteous," she hissed. "You think you're so much better and nobler than everyone else." She flicked his face, but he didn't so much as blink. "I want to cut something off you, Apollo. I want to make you hurt. But I don't think you'd scream, not for yourself. Maybe you'd scream for *her*." And she whirled, approaching me, wrapping my hair in her fist and yanking my head back. Demeter stamped on the hilt of Hecate's discarded knife, making it bounce up into her palm. She set the tip of the blade just inside my nostril. "Let's do some redecorating, shall we? Hecate has already fixed her forehead—I'll start here, with this pretty little nose."

"Leave her," growled Apollo, wrenching and bucking in his prison of vines. "Don't touch her, or I swear by Zeus's balls—"

Demeter laughed. "Swearing by the man who sold you out? How sad." She took the knife from my nose and traced my lips with it.

I clenched my teeth, willing myself not to beg, but I couldn't stop the tears from rolling down my face. My eyes were blurred with them, clouding, darkening—wait, it wasn't the tears—this was a vision, blotting out my sight and hearing. Not now, not now—

Demeter, Hecate, Apollo and the cabin were gone, yet not gone, because out of the dark they appeared again—only this time Apollo was free, and the goddess and the witch lay before him, blackened and burnt. But he wasn't the golden Apollo I knew—his eyes blazed white, crackling with lightning, and his hair glowed in a snowy cloud. A great lightning bolt, pure white and sizzling, shone in his hand.

My hearing was beginning to return. I heard Hecate's voice, dim and distant, saying, "I've sent the message. They'll be here soon. Did the girl pass out?"

"I think so," replied Demeter.

I felt pain lancing through my chest over and over as my senses clarified again. Demeter was carving into my left breast, slicing the flesh while Apollo roared curses at her. My shirt was soaked with blood, and for a second I couldn't speak, the pain was so intense.

But I had to speak. Somehow I had to tell Apollo what I had seen.

"Apollo," I choked. "Apollo, your father gave you something, or you took something. You have to use it. You're his true heir, worthier than he ever was—oh god—" I screamed as Demeter tweaked the knife deeper into my flesh. "Please, please, you have to use it now. You have to believe this of yourself, please, take it, use it—I know you hate him—"

"What are you babbling about?" Demeter wriggled her fingers between my lips, nearly making me gag. She pinched my tongue hard, pulled it out—set the edge of the knife against it—

"Not the Oracle's tongue, Demeter, for Styx's sake," snapped Hecate.

Demeter rolled her eyes, but she let my tongue go. "How about something lower down?" She reached for the zipper of my jeans. "She won't need it anymore, anyway. No chance for pleasure where she's going."

"Or you could turn her old, like you did to Persephone's hand," Hecate suggested.

"But then I'd have to look at her decrepit face." Demeter tapped my chin with the dripping knife. "You know, Hecate, I usually let you do these bloody tasks, but there's something keenly refreshing about taking things into my own hands. Perhaps I should do it more often."

I barely heard her, because despite my haze of pain, I was watching Apollo. Ever since I'd screamed at him, he'd been hanging against the vines with his head bowed, but I didn't think he'd given up. Through the pale locks half-concealing his face, I could see the hard set of his jaw, the muscle swelling there. The cords of his neck stiffened beneath the bands of vines that coiled around his throat. He was straining, trying very hard to do something, to draw on something—a latent power he didn't want to use.

"I'll take a few fingers," Demeter said coolly. "Always such fun to hear the *snap* of the little bones."

"Apollo," I said desperately. "Even if you can't, I want you to know that I love you."

Demeter's hand closed around mine, forcing my first finger out.

A pinch of pain as the knife bit my skin.

And then a shearing blade of white light, coursing through the cabin, and the vines fell away from Apollo's body. He glowed pure white, like an eternal star, and when he looked up, his eyes were filled with lightning.

"Titans preserve us," whispered Hecate. "How does he have Zeus's power?"

"Stop him, you idiot!" screeched Demeter.

"I can't," Hecate said in a tremulous voice. "The spell was designed for the sun-god's powers, not those of Zeus."

Apollo looked down at his own hand, shining like luminous snow, crackling with sparks. He raised his fist, and in its center appeared a jagged lightning bolt, a crooked blade carved of ice and starfire.

Demeter threw her hands up, sucking life from her vines, forming her green energy shield again—but when Apollo cast the bolt, it sheared straight through the shield, slamming into Demeter's chest where it stuck, vibrating with a resonance that hummed through the cabin's walls like thunder. Lightning cracked outward from the bolt, encasing Demeter in a lethal cage of electric fire. Her body jerked and juddered inside while she wailed, keening, incessant.

Another bolt formed in Apollo's hand, and he flung it at Hecate as she ran for the door. It caught her in the back, caging her in deadly arms of crooked lightning.

Apollo had a third bolt in his hand, but he held it aloft, tense, staring as the first two bolts dissolved into sparks and left smoking, blackened carcasses behind.

Demeter and Hecate lay defeated, just like in my vision.

"Are they dead?" I gasped.

"No. But the damage is too great for them to recover. They will be forced into their renewal sleep." Apollo tossed the last bolt aside, and the eerie lightning faded from his eyes. He rushed to me, ripping aside the vines holding me—not a difficult task, since they had lost their unnatural strength when Demeter collapsed.

"Shit, Cassandra," he choked, his fingers hovering over the gouges in my breast.

"I know, I look like crap. But you're looking better already. More golden."

"Hecate's suppression spell broke when she passed," Apollo said. "A curse or geas cannot last once the caster or recipient enters their next renewal. And now we need to go somewhere safe, before the Maru

Sealgair arrive. With any luck, they'll take Demeter and Hecate as their prizes and return to the Garguignol."

"Sometime you have to tell me who that is," I mumbled. "But not now, because—"

"Too much information, I know." He voiced a broken laugh and scooped me up. I whimpered at the pain.

"I'm so sorry," he said. "Hold on, my love. This might hurt."

His golden wings whipped out, and with a mighty beat and a leap, he drove us both up, through the hole he'd made in the roof, into the air.

It was night outside, chilly and somber, pricked with white stars. The heat of Apollo's bare chest kept me from shivering. We were racing fast—almost too fast for me to breathe.

"The cabin where they held you was by a lake, not far from your city," Apollo said. "I'm taking you back to the loft first. I'll have a look at you there and see how deep the cuts are. And then I'm going to see if I can summon one of the Therapeutae from Olympus, or a Fae with healing powers. They can fix the mess Demeter made better than any human surgeon. You won't even have scars."

"I thought Demeter was going to kill me," I murmured. "And you know, I really didn't mind. I'm a poison to others—I make their lives *worse*, not better. I don't contribute anything good."

"That's not true," he gritted out. "Cassandra, you can't believe that."

"Name one person whose life I've made better."

"Mine."

"How can you say that after what just happened?"

"If you won't accept my word, then think of the children you taught in school," he said. "You improved their lives."

"No more than any other music teacher could have. If I didn't exist, someone else would have taught them scales and musical classifications." I coughed, and pain shot across my ruined forehead. "Face it—I'm disposable."

"Shut up!" Apollo cried out, his radiance blazing out sudden and violent. His arms convulsed around me, a vicious grip. "Shut *the fuck* up! You mean everything to me, everything, do you understand? I belong to you, and you belong to me. You're my life-mate, my eternal partner, prophesied to me by the Fates. You're supposed to be with me through every future renewal, until the end of time. I thought you were going to die, Cassandra—I thought she was going to end you while I watched, helpless, and I couldn't have borne it. I wouldn't have survived it, not with my spirit intact."

A hot golden tear splashed onto my chest, and I reached up to touch his face, despite the painful protest of my torn skin. "Okay," I whispered, stroking the smooth line of his jaw. "Okay. I believe you. But you know that eventually I'm going to grow old and die, right?"

"You won't," he said. "Once you're healed, I'm taking you straight to Olympus."

"To live near your horrible father? No thanks."

"We can go somewhere else—maybe Neverland? Any realm but this one. When you leave your own realm, you stop aging."

"Oh. Cool. Eternal youth sounds great. Why didn't you lead with that?"

"I'm not exactly thinking straight," he muttered. "All I can think about is getting you into bed—"

I spluttered a laugh.

"Let me finish—into bed, so I can call someone to fix you." His lips clamped tight, and I couldn't help admiring the sharp angle of his jaw, the determined flex of the muscles there. He was still glowing faintly, even though he'd made his wings invisible.

"Don't get shot down," I whispered.

"That's the least of my concerns at the moment," he replied.

We couldn't risk passing through the lobby of his building, not with him shirtless and bloody and me all carved up, so he flew us to the roof and did one of his magical zap-things on the rooftop door. He carried me down a flight of stairs to his floor, bundled me through the door into the loft, and laid me down on the bed.

"I'm going to get your nice sheets all bloody," I protested.

"Like I care." He was already in the bathroom, collecting supplies and swearing in some language that didn't sound Greek. The Fae tongue, maybe? "If we were in Olympus, I'd have better supplies to work with—Fae medicine, Olympian tonics—I could repair all of this."

"Right now I'd settle for some painkillers," I said faintly. "It hurts."

He hurried back to me and sat on the bed, carefully peeling away the remnants of my shirt. "I'll get you anything you need. But first, let me look at the damage."

"Just a flesh wound," I muttered, and then I yelped as he gently prodded the edge of a cut.

"You've lost blood, but nothing vital is damaged. You're in no immediate danger," he said, relief in his voice. "I need to contact some people who can help you."

"What about you?" I caught his hand as he stood up. "You can help me. God of healing, right?"

Pain crossed his handsome face. "I told you I can't focus it. If I could, believe me, I would do it. You mean more to me that anyone else in the universe."

Flutters erupted through my belly, and I smiled even though the expression made my forehead burn in protest. "While we're on the topic, what was all that crap you said about me being your life-mate?"

He flushed, turning slightly more incandescent. "A prophecy from one of the Fates. She said the one who broke my geas would be my life-mate for the rest of my existence."

"Oh, wow." I inhaled, careful and slow so as not to jar my ravaged chest. "That's intense."

"You can understand why I didn't tell you."

"Yeah." I tugged at his fingers, and he sank onto the edge of the bed again with a sigh.

"It's too much for you to take in," he said. "Too much to ask."

"Do I have a choice?"

He swept a hand over his jaw, rumpled his blond hair. "A Fate's prophecy can be multi-layered, open to interpretation. The prediction is true, but the rest is yours to decide. You can be my life-mate and still hate me or refuse to be with me. You can be my life-mate and have other partners, like Zeus and Hera's arrangement. And like them, we could break up and then rejoin later. Though I would prefer not to model the most meaningful relationship of my existence after my father's dysfunctional marriage. But we can speak of all this later, Cassandra—right now, I need to call someone to help you."

Perhaps he was right. But physically, I couldn't let him go. My whole being sang for him, ached for him— some ancient instinct deep within me cried out for him to be with me, near me, *in* me. Somehow I felt—no, I *knew*—that his presence could soothe my pain and salve my wounds.

And his mention of Zeus and Hera had triggered a memory—Icelos, talking about how Olympian pairs sometimes unlocked new aspects of their powers through sex with their life-mate.

What if Apollo *could* heal me? Maybe he didn't even realize it yet.

"You say you can't heal me," I whispered, drawing his hand to my cheek. "But you haven't really tried."

14

APOLLO

I stared at Cassandra, hardly believing what she'd just asked me. "You want me to have sex with you while you're wounded?"

"It's an experiment," she said. "Before you call your Fae healers and your therapeutic whatevers from Olympus, let's try it. There's no guarantee they'll be able to come here, right? If inter-realm travel was easy, everyone would do it all the time. And besides, after your defiance of Zeus, the Olympian thera-thingies are probably forbidden from helping you."

I grimaced. It was a fear I hadn't voiced because I didn't want her to worry. I'd aided many realms, but when it came down to my own moment of need, the list of friends I could count on were all too few. And the list of beings with healing powers was even shorter.

Cassandra's eager expression faded. "You're making a face—oh my god, of course you don't want to do this—I'm disgusting right now. I probably smell weird—haven't showered or brushed my teeth—Can you pretend I never said anything, please?" Her tone turned desperate.

Inwardly I cursed the wretched ex-boyfriend who had messed with her self-confidence. In a past life, I used to punish humans for offending my foolish pride or claiming greater musical skill than mine. If I hadn't sworn to never again to punish someone for vengeful reasons, that bastard Ajax would be first on my list.

"It's not that," I reassured her. "You are always beautiful and desirable to me. Always. But I don't want to hurt you."

"You won't. I know this is going to help," Cassandra said softly, sliding her fingers between mine. "If you really don't mind the mess—let's just try it. Please."

I could hear her soul singing to mine, a soothing seductive melody infusing my thoughts, tantalizing my body. "Cassandra," I murmured, lifting her knuckles to my lips. "That isn't fair."

"What isn't?" she said innocently, but her dark eyes sparkled. She knew exactly how her music affected me.

"You know, the first time we had sex, you used me to unlock your powers. And now you want to use me so you can heal." I leaned in and pressed a gentle kiss to her mouth.

"I'm sorry," she whispered, penitence coloring her gaze.

She looked so pitiful, with Hecate's spell carelessly carved into her forehead and the gashes across her beautiful breast. Ragged scarlet-and-black, torn edges of flesh, blood seeping—for a moment I felt as if I was seeing the injured soul of her, the lacerated spirit bled dry by the flogging of a cruel world. And with every part of me I wanted to seal those wounds, smooth that torn skin, ease her agony.

Something thrummed inside me, heated and glowed. Not Zeus's power—I still couldn't let myself think about how I'd used his stolen energy—no, this was something else. Something new.

"If this doesn't work," I whispered over her lips, "I'm calling a healer, or taking you straight to a human medical facility."

"Fine," she breathed. "Kiss me again. It helps."

I narrowed the space between our mouths, slowly, easing into a kiss so warm and molten I felt my whole being lighting up with the power of it. Cassandra's lips parted under mine, and I slid my tongue into her, a delicate languid sweep through her mouth. She tasted like blood and darkness and bittersweet sorrow. I buried my tongue deeper, letting my breath flow into her, chasing away the bitter tang, replacing it with honeyed love. Into that kiss I pressed all my unspoken yearning, my wish for her healing.

Moving back, I let her breathe, and when I saw her eyes a jolt shot through me. Her irises shone golden for a second before fading again.

"The pain," she whispered. "It's so much better. I think it's working."

I took up a damp cloth I'd brought from the bathroom and sponged away some of the blood from her chest, as gently as I could. Then I took the zipper of her pants and drew it down. The gap revealed dark lace lying against her pale skin. Further down, the lace yielded to a softer fabric, and I probed that spot with my finger.

"Oh," Cassandra breathed, and I smiled. Slipping my fingers into the waistband of both her pants and her panties, I maneuvered them down together, over her hips, along her perfect legs, reveling in every inch of skin revealed to me. She wasn't wearing shoes, and the pants slid easily over her bare feet.

As I removed my own clothes, Cassandra shifted her legs apart, wincing a little as she arched them. The lips of her sex were damp, bare, glistening for me, and my altruistic intentions began to blur as my body reacted to the sight. But I took a moment to breathe, to control myself, to focus on *her*, on what she needed from me.

I set my mouth to that lovely place and licked long and deep, fervent slow strokes. Then I traced along her belly with my tongue, circled the pert little dent of her navel, touched my tongue to her wounded breast. I kissed the cuts Demeter had made, one by one, while Cassandra quivered under me. Into every kiss I poured my love, my longing, my curative will. The edges of the chest wounds seemed to glimmer faintly as I kissed her clavicle and her shoulder.

Cassandra seized my hair and dragged my mouth up to hers again. She whimpered between my lips, sweet soft craving. I held my body above hers, careful not to let my chest brush her injuries. And then, with excruciating control, I touched my tip to her entrance.

"Are you all right?" I whispered.

She looked up at me with glazed golden eyes. "It's working. Please."

"This isn't exactly what I promised you for our next time."

"Apollo. Hush."

I reached down and slid the tip along her folds, up and down, until she gave a pitiful mew. I nearly lost focus, because the cuts along her forehead were glimmering too—not healing, not yet, but something was happening. A bolt of delighted shock passed through my core, but I forced myself to stay centered, to concentrate the nebulous cloud of my healing aura on her, and only her.

Slowly I pushed into her, nudging into that deep warmth, the tight embrace of her body—thrills of pleasure passed up my shaft, flooding my belly, tracing along every limb. My breath caught, and I shuddered.

Not about my pleasure. Not this time. Her. All her.

I'd served women countless times, taking pride in the release I gave them at my own expense. This was a moment more beautiful, more significant. With all the tenderness I felt for her, with all the self-control I possessed, I rolled my hips, slowly, careful not to jar her body and cause her pain. Long, indolent strokes, each one a test of my endurance.

Shifting my weight to one hand, I reached down and touched the tiny nub between her thighs. The sweetest mewling cry issued from her mouth, and I circled the spot again, just one finger massaging gently while I kept up my rhythmic glide into her channel. Her insides began to flutter, and I sped up a little, pulse after pulse. I braced both hands on the mattress, and her hands clamped onto my sides. My heart nearly broke with joy at the touch of those delicate fingers on my body—I huffed a gasp and then bit it back, controlling my features, smoothing my expression into its usual calm beauty.

Not about me.

But Cassandra looked at me with eyes that glowed like mine, and she said, "You don't have to wear that mask for me."

I stared at her, my heart thundering—and then I let the Apollo I had built, the one I held so carefully upright—I let him go, and beneath him I was only myself.

The protector without a true home in the universe.

The singer with no one to listen.

The rejected son.

The man who gave to everyone while hiding the hollow craving of his own heart.

"In case you weren't sure," Cassandra said, her lashes wet, "I'm yours."

For a moment we hung together, suspended, connected, linked eye to eye and soul to soul—and then I felt the power I'd never been able to control—sensed its shape, its edges. Eagerly I gathered it, compacted it mentally—I kissed Cassandra's mouth, feral and fierce, writhing my tongue with hers—and at the same moment I plunged into her, hard and deep. With a startled gasp she came, clenching around me, her body pulsating against every sensitized nerve along my length—the trigger released, and pleasure shot through me. My spine arched, my hips snapped tight to hers as I channeled every bit of my healing power into her body.

I stayed that way for a desperate few seconds—head flung back, my limbs shaking with the blazing force of the ecstasy. Then I looked down at her.

And she was whole. Not the slightest scar on her flawless breast, not a mark left on her forehead. The finger Demeter had started to cut off was healed too. And she was shining—all of her, not just her belly. The glow faded even as I watched—soaked into her skin, leaving her exactly, perfectly herself.

With a trembling finger I traced the Fae mark and spoke the words to avoid pregnancy—for now. Someday, when she was eager for children, I would let my seed live inside her and become another Olympian—a new kind of Olympian. Someone purer and kinder than the race I knew. And I would never sell my child the way my father had sold me.

The bitterness of his betrayal rankled in my gut, souring the moment, and I hated him for that, and for so many things. I'd tried not to hate him—hatred was against my beliefs, my personal creed. But he'd put Cassandra in danger. He'd broken the last strand of my loyalty. And he must pay.

"What's wrong?" Cassandra asked, uncertainty creeping into her lovely dark eyes.

"Not you," I said quickly. "Never you. You were right—it worked." I smiled at her as broadly as I could manage, caressing her newly perfect breast.

"Don't do that." She brushed my hand aside. "You and I don't owe each other false smiles or fake happiness. Tell me what's wrong. Are you thinking about your dad? I mean, icky timing, but I understand that it weighs on you, what he did."

I moved to lie beside her, my face heating with surprise. "I'm not used being read so accurately. Except maybe by Athena, or my mother, but they've known me for centuries. You've known me for a handful of months and you already understand me."

"Lucky guess," she whispered, scooting close and pressing her face to my chest. I circled her body with my arm, drawing her in, sighing at how good it felt to lie like this with someone who cared, someone I loved. I'd been craving this intimacy.

"I love you," I murmured into her hair.

Her music answered before she did, a rush of exquisite joyful notes. "I love you too."

We lay there among the sheets, in the delicious quiet of being, for a long time. Cassandra's hand wandered my body, every ridge and slope, the grooves and planes of me. Learning me. Loving me. I lay and gazed at her, drinking in the music that was her body, marveling how my power had healed that soft beloved flesh, that smooth skin.

"Are we going to talk about you having the power of Zeus?" she said at last.

I groaned and rolled flat on my back, covering my face.

Cassandra chuckled and curved a warm hand over my bicep. "For real though. How did you do that?"

"After I rescued Persephone from Demeter, I took her back to the Underworld. But Demeter had been stirring up the Pantheon, turning them against Hades. She claimed he wasn't fit to rule the Underworld anymore, and she convinced Zeus it was time to intervene. No love lost between Zeus and Demeter, mind you, but my father was all too ready to believe that Hades was defying him somehow, revolting against the will of the Pantheon."

"And you took Hades' side?"

"I did. I stood against Zeus and the Pantheon, along with Hades and some others. When Zeus arrived and saw me there, taking a stand against him—well. I was already on thin ice. While he was confronting Hades, he began to siphon my energy."

Cassandra gasped. "He can do that?"

"Few people know about it. He can't use the unique abilities of the person he's draining, only the energy, like fuel for his own powers. When I felt him taking my energy, I was done. With him, with everything. I resisted, and I managed to reverse the process so his energy began flowing into *me*. But I had no idea I possessed his actual abilities, not just the energy. I must have inherited a version of his siphoning power, one I hadn't unlocked until now. And I would never have thought to access his abilities if you hadn't told me to."

"I had a vision of you using the lightning," Cassandra said. "I saw what you would do to Demeter and Hecate."

"You saved us both," I told her soberly. "A little longer, and you would have become Demeter's slave, while I was dragged away to the dark realms of the Garguignol."

"What is the Garguignol?"

I sighed, pulling her half onto me so that her hair tumbled around both our faces. "The Garguignol is an entity of indescribable horror and darkness, as ancient as the Titans or the Eldritch of Faerie. His territory lies beyond the edge of our realm cluster, near the nightmare world of Icelos. If I'd been dragged away to that part of the universe, I would have been little more than a slave, bound to someone far worse than Hook, Zeus, the Eldritch, or any other malevolent power in this realm cluster."

Cassandra's dark eyes were wide, her lips parted in dismay. "Hook?" she said faintly.

"I think it's time for a few more stories, my love," I said. "Stories about Hook the Realm-Conqueror, and the Fae traveler Peter Pan, and the battle of Wonderland. I'll also tell you of Jack Frost and his long war in defense of Earth against the fire goddess Auxesia."

For a moment I thought she'd recoil again, overwhelmed. But this time she nodded and slid off me, settling in against the pillows. "And tell me about Hades and Persephone, too."

"Of course."

"When you're done," she said slowly, "I have a story to tell you as well. The story of my first and most terrible vision. Hecate dug it out of my head, and in a weird way it was a good thing—I was able to face it this time, and decide how I feel about it. She said my powers are fully unlocked now. I suppose we'll find out what that means before long."

"I'll be here," I told her. "Whatever it means. No matter what evil rises or what good unfolds."

15

CASSANDRA

Apollo spun stories for hours—some of them in the bed, some of them in the kitchen while we got snacks and made microwave tea, and some on the couch while I nestled beside him under blankets. We ate crackers with cheese and watched a concert on TV while he finished the tale of Jack Frost and Emery and Auxesia. And then he lay with his head in my lap, and I played with his hair while he told me about Hades and Persephone.

Then I told him about my baby brother, and my very first vision, the one I'd ignored. I'd carried the guilt for it all my life.

Apollo sat up, eyes shining with horror and pity. "Too cruel," he whispered. "Too cruel of the Fates, to let that happen to you, as a child. You did not know better, darling. It wasn't your fault."

"Whether it was or not, I have to let it go. I have to realize that I'm not solely responsible for what I see. The paths and actions of others lead to those crisis moments—and yes, I have the chance to intervene sometimes, successfully or not—but I didn't make the choices that created those scenarios. I'm only the one who sees."

"An Oracle," Apollo said quietly.

"Yes. Maybe I can help people with my visions, and maybe I can't. But there's no way I can carry the guilt of every tragedy, so I just—won't. Maybe that sounds really callous, but I think it's what I need to do to survive. And I might have to cry sometimes, when there are people I can't save—and you might have to hold me—but afterward, I'll let it go."

Apollo leaned over, golden and naked except for the blanket draped across his hips, and he kissed me tenderly, sliding his hand beneath my hair, cupping my neck. "I'll hold you anytime you like."

I yielded to his kiss, to the blessed endorphins generated by the caress of his smooth lips against mine, the lithe probing of his tongue in my mouth. My palms grazed his hot skin, and I hummed with delight as I moved onto his lap. I pressed my whole body against him, enjoying the rush of lean muscle against my curves. It felt so good to be healed, and whole and singing inside—all of me, singing and sated. But maybe not *quite* sated, because the twitch of his arousal under the blanket sent a ripple of bliss through my belly.

I brushed the golden hair back from his forehead. "Will you get tired of me?"

Apollo regarded me for a moment without answering—the sort of look that made me feel wrapped up and comforted, even though I was sitting naked and uncovered astride his lap. "I've never had this before," he said. "There have been no lasting relationships in this renewal. And in my last lifetime, and the one before it, every relationship was brief and troubled. I can honestly say I've never heard a soul like yours, in a body like this, with a personality that I adore so thoroughly. You are my rest, and you are my One."

"I'm a mess, though," I said, tracing the line of his collarbone. "Moody, they say. Unreliable. Volatile. I go into the dark, and I don't come out for a long time. My last boyfriend—my only boyfriend—it was too much for him."

"But I'm not just your boyfriend, Cassandra," he said, with a faint smile. "I'm the man who loves you. From now until your last vision and beyond, until my final renewal. For as long as my heart drives blood through my body, until the realms fall into ruin, you and I will be an immortal duet."

Tears stung my eyes. "Okay, that was beautiful. I don't have any words that pretty—except—oh my god, the song! You have to hear my song, the one I wrote before I got kidnapped!"

I slid off his lap, ignoring his light groan as my thigh brushed along his erection. After shuffling around in my purse, I found my phone and walked back to him.

"I never post my music online," I said, tapping the TikTok icon. "But when you left, I decided I wouldn't sink into a hole again. I decided to do things that scare me, like try out for a musical and post a song for everyone to see…"

But my explanation faded as I stared at my TikTok notifications. I scrolled through them, my heart rate picking up speed.

"Cassandra?" Apollo rose, knotting the blanket around his waist. "What is it?"

"Wait," I breathed. "Just wait… oh my god. Oh my god—what is *happening*?"

"You need to explain," he said tightly. "Or I'm going to lose it."

His body gleamed hectic and bright, a frantic response to my agitation.

"It's nothing bad," I whispered. "I just—I have millions of new followers. Thousands of notifications. The song, Apollo—it went viral."

"What the Styx does that mean?"

"It means lots of people have watched it—people from all over the world," I said, trembling. "And they liked it. Apollo, they love my song."

He reached for the phone and I handed it over, helpless and stunned. He managed to turn up the volume, and music flowed through the loft—my music. My words, about him.

Apollo listened to it once, and again. And then a third time, sitting beside me on the couch, with one hand over his mouth and his eyes glimmering wet.

He played it one more time.

And again.

Finally I recaptured the phone and scrolled through the comments. Impossible to reply to them all. People wanted to know who I was, where they could buy the song, if I had an album—questions upon questions, for which I had zero answers.

And then I came to a comment that stopped me cold.

I was going to kill myself tonight, and then I heard your song and decided not to.

I replied immediately—*so glad you liked the song*—and then I recommended a suicide hotline and invited them to message me if they needed to. I typed the words, *I've been there*—and then I deleted them, and then I typed them again and posted the comment. No more hiding my own struggles, no matter what anyone else thought.

There were many comments under the initial one—offers of support and help, and then one reply from the original commenter: *Doing better, thanks everyone. Called my brother and he's staying with me for a while.*

I had no way of knowing the whole situation, but it was probable—likely, even—that I'd freaking saved someone's life. With my music.

I'd given millions of people three minutes of pure delight, made them excited about something new, lifted them out of the pain and drudgery for a little while.

My messages were full of people asking about me, wanting to talk about representation and "next steps." My wildest dreams, realized.

But suddenly, weirdly, I didn't care about any of it. I could lay the phone aside, shut out all the clamoring voices, and be back in the moment, in the quiet of the loft with the hum of the TV in the background. I could watch the changing light from the TV screen limning Apollo's bare shoulders in blue. He was sitting bent over on the couch, pinching the bridge of his nose, waves of bright hair falling around his face. I swept the locks aside and pulled his face up.

He was crying. Tears glistened on his lashes and cheeks.

"You liked it?" I whispered, my own lips trembling.

"Loved it," he said. And then faintly, as if he was scared to ask, "Was it about me?"

"Of course, you beautiful god-man," I sat down beside him and rubbed his back with my palm.

Apollo turned and gripped my head with both hands in a paroxysm of sudden passion, crushing his lips to mine. With a murmur of eagerness I reached for the blanket at his waist, plucking the knot free and tossing it aside. He had me down on the sofa in a split-second. His hands roamed my body as if he were claiming me, creating me anew with every touch. When he rolled my nipple between his fingers, a tiny spike of ecstasy lanced between my legs. Then his mouth was on my breast, sucking gently while his tongue circled the peak. I arched up, helpless, arms flung up and aside, unable to think about doing anything but living for his touch.

He took my mouth again, hot tongue lacing against mine—and then he flipped me over bodily, so my breasts were cradled in the sofa cushions. He cupped my rear, fondled handfuls of my flesh and groaned with such relish that I blushed, a fresh gush of wetness seeping between my legs. Apollo thought I was hot, and it made me hotter for him.

Grasping my thighs, he hoisted my rear higher. I tensed, unused to having every bit of me on display, rigid with concern that he'd find something wrong, something lacking. Worried that I'd fail the inspection.

His finger slid all the way through my folds, and I whimpered.

"That's it," he murmured. "Sing for me, Cassandra."

He positioned himself behind me while I waited, tremulous, one touch away from begging. The blunt tip of him rubbed along my slit, front to back, a tantalizing glide, and again I whimpered—damn it, I *mewed* for him, incoherent little cries as he repeated the motion, dipping ever so slightly in with every pass. The heat of him, the subtle vibration of his tip against my trembling nerves—I'd never been wetter, or more desperate. I came suddenly, powerfully, spasming against the hard shaft between my legs.

"Sing for me," he crooned again, in a voice rich with desire, leaning over me, cupping my quivering breast in his palm. He tucked his left hand between my legs and played with me while he kept rubbing himself against my folds, skillfully teasing until I came again. And then he slid into me from behind, and I cried out shrill, my stomach fluttering with the sheer glorious fullness of him.

Apollo held my hips and thrust deep, a jagged rhythm that told me he was long past the limit of his self-control. His raw male moans and harsh gasps drove me higher again, and my body exploded, music and fire. Three orgasms in a row—the best sex I'd ever had.

But he wasn't done with me. He pulled out before he came and turned me over again. "I want to see your eyes," he gritted out. "Look at me, Cassandra. Witness what you do to me."

I thought I might die from the beauty of him. Too much for a mortal to take, maybe—especially when he came, and lost the scant control he had left, and his radiance rocketed outward in a blazing arc. Beams from him shot beyond the wall of windows, into the pre-dawn darkness.

He hung over me, panting, his amber eyes hooded with those sooty lashes.

"What if someone saw your light show?" I said anxiously.

"We'll explain it away," he said. "Or we'll leave."

"Right—you're taking me to another realm."

"If you'd rather stay here and grow old—"

"Nope."

He grinned and gave me a quick kiss. "Can I stay inside you always?"

"I feel that good?" I whispered.

"Incredible." He sighed, drawing himself out. "Shower with me?"

After the fourth orgasm in the shower, coaxed out of me by his lips and fingers, I went entirely boneless. He had to dry me off and tumble me into bed, where we spent the most of day sleeping, and having sex, and eating takeout before having sex again. Around mid-afternoon, it occurred to me that I should probably respond to some of my messages.

When I voiced my thoughts to Apollo, he mumbled something in what sounded like ancient Greek and pulled me back down into the sheets. As I sank into the pillows, my phone buzzed from the living room.

"Could be my sister texting," I said. She'd called earlier, while I was spread-eagled on the bathroom counter with Apollo kneeling between my legs, licking me. I'd ignored the call then, but I should probably answer this time and reassure her.

"Get it," Apollo muttered, face-down and drowsy. I took a second to run my fingers through his silky locks and kiss his temple before I walked out to the living room and picked up my phone.

A text—from Ajax.

Hey beautiful. I have some good news about your audition and I thought I'd deliver it in person. I miss you. Where can we meet?

My body blazed, not passion this time, but anger. How dare he.

The bastard had talked shit about me to his team, and then he'd probably seen my viral success and decided to capitalize on it, if he could. He probably figured it would be good publicity for his little musical.

Warm male hands closed around my shoulders, and I leaned back into the welcoming heat of Apollo.

"I was too far from you," he said, kissing my cheek.

I held the phone so he could see Ajax's text. It was comical the way Apollo withdrew from me immediately, his body stiffening. "Such a dick," he said.

"He really is. But I think I'm going to meet him anyway."

Apollo glanced at me, but there was no insecurity or jealousy in his eyes, no possessive rebuke. "If that's what you want."

"What I want," I said, smirking, "is to show you off a little bit. If you're game."

A slow, brilliant smile illuminated his face. "No need to ask me twice."

I texted Ajax back and then called my sister. I didn't tell her about my kidnapping or my injuries, but I did finally tell her about the "friend" I was staying with. I made Apollo join me in the video chat and wave to Megara briefly before he threw himself on the couch to watch TV and rehydrate.

"It really is roller-coaster boy!" Meg squealed. "And where are you right now? Looks expensive."

"It is. And, um—" I glanced at Apollo, and he nodded. "We're going on vacation soon. A long trip. I might not be able to answer my phone very often."

"As long as you check in occasionally," she said. "And you should call Mom, too. She's been asking about you, worrying about—you know how she is."

"I'll call her," I said.

Meg turned aside briefly, then back to me. "Jessa wants me to ask you about some viral video?"

"Oh, yeah." Why did I feel so self-conscious all of a sudden? "I recorded one of my songs and put it on TikTok. It kind of blew up."

"Congrats, girl! That is seriously awesome. You should do that more often!"

"I plan to."

"This is so great." Meg gave a little wriggle of delight. "You're in such a good place right now. Boyfriend, music success, vacation! I'm so happy for you, Cass."

"I was really low for a long time," I said.

"I know." Her smile faded.

"No, I mean—really low. Like, I thought about ending it, low."

Pain tightened her features. "God, Cass."

"Today I've been thinking—if I'd gone through with it, I'd have missed out on all of this. When I was in that darkness, I couldn't imagine things getting any better. I just couldn't picture it. Reaching the other side seemed like the most ridiculous, impossible dream. But here I am, in this beautiful loft, with millions of people waiting on another song from me, and the sweetest man—" I glanced over at Apollo, splayed on the couch like a divine cover model, water bottle in hand. "Even if things hadn't improved in such a dramatic way, I still would have missed out on something good, something worthwhile."

"I'm glad to hear you say that," Meg said. "I hope you never get to that place again."

"If I do, I'll have someone there to pull me out." I hesitated, then forged ahead. "Listen, I wanted to thank you. Sometimes I feel like you're so wrapped up in your own stuff you barely think about me, and I probably do the same thing to you. But you made me go to Carowinds that day. You *tried.* You did something to help me, when no one else did, and I haven't given you enough credit for that."

Meg's lips pinched, and she nodded hard.

"Don't cry," I warned.

"No, no, I'm not," she said, her voice shrill with impending tears.

"Right." I laughed. "Well, I've got to go get ready. Apollo and I are meeting Ajax."

"What the fuck now?"

"We're just going to give him a little hell. Rub his nose in what he lost."

"Vengeful Cass. I like it. Have fun on your vacation."

"Talk soon."

After hanging up I sat down near Apollo's feet, which were dangling off the edge of the sofa. He offered me his water bottle and I shook my head. "We need to talk about where we're going to go."

With a sigh he turned off the TV. "Obviously my first choice would be Olympus. My powers work best in that realm, and your gifts may expand once you're there, too. Plus I want to show you things, and introduce you to people."

"But your father…"

"But my father." He nodded. "My father, whom I've served so faithfully for so long. He spied on me, drained my energy, and sold me out. He told Demeter where to find you. I can't forgive him for putting you in danger."

"Are you going to challenge him?"

"I don't know." When he looked up, I saw the dread and anxiety swirling in his eyes. "It's a huge step, Cassandra, one I can't take back. It will end with one of us being locked up with the Titans, or wounded so badly we're forced into renewal sleep."

"How long is renewal sleep? When does it normally happen, and what will you be like when you wake up?"

"Slow down." He chuckled. "It usually happens every three to five hundred years, depending on the Olympian. We sleep for twelve Olympian lunar cycles, and when we wake, we're the same, just with different personality traits highlighted. Often the deeds we've done in the previous lifetime dictate which traits become dominant in the next—but not always."

I frowned, plucking at the edge of a sofa cushion.

"You're wondering if you'll still love me when I wake up from my next renewal."

"Clever boy." I grimaced.

"It will be a change," he said softly. "My own memories of this lifetime will be somewhat softened—at least the bad ones. Memories connected to powerful positive emotions remain fairly clear. It's all about keeping the psyche from breaking, you see. We live so long that we need an extended reset, beyond normal sleep. If it's any comfort, my next renewal won't be due for another four hundred years."

"Good," I breathed, relieved. "We'll cross that bridge when we come to it."

I went into the bedroom to call my mother—not that I had anything to hide from Apollo, but some things were too private and painful to share with him just yet. Ever since he'd told me about the life-mate thing, I'd felt weirdly reassured of his love—far more comfy and secure than I'd ever been with Ajax. But I still had the nagging fear that Apollo would uncover something about me that was too troublesome, something he just didn't want to bother with.

The first thing my mother did was tell me all the things she'd been worried about lately, most of it relating to politics and conspiracies. At the end she relayed some of her anxieties about me and my finances and my lack of a partner.

"I'm okay, Mom," I assured her. "I'm fine now."

"You're fine *now*?" she said. "So you weren't fine before?"

"I've been depressed," I said. "Not sure if Meg told you. I was in a dark place. But I'm better now. I'm going on vacation with my boyfriend."

"Boyfriend?" she chirped. "Oh my god—please tell me he's not someone you met online. And double-check that he's not married—best to hire a P.I. if you need to, just to be sure. Some of these guys are real sneaky about hiding their second lives. You said you're going on vacation? If you're heading to a beach, be careful—

sharks are attacking more often nowadays. And there are man-o-war jellyfish along the coast, they say. And that's just along the East Coast—tropical waters are way more dangerous. Might as well not even risk it, honestly. Please don't go on a cruise ship, sweetie. They're just coated with diseases, and I heard about this rapist who—"

"Mom!" I cut her off. "How are you doing? Eating well? Sleeping okay?"

From there she launched into a long list of her personal ailments and dietary restrictions. She was always trying one diet or another, convinced that each one was going to solve everything for her. It took me half an hour to get off the phone, and by the end of the call I was a wreck, with my own anxiety skyrocketing and despair haunting the edges of my consciousness.

I walked straight out of the bedroom and climbed into Apollo's lap, nuzzling into the curve of his shoulder, breathing the sun-bright honeyed sweetness of his skin.

"When we've got your family situation sorted out," I murmured, "we need to do something for my mother. She needs to be—untangled, or de-stressed, or something. This is why I can't talk to her—she makes me worse."

"Sweetheart, if anyone understands a dysfunctional family and a paranoid parent, it's me." He kissed my forehead. "Once I've practiced a bit more with targeted healing, maybe I can help her. I'm not even sure I can heal anyone without—" He cleared his throat.

"Without sleeping with them?"

"Yes."

"I'm not sharing you."

"I don't want to be shared."

"No more sexual generosity from you, sir." I traced the curve of his pectoral, touching his nipple, watching it tighten at my attention. I relished the quickening of his breath, the surge of his chest under my hand.

"You're the only one I want to be *generous* with," he breathed, taking my mouth, torturing my lips with a series of short, succulent kisses.

"We don't have time for this," I panted as he kissed right below the corner of my jaw, then over the pulse of my throat. "We have to meet Ajax. And after that, you need to decide what you're going to do, Apollo. About your father. Because when Demeter doesn't come back, he'll know something's up. He might send someone else to take you out."

He moaned against my skin. "I want to hide here with you forever."

"No one understands that impulse better than I do," I whispered, cupping his smooth jaw and lifting his face to mine. "But if you hide from the problems, they just get worse. You've been letting your dad run the show for a long time now, right? Has he made good choices? Have your people and your realm become better, or worse?"

He didn't have to say it. I read the answer in his eyes. I wanted to push him further, to make him commit to a confrontation—but something stopped me. Pushing a person too far could have the wrong effect. And urging my divine boyfriend to overthrow his god-father felt like an overreach. I barely understood this new universe I'd become aware of. Who was I to start screwing around with its political dynamic?

16

APOLLO

When Cassandra and I walked into the coffee shop, I picked out Ajax immediately, before she told me who he was.

Wavy dark hair, long-lashed brown eyes. Good-looking enough, for a human male. He wore a dark gray dress shirt that gleamed when he moved, and a necklace of wooden beads, and some shiny black pants.

Cassandra had made me wear a tight pair of jeans and an even tighter T-shirt, one that hugged my biceps and made her coo with delight.

"I love your piercings," she'd added, touching each of them. "Ajax hates piercings. It's perfect." And she'd given a little wriggle of wicked pleasure that made me instantly hard.

I was still half-aroused, thrumming with lust for Cassandra and simmering with rage for everything this man had done to her, for every time he'd made her feel unworthy for being her exquisite, complex self. Violence was a last resort for me, but for Ajax, I could make an exception.

"Hi there," Cassandra said as we approached the table.

"Cassie-baby," he crooned, rising. "You look tired, poor thing. I got you a caramel macchiato, your favorite.

Skim milk, of course. We have to watch our star's figure!"

"Thanks, but I hate caramel, and skim milk, too." She smiled brightly and pulled me forward. "This is my boyfriend, Apollo. Apollo, this is Ajax."

"Oh." Ajax's whole face changed. Shock, jealousy, thwarted ambition and virulence chased each other across his features. "I thought we were meeting alone, doll. Just you and me, like old times." He laughed, light and hollow. "Boyfriend? I didn't know you were dating."

"Of course!" Cassandra's answering laugh rang with vindictive confidence. "What else would I be doing? Certainly not pining after anyone." She kept laughing, awkwardly, and shot me a look that said *help me*.

"You wanted to speak to Cassandra about something?" I said, in my deepest and most golden tones.

"Um—" Ajax swallowed, his eyes flicking down to the pecs swelling through my shirt over my crossed arms. "Won't you sit down?"

"No," I replied. "I don't think we will."

"Oh." He cleared his throat. "Well, Cassie-doll, I wanted to offer you the lead in *Cabaret*. I think you'd be perfect as Sally Bowles. And I was hoping that working together would give us a chance to—reconnect." He focused on Cassandra, pursing his lips in a look that was probably supposed to be sensual and enticing.

I stifled a chuckle. Both Cassandra and Ajax glanced at me.

"Apollo's right," Cassandra said. "You offering me the role is kinda funny, considering how *unstable* and *unreliable* you think I am."

Ajax looked from me to her. I could see his mental cogs revolving. He was trying to figure out if she knew about his conversation with the production team, the one where he'd sabotaged her chance at the role.

"Not sure what you mean, Cass," he said. "I—I may have said something that was misinterpreted by someone. Not sure who told you, but yes, I had misgivings about you taking the role. But then I realized that you're a dedicated artist with a growing audience, and—"

"You heard about my viral song," Cassandra said. "That's why you want me for your show. You want the publicity."

"Internet fame is fleeting," he said, waving his fingers as if to brush it aside. "And social media is a bunch of fools spewing their foolishness at each other. I've warned you about it before, Cassie-doll. That's why I always advised you against putting your songs on those platforms. It cheapens your art. What I'm offering is a chance for you to do serious work in the field you love."

I didn't know much about human social networks, but I didn't like the way he dismissed an achievement that had clearly meant something to Cassandra.

"What does it matter how she chooses to send her music into the world, as long as people get to hear it?" I interjected.

"It matters because—because—why am I explaining myself to you?" Ajax frowned, looking me up and down. "Who is this guy anyway, Cassie? Look at what he's turning you into." He gestured to her, shaking his head. "This isn't the best version of you. Look at yourself—you're a mess. You don't need Gigolo Mc-Biceps here. You need people in your life who actually know you and care about you."

His fingers grazed her elbow, and she jerked away.

"People who know me?" she hissed, trembling. "He already knows me better than you ever did. He takes care of me *and* he respects me. He doesn't constantly cut me down, or try to control me, or make me feel like I'm so much *less* than him, like he's settling for me."

Ajax shook his head and started to speak, but she cut him off.

"He loves my music. He encourages me, builds me up, helps me be better in the ways that actually matter. Best of all, he makes me glad to be alive. You wanna know who he is, Ajax? He's the man who doesn't inspect me for flaws." She snatched the paper cup he'd offered her, pulled the lid off, and tossed the liquid contents over Ajax's front.

"You bitch!" he screeched. "This is raw silk!"

The chatter in the coffee shop quieted, and faces turned toward us. I clamped one hand around Ajax's neck and lifted him off the floor. "Apologize. Now."

"Fuck you," he wheezed.

"Apollo," squeaked Cassandra, but she didn't stop me.

"You called her a foul name," I said calmly, lifting him higher. His face reddened, and he clawed at my hand. "Apologize to my lady."

"Sorry!" he choked. "Sorry, sorry!"

I lowered him to the floor. "I don't believe you. Say it again, on your knees this time."

"I'm calling the cops," squeaked one of the patrons somewhere behind me. I turned briefly and fixed the woman with a look. She dropped her phone back into her purse.

"This man called the woman I love a bitch," I said, raising my voice so they could all hear. "I'm simply requesting a sincere apology. Go about your business."

"You weirdo bastard," coughed Ajax. "Cassie, don't tell me you're really with this sick fucker. This guy's going to make you crazier than you already are."

I hauled him up by his collar and punched him in the face.

It was a light punch, really. Barely a love-tap from my fist, but he flew backward as if a cannonball had hit him and crashed into a table.

"Come on." Cassandra grabbed my arm. "You made your point. We've got to leave." She dragged me outside, along the sidewalk. "Ugh, why did we walk here instead of driving? We've got to get out of sight for a while in case someone does call the cops and give them your description."

"Out of sight where?"

She pulled me into a narrow passage between two buildings, and we cut across a bricked plaza dotted with concrete planters and evergreen bushes. A man passed us on his way out of a building, and Cassandra caught the door through which he'd exited before it closed.

"Yes!" she whispered. "This is perfect. Only people with keycards can get in here, like your building. They won't look for us here."

She kept towing me along, glancing back at me now and then with sparkling dark eyes that sang of freedom and vindication. Along one quiet hall, we came to a door that said "Restroom"—no gender restriction. Cassandra opened it, pulled me inside, and locked it behind us.

The bathroom was elegant as human restrooms went—glossy black tile, frosty overhead lamps, a white toilet and sink. It had the bright, stinging scent of a recent cleaning with human chemicals.

"Cassandra," I said. "Why are we in this bathroom?"

"Shh." She pressed her fingers over my mouth. "I don't want anyone to hear us. They'll be mad if they know we're in here together."

"Again, why are we in here?" I whispered.

"Because you're so damn glorious and awesome," she hissed back. "And I shouldn't have liked what you did back there, to Ajax, but—hell, Apollo, you were amazing. He was so jealous, and I loved it. Felt so good to get him back a little bit for how he made me feel." She hesitated, smirking. "Will it be too much if I send him a picture of your dick in my mouth?"

"I'm sorry, I only heard the last few words—what was the question?"

Cassandra breathed a quiet laugh, sliding her arms around my waist. As I leaned down, she rose up to meet me, and she crushed her lips to my mouth. She kissed me recklessly, ardently, twining her tongue with mine.

My hands closed around her soft body, every bit of my skin waking for her, aching for her. I groaned deep as her breasts pushed against my chest, and she broke the kiss to cover my lips again and hush me. I sucked one of her fingertips into my mouth and poured all the lust I felt through my gaze into her eyes.

"Apollo," she whispered. Her hands slid up, under my T-shirt. I felt every one of those slim feminine fingers with exquisite distinctness. She caressed my pectorals, grazing my nipples with her nails, making them tingle and peak. I felt like I had the first time she seduced me—as though every nerve ending I owned had been dormant until now, and burst into glowing life at her touch.

She kept tugging my shirt higher, so I shucked it off. As she moved in again, caressing my chest, her hip bumped against the seam of my jeans—a seam that was strained to the limit, painfully tight. The contact made me hiss, and I caught her hips, hauling her against me.

Cassandra trailed her fingers downward and popped out the button of my jeans. Slowly she raked the zipper down and parted the slit of my boxers, easing out my dick. It was burning for her, thrumming for her.

I was half a second from tearing off her pants and setting her on the edge of the sink when Cassandra loosened my grip on her waist and lowered herself to her knees.

My whole body roared with heat, every muscle taut and craving. I clasped the edge of the sink with one hand and clamped my other palm to the cool tiled wall. My length yearned up, beaded with glistening drops.

Cassandra delicately licked the tip. Her tongue was like silk fire against the thin skin and every trembling nerve beneath it. She made a little sound of satisfaction and licked me again.

When her beautiful lips parted and began to take me in, traveling farther and farther along my shaft, I swore in her language, in mine, in every dialect I'd ever learned. The wet heat of her mouth, the flexion of her lips around me—then the firm curl of her tongue against the underside—I was dying. I would die of this, of sheer pleasure.

No woman had set her mouth on me in decades. I hadn't let them, knowing I couldn't achieve a climax and that I wouldn't be able to hide the lack of one.

I'd forgotten how deliriously blissful it felt to have a beautiful woman suck on me. And not just any woman—this was Cassandra. My Cassandra. Better still—I was hers. Hers always, hers alone. Though she was kneeling, I was her devoted worshiper.

17

CASSANDRA

Apollo tasted too good for words. Why had I not put him in my mouth before? Besides the beauty of its shape, his penis glowed faintly. It was warm and silky, and it hummed on my tongue. Which was strange, but I loved it.

I let my lips pop off him. "It vibrates a little," I whispered. "Do all Olympian dicks do that?"

"No." Apollo let out a shuddering breath, but he didn't complain about the interruption. "Hades' doesn't do anything special. Hermes and Eros each have their specialties, and you don't want to know what Zeus's can do. Let's just say it's one reason he and Hera stayed together so long before splitting up. The other reason being that they're life-mates."

"And they're exes now?"

"Yes, officially at least. Life-mates can separate and go their own ways for a time, but they always circle back to each other."

"And do all Olympians have life-mates?"

"No. Only a few that I've ever heard of."

"So we're special." I licked from the base all the way to the groove right beneath the head. He couldn't answer me; he groaned, and his stomach muscles contracted with every panting breath.

I licked the full length again, and his fingers sank into my hair. Then I kissed the tip, a soft pressure before parting my lips and taking him in, slow and steady. Apollo's hands tightened against my hair, an irresistible reflex, but he didn't push himself deeper. "Cassandra," he gasped as I set a rhythm, back and forth. I almost smiled at the way he said my name, but I kept working him, lips and tongue, with my fingers stroking the part my mouth couldn't take.

I lifted my eyes, and if my underwear hadn't already been soaked, the sight of him would have done it. He'd fallen apart against the tiled wall, a broken bronze god, his golden mane tumbled around his beautiful shoulders, helpless to the surging pleasure. His body glowed brighter with every stroke of my lips.

My love for him expanded—grew wings and took flight. I wanted to make him feel this good always. I wanted to be sure he'd be safe and happy for centuries, for millennia. But how could Apollo be safe, when Zeus wanted him gone? Was a confrontation the best option? Or should Apollo stay away from Olympus, and try to find a different life? I didn't know how to protect him, how to advise him.

I closed my eyes, trying to quiet the worries, trying to focus on the rhythm, on the salty-sweet taste of him, on the tremors that had begun to roll through his length. He was close, I could feel it.

Protect him, pleasure him, always, always…

Suddenly my vision split, and I was still on my knees, sucking Apollo's silky length—but I was somewhere else too, on a circular slab of white-marble, ringed by columns, with a vista of vivid green countryside sweeping away into the misty distance. I stood at Apollo's side—and there was no Zeus, only a joyful crowd of impossibly beautiful people welcoming the sun-god, while a black-haired man with horns settled a crown of bronze laurel leaves on Apollo's golden head.

Just a brief vision—a second or two. I couldn't be sure when or how it would happen. But I'd made that vision appear—I'd summoned the assurance I needed, a glimpse of the future. Our future.

I redoubled my speed, taking Apollo deeper, harder, until he cried out and let go—and I didn't hush him, I just held him, my lips around his pulsing length, my hands on his hips. He tasted sweet, creamy, honestly delicious. Nothing like Ajax when he'd made me—I stopped myself, shoving aside those thoughts, refocusing on Apollo's exquisite moans.

At last I pulled away, with a final long lick, and I looked up at him. He was completely undone, collapsed against the wall as if he could barely stand, with his pants open and his beautiful abdomen still tightening in ripples of shining muscle. His throat bobbed between the powerful, slanted tendons of his neck. And that jaw of his—honed for cutting through a girl's walls, right to her beating heart.

"You gorgeous thing," I whispered, and I thought of more music that suited him in that moment—a weighty beat from drum and cello, pure sex in sound form, with a layer of soft sultry piano over it.

"You don't know how amazing it is just to be able to come," he panted. "Every time we're together, I'm fighting the fear that it won't happen, that I'll be trapped in the agony right before the pleasure. A hundred years of that feeling, Cassandra. You can't imagine how grateful I am that you broke my curse."

"I can imagine a little." I pressed a palm to his thundering chest. "I love doing this to you. It's so much fun."

He shed a boyish grin over me, and I took his face in my hand and pulled my tall god down so I could kiss him.

While we were kissing, he slid two long fingers under the waistband of my pants, until he touched the center of my underwear. "I thought so," he whispered.

"We have to go," I breathed. "We can't stay in here. What if someone needs this bathroom?"

"You can't expect me to leave yet, not when you're so tender and touchable. Take off your pants for me, sweetheart, and spread your legs."

I obeyed, quivering with apprehension because what if everything wasn't perfectly perfect down there— but Apollo kissed the inner thigh of my left leg, and then the hollow of my hip, and I forgot everything I'd feared. He trailed nibbling kisses along my inner right thigh next, and place a single searing kiss right on my pubic bone. Kisses, kisses everywhere, except on the anguished places where I most wanted them.

When I was practically squirming with need, Apollo sealed his mouth between my legs and thrust his tongue into me, and I nearly screamed. I clamped my jaws around my wrist, thighs shaking, feet arching. My other hand landed on his head. He lapped and lapped, until I knew I was going to scream full-voice if he didn't give me some relief. He could tell, of course—because somehow he knew me, really *knew me*. He stood up again, and he didn't kiss me but his beautiful face hovered next to mine. He watched me, watched my face, while he slipped two fingers inside me. And then a third.

He worked me quick, quick, an exquisitely violent rhythm, the heel of his hand bumping in just the right spot. I came on that warm male hand, on those strong fingers. I came so hard that I bit his shoulder to keep from shrieking.

We hung there together for a moment, mutely connected. I felt deeply refreshed, as if the last bit of grime from my relationship with Ajax had been washed away. I wasn't perfect—I didn't have to be perfect—but I was new.

When we'd cleaned up and put ourselves back together, we left the building by another back alley and spent the rest of the afternoon hiding out in the art museum downtown before going to a bar for dinner and drinks.

I hadn't drunk anything in days, and it felt good to drink casually, just a little bit, for fun—no compulsion to drown myself in alcohol so I could feel a little less awful. We found a cozy corner booth, and I sipped a white wine spritzer while Apollo savored three fingers of top-shelf whiskey. I'd blushed when he ordered it, remembering the three fingers he'd used on me earlier.

I was perfectly content, or trying to be, but the one fly in the proverbial honey was the way women kept ogling Apollo, even though he was clearly with me. Understandable, but he'd smile or nod back at them, innocently, in the friendliest way, not flirty at all— except when you're that gorgeous, everything looks flirty.

I refused to be *that girlfriend* and tell him *not* to smile at people. I needed to get used to it if I was going to be with this man for the rest of my life. He would always be beautiful, and he'd always attract attention. It didn't matter how much attention was centered on him, or from whom—he loved *me,* for more than my looks. So I would have to work on being confident in his love. Unthreatened.

Still, when another girl walked past our table and openly gawked at him while he smiled politely, I couldn't stay quiet.

"You know, you're not without your faults," I said abruptly.

Apollo lifted an eyebrow. "I'm aware."

"Like you kind of have this idea that you're God's gift to women, that women *need* a man to be satisfied, when honestly another girl or a well-designed toy can accomplish the exact same thing."

He tilted his head from side to side, as if reluctantly admitting the point. "If you like the touch of another woman, of course that's ample stimulation. But a toy? I assume you mean a device that replicates the shape and feel of a penis?"

"With vibration. Mmm." I let my eyes close. "I ordered a really good one after Ajax left me. Unfortunately it's all burnt up now."

"Do you miss it?"

I squirmed and blushed, thinking of what we'd just done in the office building bathroom, and all day today, and the night before. "No."

He grinned. "However well-designed one of those toys may be, it's no replacement for the body of another person."

"Sometimes it's less stress, though. Less complicated."

He conceded with a nod. "Have you ever been with another woman?"

"Not my thing. What about you, with guys?"

"One or two, in a distant lifetime. But with the rare exception, I've always preferred women. They're just so—" He squinted upward, as if reaching for the right word.

"Breasts?" I said.

"No." He nudged my knee under the table, looking offended, then melted into another grin. "And yes. Breasts, and shape, and their feminine aura, and something else, something truly divine. A unique strength and delicacy. And of course there's the urge to procreate, very powerful with my race." He winced. "Gets us into trouble sometimes."

"You said you had children in another life," I said. "What happened to them?"

"Demigods can die," he said simply. "And they did, in various ways, for various reasons. I wasn't the kind of man then that I strive to be now, so I wasn't as close to them as I should have been. I wasn't a good father. That will change when... if..." His lashes dipped then lifted, exposing a vulnerable, hopeful question in his golden eyes.

"When," I said softly. Not now, not anytime soon... but someday. Someday, little golden adorable god-babies.

"When," he repeated, eyes lighting. "When there's a better world for them."

We were both quiet then. I imagined he was thinking of all the ways *his* world was imperfect, while I was thinking the same thing of mine.

"I watched you reconnect with your family today," said Apollo after a few moments. "And I saw you stand up to Ajax, someone who belittled you and told you lies about yourself, lies you believed for too long. My father has done the same thing, not only to me, but to so many others. One of his most pernicious lies is the untruth that Olympians are more intelligent and more worthy than humans, and that it is our right to have human slaves. To this day, as I've told you, Olympians still take slaves from human realms, or purchase them from traders. The Fae do it too, which normalizes the practice a bit, but it isn't right. Nor is it right for the Olympian realm to remain so insular, blind to the needs of the other realms. My race has always been cruel, but now we are complacent too, and that's even worse."

I stroked his knuckles, listening.

"I've decided to go back, and challenge my father for the High Seat," he said. "I don't know whether I've taken all of his power or only a portion, but I think the display of it will startle everyone into hearing what I have to say. If it comes to an official challenge, I'll battle him. I know Athena will back me up, and she hinted at others who would. But I don't want a war, so I won't amass any forces, or bring in outside allies. It will be me alone, against him."

"Not you alone," I said. "I'm coming too."

"You can't."

"Don't give me crap about it being too dangerous," I said. "You left me behind once, and I won't let you do it again. I'm terrified about meeting your freaky god-family, but I'm coming along anyway. And I know you could stop me, but if you love me, Apollo, you won't."

He nodded heavily. "It's selfish of me, but I think I need you there. You're my strength."

"Damn," I said, forcing a smile to hide the fact my lips were trembling. "I've never been anyone's strength before. Feels good. So you don't think your dad will kill me on the spot?"

"It's not his style. He'll want to talk first. Besides, you're beautiful, and an Oracle. I can feel your power clearly now, and he'll be able to as well, the minute you pass through the Olympian realm gate. When he sees you and senses what your ability is, he'll want you, in more ways than one."

"Ew."

Apollo chuckled. "It's not going to be comfortable for either of us."

The next morning, we managed to get out the door without having sex again, a triumph we quickly lost when we found ourselves alone in the elevator. Apollo pinned me to the wall and gave me the fastest orgasm of my life.

"Okay, so I definitely don't miss my vibrator," I whispered, knees wobbling as he set me down again.

He grinned down at me, hastily zipping his pants as the elevator doors opened.

We took Apollo's car and drove out of town. He'd told me the Earth realm gate was near Baltimore, and it was too dangerous to fly that distance in the daylight, so we had our first nine-hour road trip, filled with music and snacks. I wrote another song, and we stopped in a stark-looking wintry meadow to film it. Apollo provided lighting—golden rays of sun streaming from his fingers directly on me as I played his guitar. And we didn't even need fancy equipment, because his magic augmented my voice and the guitar's sound, enhancing both so beautifully than I almost couldn't finish the song without crying. I uploaded the song while we drove, and it began taking off immediately, likes and comments rolling in.

When we were close to Baltimore, we stopped at a motel to change, because apparently we couldn't show up to the Olympian High Seat without formal attire.

Apollo also had some gross slimy things called "sluagh eyes" tucked away in his bag, which he claimed were necessary for navigating the realm gates and surviving the In-Between with our sanity intact. I managed to swallow the horrible glob, and then I nearly threw it up again—but Apollo distracted me by slipping his arms around me from behind and cupping my breasts in his hands.

"You act like you've never touched breasts before," I said. "And I know for a fact you've handled a lot of them."

"But those weren't *your* breasts," he countered, squeezing lightly. "I'm just getting to know *these*."

And so I kept the sluagh eye down, and we exerted enormous amounts of willpower and got dressed instead of jumping each other's bones. Apollo put on one of the gorgeous sunshiny outfits from his closet—it had a sort of loincloth-wrap thing beneath an open robe embroidered with suns and starbursts. The robe left the panels of his bronze chest bare. Looking at him, I felt rather small and shy, because he looked so much like a classic Greek god, like the fantasy version of Apollo from a TV show or movie.

He'd insisted I bring one of the gowns we'd purchased when we were shopping downtown. It was creamy and flowy, with a satiny under-dress draped in filmy gauze and a pair of slits up to my thighs. I felt rather like a goddess in it, honestly, and Apollo said I would fit right in.

He straightened his hair with magic, which made him look so regal and elven that I was torn between the impulse to worship him and the desire to put him in my mouth—maybe both at once.

"You should tie back your hair," he said, braiding his own, oblivious to his effect on me. "It gets in the way during flight. We can take it down when we get there."

I scraped my loose waves into a tight ballet bun, not a strand out of place, trying not to think about how many times Ajax had made me wear a bun just like this during sex. *I don't like your hair getting in my mouth*, he'd told me. *You look best when you're neat, and all that hair is out of your face.*

With the bun perfected, I turned to Apollo. "Better?"

He stepped forward, loosening the knot and tugging out a few messy tendrils around my face. He pressed his mouth to my hairline and inhaled, sighing with satisfaction. "Perfect."

It was dark when we emerged from the motel. My stomach was looping and diving incessantly because I was about to travel between *realms* to fucking Olympus to meet Zeus himself. Not just to meet him—to stand by my life-mate's side while Apollo challenged his father.

I bent over slightly, pressing a hand to my belly, fighting the residual nausea from the sluagh eye.

"Nervous?" Apollo asked.

"Hell yeah."

"Me too." He led me behind a fringe of trees and let his wings emerge through slits in the back of his robes. I'd seen the wings before, but I had the feeling I'd never get over just how beautiful they were, or how magnificent and angelic he looked with them spread wide.

"Come here, Cassandra." The warmth in his voice and eyes—the sheer tenderness—and I got to enjoy that for the rest of my life? The surge of gratitude in my heart nearly overwhelmed me, but I swallowed hard and stepped into his arms. Since my dress had slits, I could cling to Apollo face to face and hitch my legs over his hips. Sure, that left my legs entirely bare, but it was dark, and the dress covered my ass at least. I laced my arms around his neck, my fingertips fiddling with his braid.

The last time he flew with me, I'd been in too much pain to really enjoy it. This time, I felt every dramatic surge of muscle as his body contracted and extended, leaping into the air. I muffled a screech against his shoulder as we rose high, high above the treetops, higher than the peak of the tallest roller coaster at Carowinds.

Apollo's strong arms encircled me. I couldn't fall—he wouldn't let me fall. I forced myself to enjoy the vast arch of the starry sky, and the sweep of dark countryside beneath us, dotted with glimmering amber lights—and then I shut my eyes tight.

"How far until the realm gate?"

"Not far," he replied.

With my eyes closed, I became conscious of the way my center was pressed over his groin, the way his robes had parted, baring the heated skin of his thigh. I could feel that thigh rubbing against mine. With every wingbeat, Apollo's body shifted, a friction I couldn't ignore.

"Did you know I have kind of an addictive personality?" I said breathlessly at his ear. "Before I met you, I think I was becoming an alcoholic. Someone who drinks too much and can't stop."

"Like Dionysus and his followers," he said.

"Sure. Like that. Anyway—I think I've replaced one addiction with another. And that's you. More specifically, sex with you. I can't get enough." I nipped his ear lobe lightly, caressing the yellow jeweled studs with my tongue. "What have you turned me into?"

"My very own succubus, apparently." His voice was rough, and as I urged my hips tighter to his, I felt the hard length beneath his robes.

"Too bad we can't have sex in the air," I whispered.

"Who says we can't?" But then he admitted, "I might not be able to get the right leverage. And it could get very messy and awkward. Best to wait, and have something to look forward to when we succeed."

"Best to wait," I echoed quietly.

An unspoken "if we survive" hung in the scant, heated space between us.

"We should talk about what could happen," Apollo said, as his massive wings carried us higher. "If the conflict heightens and Zeus sends me into renewal sleep, you'll be in Olympus without my protection. Zeus may even try to force himself on you. He's done it with women before, in previous lifespans, and my past self did not confront him. Believe me, I carry eternal guilt for the careless and cruel things I have done, including the sins of inaction."

"I understand the heaviness of guilt," I murmured. Despite facing those memories of mine, and making the cerebral decision to let my guilt go, I'd never truly be free of it. Refusing to let it entangle and submerge me would take a thousand tiny decisions, each time the anguish began to creep up from the bottom of my soul again.

"I know you understand—though your guilt is a purer sort than mine." Apollo's arms tightened around me. "All I can say is, if the worst should happen, be strong. Trust that when I reawaken, I'll be the same person inside, though my personality may shift a little. And when I come back, I'll protect you and reclaim you. Until then, you can trust Athena—and possibly my other sister Artemis, though her loyalty is only to herself."

"Even if you change, I'll still love you." I hugged his neck and nestled my face against his cheek. "Humans change over the course of their lives too—they go through phases, up-and-down times. But some of them still manage to love each other despite all that. And trust me, I'm not about to give you up."

A relieved sigh rushed from him. I kissed his cheekbone and temple, while inside I trembled and hollowed at the thought of losing him, even for just a year. I couldn't be sure that my vision of our eventual joy and triumph was for this specific time. Granted, my visions usually applied to the very near future, but I couldn't fully rely on them. That scene could easily have been a year from now.

I didn't tell Apollo about the vision. I had this nagging sense, this twist in my gut—maybe an Oracle's instinct warning me not to say anything, not to let the assurance of success impact the choices he'd make today.

Whatever happened, I'd cling to the vision, and hope for it. I'd just been through a dark and terrible year; I could endure another one if the light of Apollo waited at its end.

Apollo's body tensed, and the beat of his wings quickened. "There is the realm gate," he said.

18

APOLLO

In this lifetime, I'd practiced concealing my true emotions. So many people around me were uneasy, panicked, or in pain, and I'd become the one who stayed calm, the one who kept a level head and a controlled demeanor. So when I took Cassandra through the realm gate of Earth into the In-Between, I pretended that it was a simple passage, free of risks. I pointed out the sluaghs and explained what they were without mentioning that they could cause madness or swallow her whole. I calmly moved us toward the Olympian realm gate, without screaming my inner panic that we'd both be attacked or imprisoned the moment we stepped through.

Everything I'd told her was true. My father wouldn't attack me without talking first, and he'd want Cassandra for himself, her body and her mind. Yet still I couldn't dispel the irrational fear that if we crossed into Olympus together, we would both die—or what passed for death in my case.

Cassandra clutched my arm as the Olympian gate sucked us through, and our feet found the top stair of the myriad steps leading from the gate to the meadows below.

Guards stepped forward the moment they recognized me. I ignored them, calmly undoing the braid in my hair and then plucking the band from Cassandra's so that her brown waves tumbled free.

"Lord Apollo," said one of the guards, with a nervous clearing of his throat. "You are to come with us at once. Zeus ordered that if you arrived, you should be brought to the High Seat immediately for judgment on a charge of treason. I must ask you, my lord, to comply. You are to sheathe your wings and walk with us to the Mount."

"And if I don't?" I smiled broadly at them. They were lesser Olympians, at least in my father's eyes—with human blood somewhere in their line. Full citizens, not slaves—but not respected or powerful, either. They wielded special weapons, spelled to defend against invaders from other realms, but I was the son of Zeus. They could do nothing against me, and they knew it.

The guards eyed each other nervously.

"I'm joking," I said. "I'll come along. But first, I'd like you to meet my friend, lover, and life-mate, the Oracle Cassandra, of Earth."

"Hello," Cassandra said, with a smile so charming I wanted to sweep her into my arms and kiss her until her knees buckled.

Instead I offered her my arm and we descended all those bothersome steps, all the way down to the smooth white pavers of the path below. I'd forgotten how long it took to descend on foot rather than fly.

Our progress through the gardens and lanes of the Olympian landscape was slow—a procession of sorts. My father had doubtless dictated that I be brought to him this way because he knew my passage would attract a crowd. The Sun God Apollo, being taken under guard to the Mount for judgment at his father's High Seat. A scandal, to be sure.

But what Zeus intended as a shame to me, I turned to my benefit—shedding my brightest smiles over the citizens, casting handfuls of tiny glittering stars for the children, releasing some of my power to make the day a little brighter, the colors a little more vivid, and the sounds a little more musical wherever I passed. I'd brought nothing with me, no weapon or musical instrument, knowing they'd confiscate it at the gate—but a woman tossed me a lute and called, "Apollo, play for us!"

I caught the instrument and began to play, a light, luscious melody that drew even more people from their homes. The guards looked nervously at the instrument in my hands, but they did not try to take it.

"Who are all these people?" Cassandra asked quietly, under the thrum of my music. "They look human. Are they slaves?"

"Not all. Most of them are servants and workers, ill-paid but free. The slaves typically work in the big houses, on the estates of the Pantheon. Many of the people you see are descendants of gods and humans, like you, except the blood is fresher in their lineage. Poseidon and Ares especially have had a habit of bringing their children, grandchildren, and great-grandchildren to this realm to live, and those descendants have married and intermingled for hundreds of years. Inter-realm travel is dangerous and expensive—more so when Hook's fleet was abroad—and some merchants from other realms decided to give up their perilous ways and live here instead. Others are also part satyr, dryad, naiad, or even Fae. The gods of the Pantheon view them all as low-class citizens, a necessary evil."

"Do they have powers?"

"Many do. The ones Zeus considers too dangerous are sealed with a mark to limit their abilities—see that man?" I pointed to a tall fellow leaning against a building. His forearm bore a silvery lightning-shaped symbol. "It's not optional. The gods will brook no rivalry from those who serve them."

"That's awful."

"It is." I kept playing, kept smiling, but inwardly I wondered if the symbol only repressed a person's ability, as Zeus claimed, or if perhaps he had drained each citizen on whom he'd set the mark. Maybe he'd been swallowing up the energy from generations of Olympians. I had no way to be sure, but judging from what he'd nearly done to me, I couldn't discount the possibility either.

The road to the Mount wound through several villages. Pretty as they were, I wondered if Cassandra noticed the hints of twisted evil, like I did. One of the lesser goddesses had two teenage girls collared and chained. She was making them crawl before her like dogs as she walked. Bellerophon, a demigod, was openly beating one of his slaves in a public square we passed. And one of Hera's descendants, whose name I could never remember, had a basket of human babies on her arm. She was trailed by a hunched, cloaked figure—her personal Unseelie spellcaster, if rumors were to be believed.

I knew what was being sold in some of the sparkling shops we passed, and I knew of the dens beneath our feet, where limbs and lives were traded as readily as wealth. Some of the upper echelon of gods still hated Fae magic, but too many of the citizens, with their natural powers removed or repressed, had turned to Unseelie craft to work their will. Others might look like bright citizens now, but come evening they would be lying in smoky hovels, lost in a daze of drugs secretly imported from Wonderland, or drinking themselves into oblivion with the heady liquor smuggled in from Oz.

I'd told Cassandra some of the sickness of my world during our drive to the gate, and she turned paler the longer we walked and the more she witnessed it for herself. My beautiful realm was a world diseased and darkened, soured and stained by cruelty. The indolence of the rich and the despair of the poor crawled through the land like a poison until, despite all that our magic could do, nature itself was becoming corrupted.

Most days I'd flown over it all, trying not to think about it. I'd told myself that Olympus was out of my control, yielded to my father's rule. The only difference I could make was elsewhere, in other realms that needed a champion.

But the longer I walked the road that my fellow Olympians trod every day, the more strength I gathered, and the more confident I became that I must act. Zeus's rule must end.

When we finally reached the Mount, Cassandra stared up at the dozens of flights of marble steps and threw me a despairing look—so I slung the lute on my back by its strap, picked her up, and mounted the first staircase, ignoring her hiss of protest.

And that was how I came to my father, in my finest robes, with my hair rippling in the breeze like living gold, and my beautiful Oracle clasped in my arms. Appearance was everything to my people and beauty was prized more than it should be. Olympus already loved me, but if I was to gain their allegiance, I needed to stoke their love higher.

I set Cassandra down as soon as we reached the plateau of the High Seat, and she smoothed her gown, shooting me a glare. "Thanks," she snapped, and I smiled, because I could tell it was half-sincere. She didn't like being embarrassed, but she hadn't wanted to climb all those steps, either.

Slowly the crowd that had followed us filed onto the platform, clustering at the edges, standing along the stairs. Those who could fly had reached the High Seat first, and they hovered nearby, a storm of fluttering wings in every hue and size—diamond-like dragonfly wings, pink-feathered wings, batlike leathery gold wings with spurs of ivory bone.

Zeus sat on the High Seat as usual, but his crown didn't flash and crackle with lightning as it usually did when he had an audience. I'd assumed his energy would replenish and his power would return; but what if it hadn't? What if, when I'd stolen power from him during the Underworld confrontation, I'd left him with nothing?

It seemed impossible.

But it would also explain why Zeus had four minotaurs in full battle armor ranged around his dais. And it would explain the presence of my half-brother

Ares, who glowered at me with more ferocity than usual. He'd been picked up by Persephone in Titan form during the Underworld standoff, and he clearly wasn't over the shame of it. Hades would have been openly mocking him by this point, and I couldn't help the tiniest smirk in his direction. Ares growled and smacked his war hammer against his meaty palm.

Hera was in her seat as well, not lounging as usual, with her lovely ochre skin and elegant body on full display—instead she was dressed in armor too. Not her favorite lightning-white armor, either—this armor was golden, gleaming.

Golden like the sun.

Was she trying to hint at something? A change of allegiance, perhaps? It seemed impossible—she'd hated my mother, and by extension Artemis and me, since before my birth.

But she'd been through nearly as many renewals as Zeus himself. In all that time, she might have changed.

"Ah, my son the traitor." Zeus's voice rolled through the space between us and into the open air beyond the pillared court.

"Traitor?" I said, with a gentle scoff. "Harsh words from the man who tried to sell me to the Maru Sealgair."

Zeus's face tightened, and his eyes raked the crowd as a shocked murmur raced round the hall.

"It's true." I stepped forward, a few steps past Cassandra, unslinging the lute so that it hung loose in my hand. "I stood by Lord Hades when he was falsely accused of failing in his duties as god of the Underworld. And Lord Zeus was so incensed by my actions that he told Demeter how to lure me, to trap me, so she could sell me to the most wicked enemy this realm cluster has ever seen."

I turned, picking out faces in the crowd, meeting their eyes, making a connection with each of them. A few of the higher Pantheon swept the bystanders aside and moved to the forefront—Hephaestus and Aphrodite among them. I was happy to see Poseidon emerge, his dark face solemn with concern. He'd committed his share of terrible wrongs, but he had also been a voice of reason and restraint with my father. I hoped he would see my side of things.

I looked back at Zeus, into green eyes blazing with pure hatred and rage. Hatred for me—for *me*. And suddenly all my posturing and strategy vanished from my mind, and only he and I existed.

"What have I done to deserve your hate?" I said quietly. "I have always tried to be a good son to you. In past lives, I've covered for you, lied for you, made excuses for you. I have let so many wrongs go unchallenged. I've been loyal to you—" My voice cracked and I halted, searching for something in his eyes—softness? Regret?

"And I would have been loyal to you still, maybe, if you had not put her at risk." I pointed back to Cassandra. "I don't know who your spies on Earth are, or how you knew about her, but you gave her up to Demeter like bait, like *nothing*. I love her, Father. She is my life-mate."

"Your life-mate." Zeus's lip curled. "She's a prophetess. A human Oracle. She should be serving in a temple. I'll see to it that she's well-placed among my priestesses."

"No." My fist curled tight around the neck of the lute—and it thrummed in my grip, a vibration beyond music—a familiar resonance, and I realized what it was. Not only a musical instrument after all. The woman in the crowd, the one who had handed it to me—under her hood, her eyes had glinted gray. My heart lifted. "No, you will not lure Cassandra into your den of priestesses. Might as well be your harem, for all the purity there is in that place."

"Worship takes many forms," Zeus said. "But enough talk of women." He descended the steps of the dais and faced me, eye to eye—I was fully as tall as him. With one large hand he gripped my shoulder, painfully tight, smiling and looking into my eyes. To anyone in the crowd, it probably looked as if he was being fatherly. But under his breath he said, "You took something from me, you whore's son. And I want it back. We can do this quietly, without bloodshed."

I knocked his hand away and raised my voice. "They don't know, do they? What you can do, what you've been doing. You've abused your power, my lord, by stealing that of others. He can take energy from Olympians," I said, spinning to face the crowd. "The marked ones among you—he didn't just repress the energy that fuels your abilities—he took it for himself, drained you to make himself greater. Yet somehow, this very act has thinned his own power, made it volatile and unreliable. That's how I was able to take the lightning from him."

My father stepped back from me, gesturing to the minotaurs to advance—but I held out my cupped hand and dove inside myself, drawing out the unfamiliar energy I'd stolen. I let the lightning collect in my palm and dance between my fingers. It traveled up my arm, jolting along my skin, crackling through my hair.

The crowd gasped, and a few people shrieked in fear and shock. Even the minotaurs drew back, startled.

"My own father tried to neutralize me—to steal my energy," I said. "But I was able to reverse the process and siphon not just his energy, but his actual power, into myself."

"It's a lie!" Zeus shouted. "A trick!"

"Is it though?" I smiled at him, and felt the lightning sparkle across my bared teeth. "If you still have your power, Father, show it to everyone."

Zeus's hand flashed. The full might of his arm struck me across the face and I fell, skidding across the marble, the lightning disappearing from my hand and the lute flying from my grasp. I hadn't been prepared for the blow, hadn't braced myself. Stupid of me. Even without his lightning, my father wielded enough brutal physical force to demolish a fortress on his own.

"I do not perform wonders at your word," bellowed Zeus. "Nor do I take commands from you, Apollo, son of the wretched outcast whore! I am your god, your king, and your father."

Father, father—what did that word even mean to me? Someone who reveled in his dominance, reminded me constantly that he was better in every way. Someone who swallowed my love and loyalty, yet never returned it. *Father* was a pain never salved, a hunger never sated, an approval never gained.

"You will bow before me," roared Zeus. "Or you will be taken to Tartarus, where the Titans will tear you to pieces. My word is the ultimate law, and I will not yield to a cowering upstart with a few sparkly tricks! You are ashamed of our people, Apollo—you always have been—and thus you are a shame to us." He stalked nearer, kicking me viciously in the stomach. "You belong nowhere. You are no one. And if you know what's good for you, boy, you'll stay down."

I glanced up, tasting blood on my lip. The faces of the people were eager and faintly malevolent, their eyes glittering with a thirst for violence. I saw no enraged fury at Zeus, no defiance on my behalf. Just the ravenous hunger for conflict.

Zeus had taken it back—the influence I'd had over the crowd for a moment. He'd taken it without any special power of his own. By the sheer force of his will and majesty, he had won. I was debased, rejected, put in my place.

My will to fight him flickered. Better not to challenge him any further—better to escape, if I could, and leave this wretched realm for good, and make my home elsewhere.

But as I half-lay there, propped on one arm, debating the obeisance my father demanded, someone stepped in front of me. My gaze traveled up white flowing skirts and a long bare leg, to a slim waist and perfectly rounded breasts, to the blazing eyes and set mouth of Cassandra.

"Get up," she said, and she held out her hand to me. "He thinks he's big stuff, but he's just another Ajax."

There was music roaring inside her, fierce and furious, a rush of cymbals and a chorus of horns, warlike and triumphant. I could pick out the strident edge of fear—she was frightened, like any sane person would be. But she was angry, too.

"Get up, Apollo," she repeated. "You're stronger than he is. You always have been."

A golden suspended moment—her gaze and mine—and then her eyes flared wide as she was yanked away from me. Zeus had her by the neck. "Enough of that," he snarled, and jerked his head at one of the minotaurs. "Take her to the temple."

I moved, fluid and quick as light, seizing the lute that lay an arm's reach from me. My fingers dismantled it in seconds, moving in a golden blur, and everything else in the world seemed to slow down—the minotaur ambling forward to obey Zeus's order, my father ducking his head to sniff Cassandra's hair while she cringed away from his touch. He tightened his grip on her nape, and she cried out—her voice echoing through the warped bubble of time in which only I existed.

I'd accessed this ability very few times in my life. It only worked in Olympus, and only when I had a desperate need to move quickly.

The lute was in pieces in my hands, pieces that floated through the golden suspension of time. But it wasn't just a lute after all—it was also a bow, crafted by clever Athena, one of many such pieces she'd made in her lifetime. She was an inventor, my sister—the best Olympus had ever known.

The curved strips of the lute's belly latched together to form the recurve shape of the bow, long as my body, and the lute-strings, once detached, merged into one long bowstring with a little help from my golden magic. The long neck of the lute straightened, stretched, and split into a dozen arrows, thin as whipcord. And the bits of hardware that held the strings in place—those were arrowheads. I lashed the arrowheads in place with golden threads and held the whole cluster of arrows while I strung the first one, drawing the bow as time sped up again, shifting, latching into place. I felt a tug along my spine, energy drained from my body. I wouldn't be able to use that particular power again anytime soon.

My father had Cassandra by the hair, pulling her head back. His bearded mouth descended toward hers, but his green eyes flashed up to mine, triumphant at first, then alarmed as I shot the first arrow.

I caught the nearest minotaur in the chest. The arrow blazed straight through his heart and out, past his body. The crowd screamed and ducked out of the arrow's fiery path as it soared between pillars and off into the blue sky—but I sent a line of quivering golden light after the arrow, lassoed it, and pulled it back to me.

I nocked three more arrows at once and let fly, and they sped to their targets—the hearts of the three remaining minotaurs. Wicked beasts they were, dear to Zeus because they shared his penchant for violence against women, and I felt no twinge of guilt as their bodies toppled from the steps of the dais and thudded to the floor.

Ares leaped forward, bellowing, eager to slam me with his hammer. I darted aside, and the sheer violence of his blow cracked the floor of the court. I slid backward, feet braced, and shot six arrows as I moved. Each arrow was tethered to the others by lines of light, and they all struck Ares, piercing him and binding him in a net of gleaming gold. He would get out of it soon, but for the moment he was held, out of my way. He shrieked swears until I flicked my finger and conjured a gag of hot glowing cords between his jaws.

I'd deal with his wrath later. My priority was Cassandra.

My father had her clasped to his chest, one large hand splayed over her slender throat. "Another step, you filthy traitor, and I will kill her."

"Zeus!" Hera rose from her seat. "The girl is not part of this."

"She is," he threw back. "She reviled me to my face, and she will pay. You've gone soft, Hera. Remember what we used to do to those who disrespected us?"

"I remember." Her voice was raw, thin, imperious. "Let her go."

I lifted my hand, and my father's power coalesced inside me, flowing into my palm, forming a frosty, shining bolt of lightning. The crowd shifted back, crying out in mingled reverence and alarm.

It was no small thing to wield a bolt of Zeus before the High Seat. Zeus's lightning had become synonymous with his position, his authority. For the Olympians, seeing that symbol in my hand could be nothing less than world-shattering.

I saw the rage spike in my father's eyes, the vengeful fury. I knew, without any prophetic vision, what he was going to do to Cassandra, the second before he did it. His hands shifted to her skull and jaw, preparing to snap her neck.

"I'll give it back!" I shouted—nearly screamed.

Zeus paused, Cassandra's head clasped between his hands.

"I don't want to win like this, with power I've taken from someone else," I said. "I'll give it back to you, all of it. Don't kill her."

My father considered me for a moment. "Drop the bow."

I sank to one knee, laid down the bow and arrows, and sent them skidding across the glossy floor, out of my reach. A foot stopped their progress, and I glanced up at its owner.

Athena stood at the front of the crowd, her silver hair and gown shining. She held a long sword, its hilt crusted with ice-white gems.

I sent her a grim, quick smile, a wordless thanks. Then I shook my head slightly, a mute request that she not intervene, not yet.

"Let Cassandra go," I said to my father. "And I'll return your power to you. And then, we should settle this as civilized societies do. You've ruled Olympus since it was created, and there may be some people here who think it's time for a change. I will not take the High Seat from you by force, but I will oppose you in an official election."

"An election?" Zeus stared at me as if I'd truly gone mad.

"Anyone who wants the High Seat can participate. As candidates, we can each share our vision for Olympus with the people who live here, and they get to vote, to decide who takes the Seat. The Fates can officiate. They're objective—they'll ensure that no one interferes with the results using powers or magic."

After a breath of strained silence, Zeus guffawed. "You've been spending too much time in the Earth realm," he roared. "You've gone completely mad. An election, in Olympus?" He kept laughing, staring around at the gathered gods and citizens.

But no one else laughed.

"It's time, Father," said Athena. "You've ruled long enough."

"Don't try it, little girl," he hissed at her. "You've always thought you were better than me, you and your fucking *wisdom*. Go suck Hephaestus's dick."

"Excuse me?" Hephaestus rumbled, his great face reddening. "Leave me out of this."

"No," Athena said, stepping forward. "None of us should stay out of it, not anymore. If we believe ourselves to be gods, ideals for mortals to aspire to, we must set a higher standard. We have fallen, and Zeus cannot help us rise."

"An election could be interesting." Poseidon's deep voice, and my heart swelled with hope.

"And you'll be one of the candidates," sneered Zeus. "Who's next, Hades?"

"Hades has no designs on the High Seat, as you well know," Poseidon said. "Nor do I. But the universe is changing, brother. You must feel it, as I do. My powers and yours are thinning and fading. The Eldritch of Faerie is fading as well. Our brother Hades seems as strong as ever, but he has his own realm to rule. Here in Olympus, it may be time to yield the Seat to a new generation."

Zeus's impotent fury was palpable, vibrating through the air like a maleficent storm. If he'd been in possession of his lightning, it would have been crackling along his body, jarring Cassandra with its lethal force.

Slowly he relaxed his grip on her skull. Cassandra had remained perfectly still and quiet the whole time—best thing she could have done.

"Give me back the power you stole," Zeus said. "And then we'll talk about this election."

"Let her go first."

Zeus scoffed. "And trust you not to attack me?"

I looked him in the eye. "I am Apollo, the high-minded and self-righteous, noble to a fault. If you can trust any one of your children, Father, you can trust me. If I betray this arrangement, Hera herself will strike me down." I nodded to Hera, and she bent her head in haughty assent. Then I raised my voice to the crowd. "You are all witness."

"We are witness," they responded.

Gritting his teeth, Zeus shoved Cassandra away from him with such brutal force that she slammed into a pillar and crumpled, wheezing in pain.

"I let her go," Zeus said, his mouth curving cruelly. "Now, return my power to me, and we'll begin executing this election scheme of yours. You've been working on this for a while, haven't you, sun-blot? And you lied to my face, saying you had no designs on my throne." He laughed bitterly. "I knew better."

"That's the strange thing," I said. "I didn't want the High Seat until you kept accusing me of wanting it. You pointed out how many allies and friends I have among the realms, all the goodwill I've generated by helping others—and I began to picture myself in that throne. I began to think of all the good I could do. A few others encouraged me toward the goal, but really it was you, Father, who inspired me to strive for this. So thank you." I gave him my most elegant bow.

"Give me my powers," he gritted out.

"We are witness, brother, that you promised to hold an election," Poseidon interjected.

"Yes, yes." Zeus glanced over at Ares, who had just succeeded in extricating himself from my net. I'd expected the god of war to come out raging for vengeance, but he looked oddly deflated, even weary. He stepped aside, taking a place halfway up the steps of his mother Hera's dais.

"What are you waiting for?" Zeus snapped at me.

"I've never done this before," I said. "Give me a moment."

My father hesitated, then said, "You have to open a channel through your target's feet, or wherever they're grounded. Push aside any other forms of energy in the way to clear the path."

Another murmur rolled through the crowd. Zeus had just admitted that I was right—that he could steal energy, and was an expert at doing so.

Balling my fists, I concentrated on the floor, the space between my father's feet and mine. I could sense the powers of everyone in the room, a general awareness like when you walk into a room full of different smells, but you don't notice them all unless you focus. My father's aura was nearly silent—empty.

I collected his power inside me, his energy. In the time that I'd hosted it, it had begun to merge with my own, so it took me a moment to separate what was mine from his. Then I began to push it toward him, all that I'd taken when he tried to drain me.

I knew it was working when he inhaled sharply, and his dark hair lifted into a weightless cloud, turned bright white as it sometimes did when he wielded his abilities. Lightning twined up Zeus's legs, over his robes. It snaked along his arms and wrists, collecting at his fingertips, and he threw back his head and laughed, exultant. Black clouds rolled across the sky, blotting out the sun, thickening and darkening while electricity speared through them in great crooked webs.

"The thief has returned what is mine," he shouted, gazing around with eyes that blazed white as stars. He grew taller, unleashing his full god-form, towering and massive. "And now—now you will all feel the wrath of Zeus! This treachery and insolence has gone far enough. When I'm done with you, traitors, none will dare to challenge me again!"

Lightning shot down from the clouds, latching on the pillars and ripping them apart, flinging chunks of broken marble into the air where they whirled for a moment, threatening, then began to crash down among the bystanders. The crowd broke, screaming, all of them trying to squeeze down the steps at once—but Zeus threw a chunk of the ceiling at the staircase and smashed it to pieces, so that all of us were trapped with him on the quaking marble disc of the court, high above the rest of the palace.

Poseidon and Athena cried out in protest—but I had expected this. For once, I'd been one step ahead of him. I let myself expand, gaining height and bulk, entering my full glory. "Stand back," I called to Athena and Poseidon. "This is between him and me."

"I hate it when people say that in movies!" Cassandra screamed. She was sitting by the pillar she'd smashed into, looking small and vulnerable, but I couldn't go to her because Zeus had turned his attention on me. Lightning bolts flew at me, each one a blade of searing, vibrating white fire. I conjured my whip of living sunlight and caught several of the bolts with it, flinging them back toward Zeus.

"Apollo!" cried Athena, and she tossed me her sword. I caught it, transforming the blade into golden fire, and I sprang toward my father with a roar of defiance.

He met my assault with a rush of electrified wind, and I was thrown back against a broken pillar. I shot concentrated rays of light at him, rays that seared through rock and left smoking lines where he dodged them. Dimly I was aware that Athena had transformed the bracelets on her arm into a gleaming shield, and she was holding it in front of Cassandra, protecting her.

With Athena's sword in my left hand, I lashed out at my father with my golden whip, splitting it into dozens of lines of light and encircling him, confining him. I'd once taken down an entire ship of Hook's with that move. But Zeus was stronger than the timbers of a ship, stronger than Ares. His body swelled against the light, crackling with electricity, and with a violent explosion he burst free, and we were both tossed back from each other.

The marble floor cracked under my weight as I landed. I leaped up again, lacing my whip around the bow and arrows and pulling them toward me, while my father began gathering a giant ball of lightning between his palms.

I vanished my whip and dropped the sword, catching the bow and arrows as they flew to my hand. My fingers flicked every arrow shaft neatly into place, half a dozen at once, and I drew the bow just as Zeus catapulted his lightning-bomb toward me with a bellow of angry triumph.

My arrows skirted the ball of lightning neatly, curving around it and aiming for Zeus. I pulled up a wall of shining light in front of me just in time, and the lightning-bomb crashed against it. The shockwave threw me backward again, and another crack branched through the floor of the court. The entire structure trembled, and people screamed.

Zeus was roaring, plucking golden arrows from his body as he advanced toward me again. I glanced around at the shaking, whimpering citizens crowding the edges of the platform, caught between our battle and the deadly dropoff. Some of them probably had enough god-blood to survive the fall, but those who didn't would be dead once they struck ground—gone forever.

And my family, the few members of the Pantheon who were present, just stood there, watching. Not caring about our people, our terrified citizens. The only one trying to protect them was Athena, and she had her hands full keeping Cassandra alive.

"Get these people out of here," I shouted to Poseidon. "Do it now!"

My uncle nodded, stirring as if woken out of sleep. He lifted his hands, and a stream of water gushed from them, forming a long chute of rippling liquid, all the way down to the ground. People began jumping into the chute, sliding down the water to safety.

Until Zeus shot a titanic bolt of lightning straight into the quivering liquid.

Guttural screams, sizzling flesh. Bodies jerked, charred in an instant. Poseidon let the water dissipate into drops, his face twisted with horror.

Hera shrieked, and her cry shivered through the darkened sky, making the remaining pillars quake.

But my father laughed.

19
CASSANDRA

Zeus was laughing, thunderous and wicked, under a sky rolling with heavy black clouds. In the flashes of intermittent lightning I saw his people cowering from him, while the Pantheon stood unmoving and watching the chaos unfolding around them. Only then did I really understand what Apollo had meant when he'd told me his world was poisoned. It was a poison of carelessness, of apathy, of misused power.

Apollo stood alone, stunned at the death toll, his glow dimming slightly.

Athena pushed me down behind her shield. "Stay low, human."

"End this!" I screamed at her. "What is wrong with you? Help him!"

"He told us to stand back—"

"Oh, fuck that!" I yelled. "Go help your brother, or at least save the citizens!" I leaped out from behind the shield, ignoring the pain in my back from where I'd struck the pillar. "Are you gods or wimps?" I shouted. "Help your people!"

Most of the winged Olympians had fled, but a few had stuck around to watch the fight. Athena shouted at them, ordering them to ferry citizens down to the ground. She threw her shield up and leaped onto it, and it carried her, like a surfboard in the air. Two by two she began to seize the survivors and carry them away.

Hephaestus took broken chunks of pillars and began heating them with his bare palms, forming new pieces and fitting them together into a makeshift ladder of stone. He beckoned to the people, urging them to climb down to safety.

Meanwhile Apollo and Zeus had engaged again, a violent whirl of yellow light and white flame. The sparks and flashes in the roiling dark were almost too much for my human eyes to bear. Apollo had taken on some kind of ultra-god form; he was taller now, and twice as ripped. He'd thrown off his robes, wearing only the wrap around his waist and thighs. His body was fluid incandescent muscle, tightening and surging with every fresh attack and parry. His hair whipped around him like a river of gold.

"I forgot to ask," Zeus bellowed. "What did you do to Demeter?"

"I defeated her," Apollo answered. "I left her where she lay. She may be there still, or the Maru Sealgair may have taken her as their prize, along with Hecate. Their fate is no concern of mine—they were guilty of dreadful things—terrors you overlooked."

"I do not judge the acts of the Pantheon," Zeus proclaimed. "I allow them freedom to pursue their own lives and desires, for they are gods. All living things should bow to their will. Have I not given you wealth and pleasure?" He raised his voice, gesturing to Poseidon, Ares, Aphrodite. "Have I not granted you ultimate freedom? And this one, this self-proclaimed noble god—he would judge your actions. He would curtail your pleasure and curb your will."

Like Ares, Aphrodite had climbed the steps to Hera's dais. She shrank behind the god of war, but neither of them answered Zeus.

Poseidon stepped forward. "Enough, brother," said the sea god. "This has gone too far."

"How weak you've become," Zeus sneered. "In the days of our glory, you did not weep for a handful of mortals and demigods. Together we razed towns, leveled cities. We incited men to war and reveled in the blood they shed, in the sacrifices they made on our altars."

"Those days are gone," Poseidon answered. "The universe is—"

But a bolt of lightning, no longer than my hand, sliced neatly between his jaws and lodged in the back of his throat. It stuck there, sparking, and Poseidon's skull turned blue and translucent with every flash of the bolt in his mouth. His head jerked, eyes smoking as the lightning spread, crawled through him and over him. I screamed and clapped both hands over my mouth.

My scream drew Zeus's attention.

His eyes, once green, now glowed white, and they swiveled toward me, two beacons of death in the gloom. For a moment, time seemed to stop. Dimly I was conscious of Athena and Hephaestus shuttling survivors away, of Hera still standing atop her dais, watching—of Poseidon, crashing to the floor so heavily that a chunk of the platform broke clean away. His body slid, along with the carcass of a minotaur, into the void below. Aphrodite screamed, and Ares shouted.

Apollo yelled and leaped forward, wielding the flaming sword of Athena. But Zeus threw a cage of wicked lightning around him, and while Apollo was slashing his way out, Zeus paced toward me.

"Prophesy for me, Oracle," he said. "Tell me, can you see your death? Because it is imminent, and inevitable."

Behind Zeus, Apollo was insane with fear and fury, hacking at the lightning that caged him. He threw himself into it, trying to push through, roaring with agony.

More of the platform was crumbling, and the sky seemed lower, like a concrete roof ready to crush me, like the great sole of Fate coming down to step on me, the tiny ant-sized human.

But I'd seen the end already, and for once in my life, all my anxiety drained away, vanished like dew under the sun.

I walked toward Zeus, my gown fluttering around my legs, my hair whipped wild by the wind of his storm. And I smiled at him, with more peace in my heart than I'd ever felt, while the world fell apart around us.

"You want a prophecy?" I said. "Here's one for you."

The god-king stared at me, chest heaving, eyes whited out and flashing. He lifted one of his bolts and angled it toward my heart.

"You lose," I said softly.

And then Apollo exploded.

A wave of light raced outward, a sheet of irresistible power, evanescing the cage of lightning that had held him. His head was thrown back, spine arched, and from his eyes and mouth and chest the light streamed in thick golden beams, slicing through the black clouds, splitting them apart, chasing them away while he roared. Sunlight detonated across the realm.

Apollo rose into the air, buoyed by his shining wings, and he turned the inferno of his blazing eyes on his father.

Zeus leaped into midair as well, carried by a tornado of wind, and I sucked in a desperate breath of relief because he hadn't killed me. I was alive, and Apollo—Apollo was unleashed.

Apollo's fingers were alight, lethal rays streaming from them. When Zeus threw bolts at him, he batted each one away as if they were moths. He slashed at his father with those claws of light, and great gashes opened across Zeus's chest, arms, and legs. Then Apollo opened his mouth, and a great ball of sun-fire shot from his open throat, catching Zeus full in the face.

Apollo kept slashing, kept disgorging whole suns at his father, over and over and over, until Zeus was a writhing, molten, formless figure. His blood sprayed through the sky, turning to mist in the heat of Apollo's attacks. Even after Zeus crashed to the platform, Apollo hovered above him and bombarded his father's body with volley after volley, slice after slice from those golden laser claws.

I collapsed on the floor, shaking, cupping my mouth. I couldn't think of how to make it stop, how to pull Apollo back into himself. Maybe he needed to express the pent-up rage and sorrow of lifetimes this way. Maybe his father deserved it. But it was horrible.

I closed my eyes, cringing at repeated explosions and whistles of searing light. I could smell the dust of broken stone, the heat of molten metal, the acrid stench of burning flesh. I heard Aphrodite sobbing quietly, and Ares swearing, and the hum of Athena's shield as she soared back up from dropping off the last of the citizens. I heard Hephaestus breathing heavy and slow, with a hitch of emotion breaking the cadence now and then.

I heard the soft click of Hera's footsteps descending from her dais.

And I wove it all together in my mind, picking out the rhythms and selecting the instruments, winding a melody, soft and sure. A calming, sinuous thread of notes sliding out to Apollo, slipping past the gale of his anger, gliding into his mind. It was the melody I'd imagined while we sat in the food court, the one that impressed him so deeply, only it was different now, deepened by my understanding of him and his vivid, beautiful, terrible world, of his divine, dreadful family.

The crashing rhythm of his attacks ceased, and there was no more whining whip of light slashing the air.

I kept my eyes closed, kept singing the melody in my mind, layering it, shifting it into a new key.

And I waited in the dark, waited until I smelled sun-warm grass and honeysuckle—his scent, discernible through the stench of fire and death.

Apollo's hands smoothed across my cheeks, and I opened my eyes.

There he was, beautiful and bloody, but restrained again, his normal size, with his usual calm and compassionate gaze.

"Thank you for the song," he said quietly.

I struggled upright and I reached for him, pulling his great tall self down to me so I could kiss his mouth. It was a dry, desperate kiss, a "we-almost-died" kiss, a "you're-really-intense-but-I-still-love-you" kiss. His mouth was hotter than usual, and his tongue scorched mine a little.

"Take it easy, spitfire," I said, pulling back.

"I'm sorry." He pressed his forehead with his fingertips, casting a sideways glance at the smoking corpse that was his father.

"Will he survive?" I murmured.

Hera bent over her ex-husband's body. "He'll be renewed," she said. "It will take time. Usually I'm the one who governs in his stead, but—" She straightened, meeting Apollo's eyes. "I think this time, it should be you."

"What about elections?" Apollo began.

"It's a noble thought," she interrupted. "But our people are not ready for that, not yet. Take the High Seat, and when your father wakes, we'll help you hold it. Then, when the time is right, you can introduce the idea of a democracy."

"You'll help him hold it?" I scoffed, but my voice trembled. "Why should he believe you? None of you took his side today, except Athena. And Hephaestus and Poseidon a little bit."

Hera stared me down from her goddess height, looking so divine and resplendent that I shifted a little closer to Apollo. "You can believe the word of the Olympian queen," she said. "Or should I say, the former queen. Perhaps you will be holding that title in future. A good day for you, isn't it, little human? From Earth child to Oracle to consort of the High Seat."

"I didn't ask for that," I whispered.

Her gaze softened a little. "The worthy ones never do." She turned to Apollo. "Take her below, and tell everyone what has happened. I will begin arrangements for your father to be laid to his renewal rest. And you there—" she waved an imperious hand to Athena, Hephaestus, Ares, and Aphrodite. "If Poseidon did not survive his fall, we must lay him down for renewal too. You will all help me. And send for Iris. She and her messengers must carry this news through the realm. I'll write an announcement—"

"If it's all the same to you," Apollo interjected. "I'll write the announcement."

Hera hesitated a moment, then nodded, with a faint smile. "So it begins. A new era."

Apollo flew me down to the ground level, where he proclaimed Zeus's temporary death and his new position on the High Seat. No one objected—in fact, they cheered for him, despite the dead and wounded littering the ground.

The next several hours went by in a blur of unfamiliar medicines and healings and rituals for the injured and the deceased. I helped write the announcement of Zeus's renewal and Apollo's ascension, complete with Apollo's first act as High Seat—the freeing of all slaves, whether human, Fae, or any other kind. Iris used magic to multiply the message and sent it out in the hands of her harpies.

"One of the daughters of Proteus was spying on you on Earth," Iris admitted to Apollo. "She's very good at assuming human aspect and blurring her power aura. You'd never have noticed her. She would report to me, and then I'd report to the High Seat. Only doing my duty, you see."

"I understand," he said stiffly.

"Anything else I can do for you, Lord Apollo?"

"I'll let you know," he said, and when she skittered away he muttered. "She's certainly changed her tune where I'm concerned."

"You're the boss now." I nudged him. "She's gotta show some respect."

He chuckled, then sobered. "The way I was today, at the end—I've never been like that, except when I was alone, in the In-Between, where I couldn't hurt anyone. I've never let myself use that much power, not even when I helped Pan fight Hook."

"Maybe you should have."

"Maybe. But as you saw, it's tough to control. Hard to rein myself in." He takes my chin in his fingers. "I owe you, Cassandra. You saved me twice today—you helped me find my strength, and then my restraint."

"I think that's what life-mates do." I shrugged, giving him a small smile. "I've got no experience, I'm just guessing."

"Good guess," he whispered, brushing his lips to mine. My eyes drifted shut, and I sank into the heady warmth of the kiss.

But there was no time for much kissing. The two god-brothers had to be laid to their renewal rest, with much fanfare and ceremony. Hades and Persephone even showed up, on very short notice, because of course

Hades had to be present at the laying down of his brothers.

I was so nervous about meeting Hades and Persephone that I felt sick to my stomach, but they were much more personable than I'd imagined. Sure Hades had horns, but other than that he reminded me of a very hot, kind of goth, college frat boy. And Persephone was, in a word, adorable—pink-haired and pretty, with an innocent glow about her face even though, as Apollo had told me, she was one of the most powerful beings in the universe. She embellished the decorations for the renewal ceremony with a casual kindness that made me think of Apollo's generosity.

"I'm sorry about your mother," Apollo told her soberly.

"It's fine," Persephone replied. "Demeter was a bitch. I hope never to see her or Hecate again. Are we sure the Maru Sealgair took her?"

"No," said Apollo. "But one thing is certain—both she and Hecate would have entered renewal sleep after injuries like that. And judging from their history, they won't wake for several lunar cycles, maybe more."

"Good." Persephone tucked her arm through mine and said, "Let's go see if we can find a drink, Cassandra. I like Faerie wine especially. Have you tried it?"

"Not yet," I said cautiously.

"Just a sip for you then," she replied with a grin. "It has a very strong effect on humans. So you're from Earth? Hades and I are big fans of Earth TV."

As she and I walked away from the men, I heard Hades saying to Apollo, in a low voice, "Anything you need, sun-spot. It's going to be a big job, and I've got some experience ruling a realm. Just say the word, and I'll help out wherever I can."

Relief flowed through my heart, soothing an anxiety I'd barely had time to register. We'd have help, Apollo and I. There were people in the universe, good people, who were Apollo's friends, and could be my friends. People like Peter and Wendy, whom I desperately wanted to meet. Like the pink-haired goddess holding my hand and chattering about "How I Met Your Mother" like we were BFFs already.

My sun god and I—we would be okay.

Zeus and Poseidon were laid in a vault of the palace for their renewal sleep that night, and the next day, my vision of Apollo's coronation came true. I stood at Apollo's side, while a joyful crowd of impossibly beautiful people cheered for him and Hades set a crown of bronze laurel leaves on his golden head.

I was truly, thoroughly happy for Apollo, but I was exhausted. Too much had changed, too fast. One week I was normal Cassandra, adjusting to the idea of having a Greek god for a boyfriend. Then I was kidnapped and nearly killed. Then I was a TikTok sensation with a huge new fanbase. And now, somehow, I was the "consort" to the High Seat of Olympus.

A girl could only handle so much change at once without collapsing. I was only human, after all.

Somehow I managed to keep a smile plastered to my face throughout most of the coronation feast, but as it drew to a close, I whispered to Apollo, "I got a few hours of sleep last night in some room of the palace I barely remember. Is it possible to get some actual rest somewhere, before I dissolve into tears of exhaustion?"

"Of course," he said. "I'll send you to my estate at Delos. I have so much to do here—" He hesitated, probably reading the sadness in my face.

Hades leaned over. "Realms take a *long* time to get in order, Sunburst. Take my advice—enjoy life, and don't overwork yourself. Oh, and *delegate*. Delegating is the best."

Persephone rolled her eyes and shoved his shoulder lightly. Hades just grinned and downed another cup of wine. "Athena looks like she's aching to share some responsibility. Goddess of wisdom and all that. Let her take over for a few days while you show Cassandra around. Olympus was basically running itself anyway— Zeus did precious little to manage it—so it'll be fine without you."

"But I just took the High Seat," Apollo protested. "And I have so many plans—"

"Listen, bud. If you do too much change at once, all these cheering crowds—" Hades poked a beringed pinkie toward the jovial guests— "they're going to get pissed. Things have operated the same way in this realm for a long damn time. Take it slow. You've already made one huge change with the slave thing—the rest will come. Go be with your girl, and take care of her.

Styx knows she deserves it, for getting you to finally make a move against Zeus." He grinned and winked at me, picking up another brimming cup of wine. "Cheers, Oracle."

I couldn't help smiling back at him, and I clinked my own wine cup with his. Toasting with the freaking god of the dead. Yeah, I'd reached my limit of weirdness.

"Persephone's making you wiser," Apollo said to Hades. "I'll heed your advice. Cover for me while we sneak out early?"

"Covering for sneaky people is my favorite thing to do," Hades replied. "Come on, Persephone darling— let's make a scene. Apollo—music, if you please."

Apollo sent threads of golden light racing toward the musicians, and they began to play faster, an irresistible dance tune. Hades swept Persephone out of her seat, away from the feast tables, and into the center of the enormous hall. Enormous was an understatement—the scope of the place, the sheer height of the columns and ceilings made me feel like a toddler in a cathedral. Apollo had created a multitude of tiny golden stars to light the feast, and between those glimmering orbs and Persephone's lavish decorations, I had never seen anything so beautiful.

The crowd left their tables, streaming out to join Hades and Persephone in the rather erotic dance they'd begun. Apollo took my hand and led me out of that huge space to a quiet hall with arched windows open to the cool night air. A garden courtyard lay below, the tops of its trees silvered by the moon.

I inhaled the sweet freshness of the night air, feeling the stress easing out of me. The debris of the broken sky court was far away, in another part of the palace, and here everything was pristine and peaceful. Here, I could finally face the fear I'd been too busy to name.

"Apollo," I murmured, running my hand along the smooth stone.

"Hm." He slid his arms around my waist, palms against my lower stomach, his chest pressing my elaborate hairstyle.

"I'm afraid I'm not the best person to be your consort or whatever. This has all felt like a really weird dream. I've managed okay, but you know I'm not the most even-keeled of people. I don't know if I can do whatever this is."

His hand pressed lightly on my stomach, so that my rear bumped against him. I felt a tingling heat grazing my skin, starting at the curves of my ass and traveling down between my legs. "Are you trying to turn me on?" I whispered. "I'm being serious here."

"I know." He chuckled softly. "And you don't have to do anything you don't want to do. As Hades said, Athena will be all too happy to partner in the actual ruling of things. You don't know this realm, and brilliant as you are, ruling it takes experience, and knowledge. So for a while, you don't have to be anything at all as far as the rulership goes. Just be your wonderful, musical self." He kissed my hair. "Do you know, there are children here who need a music teacher like you?"

"Olympian children?" My stomach dipped. "But— aren't they—I mean—"

"They have their own unique challenges, like any other children. And I know they would love you. There's a particular village I'm thinking of, between here and Delos, where the school lacks musical instruction."

I swallowed. "So I'm going to live here. With you."

"We can return to Earth whenever you like," he said. "It's possible to do it without aging at all, as long as you keep the visits short. Since you're an Olympian, all you need to do is drink some ambrosia before your trip, and limit your time there to a day or two. The ambrosia will prevent any of the natural changes that would otherwise happen to your body in your home realm."

"That's a relief." I sighed, nuzzling between the folds of his robe until my cheek rested against his bare skin. His heartbeat thumped quietly through his breastbone, into my ear.

"This way you can pursue your musical career on Earth, too," he said. "And we can visit all the cities on my list. The passage between realms is dangerous, but if I'm with you, you'll be all right. And if we take my chariot, we won't have to swallow any sluagh eyes. I like them as little as you do." He chuckled, and I groaned with relief.

"Eventually—not anytime soon, but someday—I want to visit other realms, too," I said. "I was thinking, if we go together and spend a little time in each realm, maybe I can perceive disasters before they happen, and you can help me prevent them. Things like floods, fires, terrorist attacks, assassinations."

"Apollo and his Oracle, the emissaries of peace, bringing aid to the realms," he mused. "I like the sound of that. And now, my love, it is time to take you to bed."

He lifted me and stepped onto the windowsill in one fluid motion, ducking outside and unfurling his wings just in time to catch our weight as we dropped. I gasped, clinging to his neck, and he laughed. He seemed unburdened, weightless, joyful, and his happiness wriggled right down into the soul of me and glowed there.

Olympus was just as beautiful at night as it was during the day, and from above, we didn't have to witness any of the sadness or depravity below. The sky was clear except for a few stray clouds. Constellations I'd never seen pricked the night, while glimmering lamplit villages dotted the dark hills below. We flew lower, over a lush forest, and then into an area of tall craggy landforms that spilled glistening waterfalls over each other and sent cool mist across our cheeks. We soared past a cliff and darted under a gigantic rock bridge the length of a city. Beyond, in a hollow between mountain and hill, lay a white mansion surrounded by gardens and pools. Walls encircled it, gleaming faintly golden, and I felt the press of something as we approached.

"Is there magic around your house?" I asked.

"You can feel it." Apollo sounded pleased. "Your sensitivity is improving."

"Guess so."

"I've warded the place and added Fae spells into the mix," he said. "As well-liked as I am, there are people who wouldn't think twice about hurting my mother. Her affair with Zeus was messy, and Olympians have long memories."

"Hera?" I asked. "Hera would hurt her? But she seems kinda mellow."

"She does seem different," he agreed. "Almost as if she's been maintaining a façade until someone actually challenged Zeus." He pursed his lips. "Only time will tell if she has changed."

I reached up to brush his lips with my fingertip. "I love your mouth. I love all the things you do with it."

He beamed, and I shook my head, laughing. "I didn't mean that. I meant your expressions."

"Sure you did." He nuzzled his nose with mine and kissed me. We were descending, passing over lawns, and Apollo set me down long enough to lift his hands and open whatever veils of magic he'd thrown over his estate.

We entered the gate together, and the first thing I saw was a golden, glowing, winged horse prancing through the garden on my right.

"They wander at will," Apollo said. "You're not afraid of horses, are you?"

"No," I squeaked. "I mean—he's big, and magical—but no."

Apollo laughed and pulled me on through the gardens at a half-run. "We'll explore out here tomorrow. First I want you to see the house. Your new home."

"My home," I whispered, and I ran with him, tired as I was, because every girl secretly dreams of a beautiful mansion to call her own.

And it was more than beautiful. Stunning, stately, with a hundred tiered balconies and arched windows and decorative moldings. The eaves and ledges dripped with hanging plants, and fruit trees clustered at the corners. Pillars laced with blossoming vines lined the front entrance. The doors stood open, golden light flooding over the front steps.

Apollo guided me through the immense front hall, pointing out his most treasured possessions in their cases or brackets along the walls—beautifully carved golden bows, arrows that glistened like sunbeams, Fae arrows with iridescent feathers, and an ancient-looking, battle-beaten short sword with a broad blade. "From the Trojan War," he said grimly when he noticed me staring at it. "And so is that arrow over there. I guided it to Achilles' heel. I keep it to remind myself of my past mistakes."

"We've all made mistakes," said a voice, and we both turned. In a doorway stood a woman, thin and birdlike, with pale blond hair. She wore a white dress, gold-embroidered, that plunged low between her breasts.

Behind her stood a curvy, beautiful woman with rosy cheeks, sparkling blue eyes, and hair the same glorious gold as Apollo's. Her arms were magnificent, thick with muscle. She had a wide stance, and her short skirt brushed thighs just as powerful as her arms.

"Cassandra," Apollo said. "This is my mother, Leto, and my sister Artemis, goddess of the hunt."

"A pleasure to meet you," I managed, and I sank into a brief curtsy. I'd never curtsied in my life, not since I'd been a little girl playing princess, but it seemed appropriate.

"I was hunting in the Western Reaches, so I didn't witness your glorious overthrow of our father," Artemis said. "I only just returned and heard the news. But I wish I could have seen it."

"You'd have backed me, of course." The sharp twist in Apollo's voice made me think perhaps he wasn't on the same good terms with his twin as he was with Athena.

"Oh, I didn't say that," she retorted. "But it would have been fun to see you stir the old man up."

"Don't argue, children," Leto said, gliding toward me. Her pale bare feet were soundless on the marble floor. "Cassandra, we're so pleased you and Apollo found each other."

"It was fate, I suppose," I said, catching his eye.

"And a bit of luck from a friend," he replied. "You two can get to know Cassandra tomorrow, and in the days after, but she's been through a lot, and we're both tired."

"Of course." Leto nodded. "You must rest. And son—" She stopped him with a hand on his arm. "Well done."

Apollo let go of my fingers long enough to clasp her in a hug. Then he caught my hand again, and led me deeper into his lovely house.

The halls were the perfect kind of gloomy, blue with shadows and amber with lamps, with enough cushioned nooks and book-lined alcoves to make you feel cozy despite the vast rooms. There were entire chambers filled with instruments and art, like endless galleries in the best and most interesting museum in the world. I found myself wanting to squeal with delight, so I did. Apollo's answering laugh was everything I could have wanted to hear. Music for days.

His suite was a forest white pillars and golden trim, with a bed like a cloud and furniture lavish enough to make a French king envious. We shed our clothes on the way through to the bathroom.

"I feel like I'm dating a billionaire," I said as I sank into a foamy bath that he heated with his own power.

"What's a billionaire?" He tilted his head curiously, immersing his lovely body in the water.

"Someone very rich and powerful."

"Ah. Well, then I suppose you are."

"Except you're nicer than any billionaire." I scooted toward him through the ripples. "You're the sweetest man I've ever met. And I've never called a guy 'sweet' before."

"I've never shared this bath with anyone before," he said.

"Never?" My eyes popped wide.

"Never."

Knowing how long he'd lived and how many lovers he'd had made his words infinitely precious. I thought I might cry, overtired as I was.

But then he splashed me in the face, grinning, and I forgot about the tears.

After the bath, we made love slowly, drowsily, and fell asleep naked and entangled.

For several days it was like that—exploring the house with Apollo, christening every room with him. When he had to return to the High Seat for some reason, I spent time with Leto. I truly liked her, and she seemed to enjoy teaching me all about Olympus and its people.

I hadn't had a vision in forever. I began to fear— and hope—that they were gone for good.

One morning, Apollo and I were idly playing an impromptu duet. We'd discovered we could play together in this way, unplanned, a meandering melody born from the synchronization of my inner song with his knack for inspiration and improvisation. It felt like talking, like communing without words, and we both loved it.

But then my sight began to cloud and fluctuate. I could feel the oncoming vision creeping at the edges of my mind, pressing inward. I pushed against it, just to see if I could hold it off, and I found that I could. Firmly I held the darkness away, but I couldn't do that and keep playing. My fingers struck an off chord on the keyboard and Apollo made a harsh sound of pain. He had that reaction to dissonance sometimes, especially here, in Olympus.

"Sorry," I said. "I can feel a vision coming, and I was trying to see how long I can hold it off. If I can learn to control when it happens, maybe I'll still be able to drive safely while I'm on Earth."

He nodded. "Don't keep it at bay too long. We don't know what the resistance could do to your psyche."

I struggled with the vision for several more minutes, long enough for a person to pull over a car safely. And then I let go, and the darkness flooded over me, blotting out sight and sound.

I could see five identical human men—young and beautiful, copies of a real human slave Demeter had owned. Apollo had told me about these five clones, how Persephone was forced to create them when Demeter was holding her captive. In my vision, the boys were beating several humans, smashing their bodies into gooey pulp with spiked clubs. In the background, three males watched, laughing. The mocking males didn't look quite human—demi-gods, maybe. Clearly they'd discovered that the clones had little free will of their own and could be commanded to carry out almost any task. And they'd used that knowledge to commit mass murder. At the edge of my vision I could see more naked bodies, broken limbs askew.

When the vision ended, I explained everything to Apollo. He looked just as horrified as I was.

"I'll deal with this," he said. "From your description, I think I know who the three instigators are. I'll lock them up until Athena can share a little *wisdom* with them."

He said it so grimly that I suspected this particular brand of Athena's "wisdom" would involve more than a therapy session.

"I'll also have the five boys Persephone copied put somewhere safe until she can return here and work with them," Apollo added. "Since she's been with Hades, her powers have expanded, and she's developing a way to give her creations free will and empathy, something Demeter wouldn't allow her to do before. She can fix the boys, I think. And if not, we will put them in the care of someone we trust."

He didn't suggest bringing the clones to Delos. Over the past week I'd learned that he liked to keep his home mostly empty of people, a sanctuary for his art, his music, and his archery. It was a relief to know that no matter how many parties or events we might attend at the palace of the High Seat or elsewhere in Olympus, we would always have this quiet, luxurious mansion waiting for us.

Apollo left almost immediately to prevent my vision from coming true. He was gone for the rest of that day and most of the next. Leto wasn't around, either— Apollo and Hera had made an official truce, so Leto was venturing beyond the protection of Delos for the first time in centuries. The servants did what little work needed doing and then left, so I wandered the huge empty rooms and echoing halls alone.

My vision had saddened me, that people could exist in a gorgeous realm like this and still be wicked to each other. I kept trying to remind myself of all the good things in my life—the new music I was writing, the fans waiting for me back on Earth, the students I'd begin teaching soon, the fact that I'd never have to worry about money again, my new agelessness, the absence of our enemies—and above all, my beautiful Apollo. So many wonderful things.

But I kept sinking inside, lower and lower. It didn't help that the day was dark and cloudy. Rain splattered along the edge of the balcony, past the overhang under which I stood. Even the loveliest of realms had its dreary days.

I wandered closer to that little fall of rain, and I put my fingers into it. Then I stepped whole into the streaming drops, letting the rain soak into my gown and turn it transparent, melting down until I sat on the cool wet stone, my hair drizzling water.

"Cassandra."

Apollo stood in the doorway to our rooms, bronze and gleaming, the epitome of beauty and light and love, while I crouched miserably in the rain. And suddenly I feared that he and I couldn't last. When Apollo saw the charred, ruined side of my soul, he would realize what a terrible mistake he'd made. Our relationship would end in pain, like my relationship with Ajax, only this time it would hurt so much worse.

"We confined the men from your vision, for now," he said quietly, as if me sitting in the pouring rain was a perfectly normal thing. "But since they didn't actually commit the murder, we'll have to let them go at some point. Athena believes she made progress with them, but there's no telling what further evil lies in their hearts."

"Maybe no one can help them," I said. "Maybe some people are too messed up inside."

A heavy sigh rolled from him, and he ran a hand through his hair. "Maybe. I've wondered that about my father. I hope he wakes a better man, but we have no way of knowing. Same with Demeter and Hecate. Iris went to the cabin where we left them, by the way. She found a lot of shriveled vines, but no bodies."

"So the Maru Sealgair did take them. Good riddance."

Apollo looked as if he wasn't quite satisfied with the outcome, as if something else was bothering him. But I couldn't muster the energy to ask about it.

He kept watching me. I could feel his gaze, but I couldn't look at him because I knew what I would see— the aching compassion of his big beautiful heart.

He took a step forward, but I held up my hand. "Please—don't touch me. I can't be touched right now, not by you, not by anyone."

"Whatever you wish." He sat down cross-legged on the balcony and waited.

But I couldn't resist, not for more than a few minutes, no matter what the despair in my heart said. I crawled to him, and he pulled me in, folding me against his chest.

"I sh—I shouldn't feel like this," I gasped, my breath hitching. "I'm *here*, in this beautiful place, with everything I could ever want, both in Olympus and on Earth—my powers are unlocked—and I have *you*—so why do I still get this way? Why am I still *wrong* and *broken*?"

"Cassandra." Apollo stroked my upper arm with a warm palm. "You may one day come into a place where you don't feel like this anymore. Some people find that place through therapy, medication, professional satisfaction, meditative rituals—even a special person. Others find faith in God—or gods." I could hear the faint smile in his voice. "But nothing is ever perfect, and if you keep expecting perfection of yourself and everyone else, you'll be disappointed. I can't promise never to fail you. I can't promise to fix you—because, love, you're not broken. You are exquisitely yourself. What I can promise is to *be here*. I will step aside when you want to be alone—but when you want to be fed, or pleasured, or taken somewhere new, trust that I will always be standing ready to deliver anything you need that's within my power."

"God, you *are* perfect," I sniffled. "It's so freaking annoying and wonderful. Speaking of things I need—do you have tissues in Olympus?"

Chuckling, he pulled me to my feet and drew me inside the room. He reached to one of the side tables and opened a gold-enameled box, in which lay a stack of thin white cloths. "Here."

"Fancy," I muttered.

He kept holding me while I wiped my eyes and then my nose.

"I'll be *here*," he said again, low. "Always here, loving you. You never have to smile for my benefit. You never have to feel guilty for showing your feelings. Do I want you to be gloriously happy? Of course. But in your sadness I cherish you just as deeply."

He scraped the wet hair back and kissed my forehead while I stood in his embrace, drinking in his presence, his love. Trying to comprehend it.

"I love you." I shaped the words like talismans, like flaming tokens held against the darkness. And they helped. A little.

"I love you, too."

"And I also just want to curl up and watch some TV and eat Earth snacks. But I can't do that here."

A mischievous light gleamed in his eyes. "Before Persephone left with Hades, I asked her to make some things. I had them brought here, and I hid them from you. I hope you can forgive me."

"Depends on what they are." I eyed him. "Are they—sex toys?"

"Styx no. Come on."

He led me to a corner of the room and swung aside a heavy painting in a gilded frame. Behind the frame was a door.

"No way." I gaped at it. "There's a secret room in your bedroom?"

"Yes. It has served many purposes over the centuries, but I think this is my favorite."

He pushed the door wide.

Beyond it was a cozy room, outfitted with a deep, plush sofa and plenty of cushions and blankets, all emblazoned with sun emblems. Shelves all around the room held plastic cases—hundreds of TV shows and movies. And facing the couch sat a large TV.

"Persephone and Hades are fans of Earth entertainment," said Apollo. "Persie created duplicates of every show and movie she's seen, both from Hades' collection and the one in Neverland."

"How does that even work?" I breathed.

"She's the most powerful goddess I've ever known," he answered. "A true creator, like the Titans who formed the realms, only better."

"And she made me a TV," I breathed.

"She did. And I made it a power source. See?" He pointed to an orb of golden energy behind the flatscreen. The ends of the power cords for the TV and Blu-ray player were floating suspended in that tiny sun.

"Weird, and awesome."

"It gets better." Apollo darted to the cabinets under the rows of movies and showed me a mini-fridge stocked with drinks and cupboards full of snacks. Some of the snacks and drinks were clearly from other realms, but there were several Earth options.

"I know this has been strange," he said, anxiety and hope mingling in his gaze. "I wanted you to feel at home. And I've been saving this for a moment when you really needed it."

I choked on a laugh that was also a sob, more tears slipping down my cheeks. "I really needed it. Thank you."

He lunged for me and lifted me right off my feet with his hug. "Now before we enjoy this together, there is something else we must do."

I narrowed my eyes at him. "I'm afraid to ask."

Apollo led me back into the bedroom and stepped to the balcony, stretching out his arms. A flood of sunshine broke over the landscape, and the clouds scudded away before it like bats shrinking from the day. Long shafts of translucent yellow light struck the lawn and gardens of Delos, making every wet surface sparkle.

Apollo whistled, clear as a bell, a beautiful sequence of notes. Within moments, four shining winged horses leaped through the air toward us. A chariot soared after them, lines of golden light unspooling from it and settling over the horses' backs and noses. They were magically harnessed in the blink of an eye, and Apollo hadn't even touched them.

The chariot floated just beyond the balustrade, and Apollo turned back to me, a radiant smile on his face. He sent a whirl of warm sunshiny air around me, and suddenly my hair and clothes were dry.

My jaw dropped.

"I have more powers here," he grinned with a shrug. "Now we might not have rollercoasters in Olympus, my love, but we have something nearly as exciting. Care for a ride?"

I hesitated. In spite of his sweet surprise of the TV room, my limbs felt weighted, and my mind was sluggish and sorrowful. "I won't be much fun."

"There is no obligation to cheer up, or to have fun." He held out his hand. "All I'm asking for is your company, if you feel strong enough to give it. One brave little step, love, and I'll do all the rest."

I could do this. I could take a step, so I did. And then I took another, and a few more until I reached him.

He lifted me into the chariot, which had a padded seat that was surprisingly comfortable. After conjuring lines of golden light across my hips and shoulders to secure me in the seat, Apollo stepped to the front of the chariot. Gleaming reins floated into his hands.

He spoke to the horses in Greek, and they jumped higher into the air, as if they were bounding up non-existent steps. Blue-gray clouds clustered thick and heavy around the sunny gap Apollo had made over his estate, and the sun streaming down through the hole made me think of heaven. No such place, perhaps, but this was as close to paradise as I could ever have hoped for.

And still the horses climbed the crystal-bright air.

"How high are we going?" I asked nervously.

"A little higher."

"Is it safe?"

Apollo glanced back. "Hades told me he did this with Persephone. I guarantee my chariot is prettier and safer than his."

"Well, if Hades did it—" I muttered. "Damn, Apollo, we're really high up. Your mansion looks like the cutest little dollhouse. Are you sure—"

But Apollo gave the horses a sharp command and they dove straight down through the clear air. I almost screamed, but I held the sound in. Down, down, and then a sharp swerve to the right, and then up again. The horses' manes and tails streamed with flaming sunlight as they galloped up an invisible mountain. Wind bathed my face, rushing past me, raking through my hair.

I realized I was smiling outside, shining inside. The burst of speed, the sun, the thrilling drop—it was actually helping.

Or maybe it was just him.

Another sudden halt, high up in the clouds—a moment of terrifying anti-gravity—then another dramatic plunge. This time I let myself scream, shrill and free.

Apollo's laugh was like sunshine blended with music. Just above the treetops, he pulled the horses out of the dive and leveled the chariot again.

"I love hearing you scream," he said, twisting to look at me over his shoulder. When he saw my face, his grin brightened, and delighted triumph shone in his eyes. He didn't comment on my smile though, just seated himself beside me, reins still in hand. "I know a very high waterfall near here. Lots of spray." He winked at me. "Should we ride through it?"

"Or down it," I answered. "You'll catch me, right? If I happen to fall?"

Apollo's eyes glowed into mine, molten tenderness. "I'll catch you, Cassandra," he said. "Every time."

REBECCA F. KENNEY
BOOKS

The SAVAGE SEAS books

The Teeth in the Tide (Savage Seas Book 1)
The Demons in the Deep (Savage Seas Book 2)

These Wretched Wings (A Savage Seas Universe novel)

The KORRIGAN trilogy

Korrigan (Book 1), *Druid* (Book 2), and *Samhain* (Book 3)

The Monsters of Music (a gender-swapped Phantom of the Opera retelling)

Her Dreadful Will (coming April 2022)

The ASHTON SHIFTERS adult fantasy romance series
Lion Aflame
Panther Ensnared

The DARK RULERS adult fantasy romance series
Bride to the Fiend Prince
Captive of the Pirate King

The IMMORTAL WARRIORS adult fantasy romance series

Jack Frost

The Gargoyle Prince

Wendy, Darling (Neverland Fae Book 1)
Captain Pan (Neverland Fae Book 2)

Hades: God of the Dead
Apollo: God of the Sun

The Horseman of Sleepy Hollow

The PANDEMIC MONSTERS trilogy

The Vampires Will Save You

The Chimera Will Claim You

The Monster Will Rescue You

Interior Design for Demons

Lair of Thieves and Foxes

Printed in Great Britain
by Amazon